Promptly at eight o'clock, forty-seven male and three female uniformed officers assembled in the large, bile-green muster room on the second floor of the 53rd Precinct.

Sergeant Sam Turner read the roll, glanced at his clipboard, and discussed the cases and priorities facing the officers. When that was done, he said, "We have a survival tip today, courtesy of an officer in Cincinnati, who owes his life to it.

"He was involved in an armed confrontation with a perp in the street. He reports that he and the perp shot at the same time, and he felt himself shot—in the chest. He had missed the perp, and he figured he was dead, because he was shot in the chest.

"But he had only gotten off two shots, and decided to squeeze off the rest. Maybe he wasn't dead.

"He did that, and the perp went down—he was dead. Later the officer learned that his wound was not in a vital area. His original inclination was to give up, but he had not. The tip is this: Just because you're shot, don't assume you're dead. Squeeze the trigger until all your shots are fired."

The meeting was over. A few minutes later, the men and women of the 53rd Precinct hit the street.

Also by Tom Philbin in Sphere Books:

UNDER COVER

PRECINCT: SIBERIA

Tom Philbin

SPHERE BOOKS LIMITED

For Bob Feuchter

A MESSAGE

To Joe Elder, my agent; Tom Kenny, Det. Sgt., NYPD; John Carlton, Det., Ret., NYPD; Richard Milner, co-author of the classic *Black Players—The Secret World of Black Pimps*; Jack Sturiano, P.A., Suffolk County ME's office; Eddie Meagher, NYPD; Ruth Gold; Mike Philbin; Dan Zitin, Editor: Thank You.

SPHERE BOOKS LTD

Published by the Penguin Group
27 Wrights Lane, London W8 5TZ, England
Viking Penguin Inc., 40 West 23rd Street, New York, New York 10010, USA
Penguin Books Australia Ltd, Ringwood, Victoria, Australia
Penguin Books Canada Ltd, 2801 John Street, Markham, Ontario, Canada L3R 1B4
Penguin Books (NZ) Ltd, 182–190 Wairau Road, Auckland 10, New Zealand

Penguin Books Ltd, Registered Offices: Harmondsworth, Middlesex, England

First published in the United States of America by Ballantine Books 1985
First published in Great Britain by Sphere Books Ltd 1989
1 3 5 7 9 10 8 6 4 2

Copyright © 1985 by Tom Philbin
All rights reserved

Printed and bound in Great Britain by
Richard Clay Ltd, Bungay, Suffolk

CHAPTER 1

Sixty-one-year-old plainclothes police officer Leo Grady sat by the window of the master bedroom in his Queens apartment and polished his shoes carefully, a ritual he had done almost every day of the thirty-four-plus years he had spent in the New York City Police Department. There was perspiration on his temples and forehead and a fluttery feeling in his stomach. Part of it was due to drinking the night before—and so many nights before that—but part was due to the prospect of another day, God save us, at the 53rd Precinct in the Bronx, more commonly known as Fort Siberia.

Grady was on the homicide squad and was wondering—his stomach was wondering too—what they would catch today. So far, in the month since he had been transferred to Fort Siberia, he and his partner, the squad commander Joe Lawless, had caught three homicides, two shootings, and a knifing.

"But we're slow now," said Frank Piccolo, another member of the squad, who Grady thought was insane. "Wait till the hot months—July and August. That's when we really get the numbers. It's open season on one another for these spics and niggers," he had said enthusiastically.

Grady's fluttery feeling enlarged thinking about it. It was now June 17. He had arrived May 15. Three homicides. He had looked up the numbers. The average of the precinct, highest in the city, was 1.5 homicides a week—but that was average. Half of them occurred during the long, hot summer.

He picked a Kleenex from a box on the window and dabbed his head, including his bald dome, which had also become sweaty. His stomach gurgled, and he suppressed the urge to pass wind. He had been drinking, more or less steadily, for six months; after six months of drinking you suppressed passing wind.

So far, whatever came, Grady thought, Lawless would help him. He had helped him so far. He hadn't made him go to any of the autopsies, and Grady got a sense that he was watching out for him.

Thus far, too, the homicides hadn't been all that gruesome or upsetting, either in terms of gore or the people who had been killed. Two were drug dealers, one a man who had been beating his wife for years.

"When that fucker sleep, I pin him to mattress," the wife said. "He don't beat me no mo'."

Any way you cut it, he thought, humorlessly aware of the pun, it was not going to be easy. One homicide more, or a hundred, it was violence. Grady was just not built to tolerate it well. And he knew, on the face of it, that it was ridiculous. A cop who couldn't stand violence? It was like a surgeon who couldn't stand blood.

Then why was he here, the most violent precinct in the city?

Grady had first learned that he might be transferred— but not to the 53rd—around four months earlier, when he was called into the office of Horace "Iron Balls" Callahan, chief of the records section, where Grady was a clerical man.

"Last warning, Grady. Stop your boozing or I'll put you on the street."

As usual, Grady had been half drunk when Callahan told him that, but the words had cut through the vodka to his belly.

The street? He was a clerk, a clerical man. He was not cut out for it physically, for one thing, standing just a shade over five-five, weighing about one-fifty—a good hunk in a paunch—and one year away from the age when they gave you Social Security. And then, of course, there was the emotional thing he had known about himself for such a long, long time.

In fact, just a few weeks after he got out of the Academy he had gone on two runs to vehicular accidents, and one homicide. This plus an acute aversion to autopsies told him all he wanted to know. For a long time before he went on the job he thought the violence would be like movie violence. You could take it. But real violence, he learned, made you get cold in the belly, made you throw up, even made you cry.

The idea of throwing in his papers presented itself. And as the days went along he became more and more depressed, because he knew it must end that way. He knew he would quit, he had to quit, but when he put the badge on the desk his dream would die, a dream, a fantasy, of being a policeman since he was a little boy. To be a POLICE OFFICER: brave, respected, full of pride, someone who did good things—because that's the way it was when Leo Grady was just starting out, and all across the years of his youth.

His depression was at its blackest, he had done all the preliminary paperwork, and he was just one day from quitting when his wife, Rita, came up with a miraculous idea—"I prayed to St. Jude for it," she said later—based on a skill Grady had which few cops had. Indeed, which few people, male or female had.

He could type like Superman, seventy to eighty words per minute without shifting into high gear, and hardly ever made an error. He was neat and organized, and details delighted him. "You are," his wife said triumphantly, "a born clerk!"

They got a postponement. They got hold of a "rabbi" downtown known by a friend of a friend. And Leo Grady was appointed a clerk at headquarters, then down on Centre Street. It worked out wonderfully.

Unlike most cops, Grady had regular hours instead of rotating tours, he was not far from the apartment in Queens, and he felt that yes, he was making a contribution.

But most of all, he carried around inside him the deep, pride that he was a police officer. He carried a gun and a badge, and when someone asked him what he did for a living he could say, very matter-of-factly but bursting inside, that he was a cop.

So Leo Grady lived his life. And he and Rita raised two lovely girls, and saw them married to good men, and were blessed with two grandchildren, and more to come, and more days to come.

And then, on a gray, bitterly cold day in January, God came and took Rita home to Heaven, and it opened a chasm of loss and loneliness and pain inside Grady so vast that he went to Mass every day and prayed and begged God to make the emptiness go away. But God did not, and then the only way to fill the void was to drink.

He started at night, taking a few shots of vodka, then more shots, and then he started secret sipping during the day. And, of course, everyone knew it. Grady was the last to know.

The first time Callahan called him in he told Grady to get counseling, which was available through the NYPD free to members of the force. It was a good program, and Grady plunged into it and was able to stop cold turkey for a while; but then he started to sip again at night, just enough to get him to sleep, and then some more to get him through the day, and then just around the clock.

The second meeting with Iron Balls, the "last warning" one, had indeed scared him. And it kept him away from the vodka for a couple of weeks. But in the end, it was the night that won, and he started again.

When Callahan called him in the third time, Grady knew it was over. And he was ready. The meeting was for two o'clock. Starting at nine o'clock that morning, a Tuesday in late April, Grady consumed a fifth of vodka. By around one o'clock he was joking to himself that you could tell him his behind was on fire and he wouldn't care.

4

And he knew what he was going to do. Go for thirty-five years in, whether Callahan put him in the street or not. He had only five months to go. Yes, with a nip here and there, and a prayer here and there, he could make it.

Promptly at two, Grady went in and stood before Callahan's desk. It was during confrontations like these that Callahan earned his nickname. "When he's really enjoying himself," someone once said, "you can actually hear his balls clicking together."

"You've got two choices," Callahan said. "Retire or be transferred to street duty."

Retirement, Grady thought. That was a new alternative.

"I can't retire," Grady said, feeling as calm as a lake and sharp as a tack. "I'm too close to thirty-five. Just a little over five months."

"So what? You're talking about a hundred and fifty a year difference in pension."

Callahan didn't understand. Guys like Callahan could never understand.

"But it's *thirty-four*, not *thirty-five*. Don't you see, sir? What will I say when someone asks me how come I put in thirty-four and not thirty-five?"

"We could fire, you, Grady," Callahan said. "We're being considerate."

Grady said nothing. The vodka stood between him and Callahan like a wall. Yet there was something ominous that he could almost feel. A hint of a smile on Iron Balls's face. Click, click. He had something in reserve.

"The Five Three," Callahan said, "is all that's available."

It almost took the wall down, but then Grady was a lake again, because he realized instantly that the only alternative now was to retire. The Five Three? That wasn't the Five Three: it was Fort Siberia.

It was places, precincts like the Five Three, that cops dreaded being sent to. Actually, you weren't sent; you were sentenced, and at any given time there was always a Fort Siberia. In the fifties and sixties there was Fort

Apache. Before that there was Staten Island; there was a precinct in Harlem, one in Bed Stuy. It was punishment duty, except for cops who had the misfortune to be assigned there after the Academy. It was for misfits.

Alcoholics who couldn't be helped, homos, psychotics, grass-eaters, drug users, malcontents, thieves who couldn't be nailed, wheeler-dealers, cops who messed with the wrong people, and old cops who should retire but who wouldn't and, like old Indians, were put out on the plain to die.

Grady had seen paper on it many times. It was in the Fordham Road section of the Bronx, well over 80 percent black and Spanish, and it was funny to talk about.

"South of Fordham Road," a cop had said to Grady once, "they call Death Valley. When you go there in July on a four-to-twelve, there's only one acceptable mode of travel—armored personnel carrier."

"They got no rats," another cop had said, and Grady had laughed heartily at the time. "The rats are too afraid of the people."

Grady's instant reaction was to tell Callahan that over the next week or so he would put in his papers. But he did not. Just standing there, remembering maybe all the other clerk types that Callahan had terrorized, hearing his balls click, Grady could not say it. What he did say was "I'd like to think about it, sir. I need some time."

Callahan looked incredulous. He lowered his eyes. "Get back to me Friday."

The meeting was over.

Grady could not bring himself to say, "Yes, sir," either.

The evening of the last meeting with Callahan, Grady sat in his living room, the light starting to fade—and Grady with it. He had worked his way through another fifth of vodka. Two in one day.

But even with two fifths in him, reality roared at him. He would not go the the Five Three; he simply could not make it. It was not silly; it was ludicrous to think he

6

could make it. Five months at Fort Siberia would be like five years, at least from what he had read and heard.

And then he started to realize something else: He could probably not make it anywhere. He was no cop. He had been fooling himself all these years. He was just a clerk.

And then the tears started to roll down his cheeks and he also realized what Iron Balls was doing: he just wanted to get rid of him, one way or another. Callahan knew he couldn't take Fort Siberia. That was what the NYPD thought of him after all these years.

The tears came harder, and then he thought of maybe "eating his .38" as cops say, but no, he couldn't, because they don't allow you in Heaven if you kill yourself.

"I can't make it, Rita," he slobbered out loud as the last light of the sun left the room. "I can't make it. I'm no cop. I'm just an old washed-up clerk, right?"

He did not, of course, expect her to answer. He had spoken to her before, at night, on many nights. And she never answered.

This time she did.

"Oh no you're not," he heard her soft voice say inside his head. "You're Leo. You're my knight in shining armor. And you're going to do it for me. And for you. You're going to Fort Siberia."

"You think I could?"

"I know you could! Remember who you are. You don't look like a lion. But you are a lion!"

It occurred to Grady that at five-five he did not look like a lion. But he was. He would go to Fort Siberia! Then he vomited all over himself.

The next day, Grady remembered nothing about his conversation with Rita. And he was sure that when Friday came he would put his papers in.

But just to satisfy his curiosity, or maybe to get his mind off the pounding headache he had, he looked up the stats on the Five Three just to see exactly—currently— how bad they were. The numbers seemed false, an aberration, they were so out of line with all except a few precincts. Only Harlem, Bedford-Stuyvesant, and three other precincts were in the same league.

The Five Three led the city in homicide, rape, assault—crimes of violence. The number of drug-related offenses was immense. In sum, it was an Everest of crime.

The other statistics he looked up were related to the crime ones, and were as predictable as night following day:

Most of the inhabitants of the Five Three—a whopping 73 percent—were on some form of public assistance.

Out-of-wedlock births were usual, in-wedlock births unusual. The average age of the mother was fifteen.

Many buildings—probably most—in the precinct had been abandoned; many others were victims of what cops called "Jewish Lightning"—arson.

Last year, three cops in the precinct had been critically but not fatally injured. One officer had been knifed to death while attempting to break up a family dispute.

It was lucky, Grady thought after finishing his perusal of the statistics, that he wasn't going to go there.

Still, a stubborn ember of curiosity remained.

Could it really be as bad as the numbers said? Grady had been dealing with numbers his entire professional life, and he had been involved in more than one statistical report that had proven to him that numbers could be made to lie.

He decided, not a little tremulously, to visit Fort Siberia himself, on Thursday, to see what it was really like. Then on Friday he would go tell Callahan that he had decided to retire . . . unless there was some great reversal, in person, of everything he had read and heard.

On Thursday, at around eleven A.M. he rented a car and drove to the Bronx, his .38 in his shoulder holster (though he wondered if he could ever use it if it came to that), and a large flask of vodka in his suit jacket pocket.

He decided to start his survey at 200th Street, the northernmost boundary of the Five Three. He took a slug of vodka and started driving south.

At first his route was flanked by apartment buildings, some burned out, some abandoned. Curiously, he would occasionally see a gaily colored material, usually either pink or bright red, over some windows of an abandoned building, and he did not know what they were until he finally realized, incredulously, that they were shower curtains and that there were human beings living in the "apartments."

Most of the buildings were marred with graffiti, obscenities written in Spanish and English. There were a few pedestrians, colored or Spanish. They looked at him with eyes that were not particularly hostile but asked what the little white dude in the First Holy Communion suit was doing in Fort Siberia.

At 194th Street, traveling down Creston Avenue, the area to his right opened up. It was St. James Park, a vast area of grass and trees, now coming into full bloom.

The streets were dirty, but Grady had seen worse. He kept driving.

So far, the Five Three hadn't given any indication that it would live up to its reputation, though Grady realized that it was only noon. But he had high hopes. Maybe it wasn't bad.

As he crossed Fordham Road, Grady saw something that startled and saddened him. It was an abandoned church, its roof caved in, windows broken. A House of God desecrated.

"Mother of God," he said to himself, and made the sign of the cross.

He realized that he had crossed over into Death Valley. There were more people on the streets, mostly clustered on corners. Beer cans and bottles were openly shown, and he got a queasy feeling as almost to a person they seemed to stop, turn, and eye him—hostilely—as he went by. Young men, old women, pregnant women, young and old women wearing skin-tight outfits that left little to the imagination.

The buildings were more broken-down here than above

Fordham, and more were burned out. Something oozed through the car to him: a sense of chaos, despair, and brooding violence. He felt clammy. He wiped first one hand, then the other, with a handkerchief. He turned the air conditioning up to maximum.

As he went deeper south, the streets got narrower—there were many cars parked illegally on both sides, and he had to slow down.

He was traveling slow anyway. Kids were playing on the sidewalks and in the streets. He didn't want to hit one. They would probably lynch him on the spot.

At each intersection, even if the light was with him, he stopped and looked both ways.

At 184th Street, this practice paid off. A souped-up, fire-engine-red Trans Am with big back wheels roared across the intersection doing about fifty. He would have clobbered Grady broadside.

At 183rd Street he stopped for a light, glanced around and in the rear-view mirror, and took a long swig of vodka. He was sweating freely, despite the air conditioning.

He watchfully made a turn onto Ryer Avenue, and immediately saw the station house. It was halfway down the block, on the left side, blue-and-whites parked in front of it.

The building had nothing near it except a rubble-strewn lot on one side and an abandoned building on the other. Indeed, most buildings on the street were empty. He understood the Five Three's other nickname, "Little House on the Prairie."

As Grady got close, he thought the Five Three should be torn down too.

The building had to be at least seventy-five years old. It was made of bricks, but they were badly stained. Mortar was missing, barred windows were rusting out, paint along the roof trim was peeling off.

He went by. There was no one in sight, and he couldn't see a light through the old scarred wooden entrance

10

door. Maybe, he thought, it had been abandoned, or everyone was dead.

He turned off Ryer Avenue and stopped the car. There were only a few people down at the end of the block. He took a short swig of vodka.

In fact, he thought, he had not seen any violence or evidence of violence, just an area where it could certainly occur.

He started the car again, moving east, then turned south again. He wanted something more concrete.

Then, in the distance, he saw the top of what he knew was Morrisania Hospital. He decided to stop there. They would have a feel for what happened in the precinct.

He parked near Emergency. It was ominous. Filled. But it was more than that: there was a Cyclone fence, topped by razor wire, around the entire hospital. To get in he had to show his badge to a guard at the gate.

The waiting room in Emergency was filled too. Mothers with kids, an old guy with his hand on his chest, a couple of kids who had their heads bandaged, many others, either patients or visitors.

Leaning against a wall near the door to the emergency room, a small Indian doctor dressed in a green cotton surgical uniform was smoking a cigarette.

Grady approached, took out his shield. He put his John Wayne image forward.

The doctor turned as Grady came up. He had large liquid eyes and a splayed nose. He looked like he hadn't slept in ten years.

Grady almost forgot he had his shield out. He showed it to the doctor.

"How are you, Doc," he said. "I'm new in the precinct. I'm trying to find out what kind of action you get."

"Everything," the doctor said with a slight English accent.

Grady smiled. "Leprosy?"

"Two cases since the first of the year."

"You're kidding, right?"

The Indian doctor shook his head.

"Everything. Plague, TB, AIDS . . ."

"Violence?"

"Violence?" The doctor smiled. "A madhouse."

Just then a bloodcurdling scream came through the door from the examining rooms.

"What was that?" Grady asked, needing a swig of vodka.

The doctor smiled, his yellowish-tinged, bloodshot eyes twinkling. "A woman's in labor."

At home the night of the day he visited Fort Siberia, Grady considered what he would retire to, and then he drank himself into an absolute stupor.

The next day, as required, he reported to Callahan. He saw him about nine-thirty. He wanted to get it over with fast.

He entered the office and stood in front of the desk while Callahan, who had not greeted him, busied himself with something.

And there, upside down on Callahan's desk, Grady saw a series of retirement forms that Grady would fill out.

Callahan knew what Grady was going to do.

Finally, Callahan looked up. Click, click. He said nothing.

"I'll take the transfer," Grady blurted.

Iron Balls looked incredulous. "This is the Five Three, Grady. Not Wall Street."

"I know," Grady said.

"You know? You're a clerical man. You know nothing about the street."

"I'll do the best I can."

"Your best is not going to be good enough."

You don't know Leo the lion, Grady thought.

Grady was almost ready to leave for Fort Siberia. He stood in front of an old chiffarobe and looked into the mirror. As always, he had on a white shirt and dark tie, slimly knotted and pulled up tight. He had been dressing like a clerk for a long time, and he couldn't change now.

With repugnance, he took his .38 off the chiffarobe and nestled it in a holster under his left arm. At the Five Three a gun had a new meaning.

He slipped on his dark suit jacket and buttoned it up. He was not, he knew, exactly a fearsome figure.

He wished he could be like Lawless, who didn't seem to be afraid of anything, though he never went around trying to show how tough he was. You just knew it. He reminded Grady of the late actor Steve McQueen. Looked a little like him too, with short blond hair, very blue eyes, and kind of battered features. Lawless just seemed to be able to eat anything, and he had this sort of inner tension, like a coiled spring.

He was the kind of cop Grady had wanted to be so long ago.

Grady buttoned up the suit jacket.

He was glad he had told Lawless about his fears of violence, and that for some reason he just wanted to make it to thirty-five.

All Lawless had said was "Bledsoe should have put you inside, but that's the way he is. We'll see what we can work out."

Grady was glad, too, that Lawless didn't know about his drinking. That would have embarrassed him.

Okay, Leo the lion, he told himself, let's go.

He went out of the room, and as he did he patted his suit jacket pocket. In it were his flask and his rosary beads.

He went through a short hallway, then through the living room, which was filled with ornate furniture that he and Rita had bought in 1945, when they married and moved into the apartment.

At the front door he disassembled four locks, including a bar-lock which he had modified so it couldn't be beaten. He opened the door and glanced back across the living room. Through an open door he could see the

13

sun-filled kitchen and part of the plastic-laminate-topped table which they had owned for most of the years of their marriage.

For a moment he thought he could smell Rita's cooking. In his mind's eye he pictured the two girls, Jean and Jennifer, and him and Rita sitting around the table, everyone happy on some spring day long ago.

His throat thickened. Now Rita was in Heaven, and Jennifer and Jean were gone, building their own lives.

He swallowed hard and stepped into the hallway. The heavy garlic smell of Spanish cooking jolted him into the present. It was the smell of change. This building would be gone soon too, grown too dangerous to live in. Maybe he would move away and . . . It was something he would think about when the time came.

On the street, he noticed for the first time that it was a beautiful day.

He walked toward Queens Boulevard, then made a right and walked to Ryan's Pub. He entered the cool dark interior and found the smell of bathroom, booze, and disinfectant strangely comforting.

Ray, the cadaverous owner, had Grady's breakfast, a double screwdriver, on the mahogany when he reached it. Leo whacked it down and set the flask on the bar. Ray took away the empty glass and flask to fill while the two men exchanged pleasantries of the day.

Grady slipped the filled flask back in his pocket, then turned toward the plate-glass front window. He sipped his drink. In his pockets, in addition to the rosary beads and flask, were Sen-Sen and Binaca. He bought good-quality vodka that didn't leave an odor on your breath, but he wanted to be sure.

He reached in with a free hand and touched the rosary beads. Maybe today he would be lucky. Nothing would happen. And he would be that one day closer to thirty-five years.

14

CHAPTER 2

As Grady sat in Ryan's Pub, Captain Warren G. Bledsoe, commanding officer of the 53rd Prècinct, stood in the darkened bedroom of his Riverside apartment in the northwest Bronx, buttoning his uniform shirt and looking at the large mound of his wife, Holly, under the covers in one of the twin beds. There was a smell of alcohol, methanol, and nicotine in the room.

What a son of a bitch she is, he thought. Drinking all the time, not taking care of the house, and with a tongue like a stiletto. It was why, he thought, he spent as little time as possible at home. He only wished he didn't work in a hellhole like the 53rd; he would spend even more time away.

A hot spasm raked his stomach. He could almost taste bile. If only he had succeeded downtown. If only his move to oust that stupid bastard Jeffries . . . But it hadn't, and Jeffries was behind his being shipped to Fort Siberia.

He picked his uniform jacket out of the closet. There was no attempt to be quiet—he just pulled it roughly off the hanger—and headed into the kitchen. He made himself a cup of black instant coffee, sat down by the window, and thought about the day ahead of him as he watched the traffic streaming down the Major Deegan Expressway. On the horizon he could see the gold dome of Manhattan College, glinting in the sun.

Just yesterday he had received the new stats on the precinct. Everything was up; clearance rates were down.

15

Today he would start getting the calls, the ball-busting ones. He hated it.

He ground his teeth. No one could control what was happening at Fort Siberia. It was just a bunch of crazy spics and niggers killing each other.

Jeffries must be laughing his ass off, really getting his rocks off. He would love to see that bastard die.

Police Officer Andy Fletcher, Bledsoe's driver and assistant, picked the captain up outside his apartment at seven-thirty. Fletcher immediately saw that Bledsoe had not one but two rags on.

As they drove downtown, Fletcher's eye flicked into the rear-view mirror. He caught a scowling eye, a furrowed forehead, a jumping jaw muscle. Every day was a good day not to get too involved with Bledsoe, but today was a day he would have to be extra careful. Bledsoe was looking to ream somebody, and he could be a Class A prick.

Fletcher was good at surviving. Before Bledsoe the CO had been a guy named Flynn. He took Siberia for two months before putting in his papers.

Before Flynn was Grunwold, a mad kraut who drank schnapps around the clock. He retired on disability, his liver the size of a medicine ball.

Before Grunwold there was Bailey, who, Fletcher found, was easiest to handle. The main reason was that he was out to lunch. They said he had accidentally killed himself while cleaning his sidearm, but Fletcher would give odds that he had eaten it.

Bledsoe's anger seemed to increase the closer they got to Fort Siberia. Fletcher drove carefully, and kept conversation to exactly zero. He wondered who Bledsoe was going to ream today. There was no question that he would. Just who.

CHAPTER 3

Arnold Gertz, dressed only in tight green shorts, opened the door to the refrigerator in his Freeport, Long Island, home at about the time Captain Bledsoe sat down with his cup of coffee.

Arnold took a milk bottle full of a vile protein concoction and slugged at it. His wife, Naomi, a small, plain woman dressed in a housecoat, was standing by the stove, cooking eggs. She glanced at Arnold. She loved him dearly, but hated that drink, and she always made sure he brushed his teeth after it.

Looking at the two of them together, one might wonder why Naomi was not dead. Arnold was immense. He dwarfed Naomi, and would seemingly kill her in the sex act. Indeed, Arnold dwarfed the kitchen. He stood six-three and weighed about 260. A weightlifter since he was twelve—he was twenty-seven now—Arnold had the kind of body that drew looks from women and men. He had a 58-inch chest, a 31-inch waist, 22-inch arms, and 18-inch calves. He was balding and had a pleasant face with thickish features, but he did not like the idea that his head seemed small in comparison to the rest of his body.

Arnold's weight had not varied much since he was around nineteen, because though he wasn't in active bodybuilding competition, he trained as if he were. He ate small meals to avoid becoming digestively and systemically overloaded, as they said in builders' magazines, and he ate things full of protein—meat, cheese, eggs. The protein concoction he had swigged contained peanut butter, raw eggs, soybean oil, protein powder, and tiger's milk—small wonder that Naomi insisted on the teeth-brushing.

Arnold Gertz was a Detective Third Grade, at the Five Three, and there were four jokes about him.

First it was rumored that he had once been on the mounted force and was great at crowd control—without a horse.

Second was that he had succeeded at making detective because when he busted down a door at a former precinct, the Six Three, he tranquilized everyone easily. They all died when they saw him.

The third joke was that his intelligence was in inverse proportion to his size.

The fourth joke was that before you told Arnold the third joke—have your will drawn.

Arnold left the kitchen and rumbled down a short flight of stairs to the basement. His twin four-year-old boys, Aaron and Jude—budding musclemen in green shorts like Arnold—were watching cartoons on television.

Arnold stopped and watched the TV. He never admitted it to anyone, not even Naomi, but he liked cartoons. He had been watching them faithfully since he was a little boy. He knew a lot of them by heart. Sometimes when he was alone he would turn on the TV and watch them, feeling a little guilty and embarrassed but soon lost in the fun, laughing out loud, becoming excited and involved the way other people might be affected by a movie. Cartoons were easy to understand. He particularly liked the older Bugs Bunny ones. Not the newer ones. The new Bugs was meaner and not as funny as the older one.

There was a Road Runner one on now. Arnold liked Road Runner—that poor coyote—but he knew he had to get going. He would have time for ten minutes of working out, a quick shower, and then he'd have to leave for the precinct.

Arnold had converted half the basement into a work-

18

out area. He had weights and some tension equipment, but nothing fancy.

He grabbed one of the 100-pound weights and did some curls, his muscles rippling but his face showing no sign of strain. Arnold's face showed strain when he got up to around 250 pounds.

As he worked out, he thought about what he would be doing at the station today. Captain Bledsoe never gave him much to do—maybe do the battalion mail run or go on errands all over the city, or sometimes he was assigned to station house security.

Arnold knew why. Bledsoe didn't trust him to do much of anything else. Probably thought he wasn't smart enough.

It pained him to think about it, but he did: the reason he was sent down from the Six Three to the Five Three.

They had been on a stakeout of an apartment—a drug deal was supposedly going down—when they broke it to respond to what seemed to be a homicidal family confrontation in a building adjacent to the one they were watching. There was a mix-up, a lot of confusion, and Arnold, right in the center of the action, had fractured the skull of the perp, the man the woman said was killing her husband. The only problem, it turned out, was that the real perp got away and Arnold had fractured the skull of the husband. What was more, the papers had had a lot of fun with it.

When it comes to image, police brass have no sense of humor whatsoever, and Arnold was sent to Siberia. "You're lucky you weren't flopped back to uniform," his CO had told him.

At the time, Arnold had felt lucky, but as the days went by—he had been at Siberia four months—he didn't feel lucky anymore. All the old feelings—the ones that had started with his father calling him a "big galoot" —returned. He felt like a big dumb ox, and it killed him when, one day, watching a Popeye cartoon, he started to feel like he was Bluto.

But deep down Arnold believed he was smarter than

Bledsoe thought. He had never done well in school—but he did get his diploma from a technical high school, and he did pass the police exam with the help of the five points he got because he was a veteran. He knew that most of the men at the station laughed at him behind his back—or at least some of them did. Bledsoe treated him as if he didn't exist.

Arnold cut off the thoughts, which were starting to upset him badly, and concentrated on the curls with a vengeance. He would show them what he could do, if only he was given a chance.

CHAPTER 4

Arnold Gertz was going through the front door of the 53rd Precinct at the same time that Barbara Babalino was coming down the stairs onto Jerome Avenue from the IRT train station at 161st Street and River Avenue.

As she started up the block toward the Concourse, a Hispanic male standing at a newsstand eyed her with carnal interest. As well he might. Though she was dressed conservatively, in a plain light cotton skirt, blouse, and jacket, she could not hide a lush figure that moved sensuously under the fabric as she walked.

She did not look like what she was, a police officer assigned to the Five Three.

She was heading toward the Bronx County Courthouse, and she was nervous. She was hoping very badly that Laura would show—not only to press the complaint, but also for Laura herself: psychologically, it would be a real beginning for her. A giant step out of "the life," as they euphemistically called prostitution, and a giant step toward a better life.

She would be there. Yes, she would. Barbara was nervous, but she believed it.

Barbara had first come into contact with Laura about three months earlier. She was on a four-to-twelve tour, doing busywork inside the station, when the call came through from the hospital. A young girl, maybe seventeen, had been brought into Emergency at Morrisania Hospital. She had been found on Webster and 181st, deep in Death Valley. She was nude, she had been beaten badly, and her head was shaved.

Laura was still being treated in Emergency when Barbara got to the hospital. Through swollen, bloody lips and loose teeth, her narrative interrupted by tears and cursing, she told Barbara the story.

She was, she said, a "ho" in the stable of a gorilla pimp named David—who ruled by fear. He had four girls in this stable and worked them as "flatbackers" —they would take anyone on, one after another, fifteen, twenty tricks a night, and it didn't matter if the girls were sick, menstruating, whatever: they had to work—and turn all the money over to David, who gave it back to them, as most pimps did, in the form of little presents and clothing according to his whim.

It was his beating that got to Laura. No matter how good she or the other girls were, David enjoyed beating them, and would look for any kind of minor infraction of his rules to do so.

Laura resolved to leave, so she started to squirrel trick money away, a dangerous thing to do with any pimp, but especially a gorilla like David.

Then two nights before she was to leave, a little drunk and feeling gay at the prospect of getting free of the sadist, she told one of the other hos that she was going "on the fly."

The other ho told David.

In the apartment where he lived with his hos on Webster Avenue, and in front of the other hos, David gave

Laura a classic pimp send-off. He beat her savagely with his fists, then with "pimp sticks"—wire hangers wound together—shaved her head, and told her she was lucky she hadn't been "wasted."

Barbara got Laura's statement—her full name was Laura Hutchens, and she was eighteen and from Minneapolis—on tape, and Laura agreed to follow through with a complaint. That should have been that.

But as she had listened to Laura's story, Barbara realized that the girl would probably end up back in the life. And one day Barbara might meet her again—in the morgue.

Laura was one of the losers of life. Prostitutes, bums, bag ladies, and the rest.

Well, Barbara thought, maybe she would end up badly, but not because I didn't try to help her.

Barbara promised to visit Laura the next day. Laura didn't seem to care either way, but the next day she showed up, and happily, she was feeling a lot better. She had no internal damage.

The girl seems surprised and pleased to see Barbara. They talked about mundane things—the food in the hospital, the service, the weather—and throughout, Barbara could read something in Laura's eyes: suspicion. Just what, she must be wondering, did Barbara want of her.

Barbara had decided to be direct.

"You're wondering what I want, aren't you?"

Laura said nothing.

"It's simple. I'd like to see you free of the life."

Laura looked at her and smiled, but it was a bitter smile. "I've been in it since I was fourteen," she said.

For a moment, Barbara had an image of her own Sweet Sixteen party, and her father kissing her gently on the cheek. Fourteen? Laura was eighteen now. Jesus.

"I'll help you get out if you'll let me."

To another person, Laura's automatic response would have been to forget it. In fact, she had already been planning what area of the city she could stroll when she got discharged. But there was something about this woman, about her large, intense dark eyes.

"How?" Laura said.

"One day at a time. We'll figure it out as we go."

Laura looked down. "I can try," she said.

Barbara reached over and took one of Laura's hands in her own. "That's all anyone can do."

The courthouse loomed into view, a massive gray structure with immense fluted columns, surrounded on three sides by wide, sweeping steps.

Barbara turned the corner to the front of the building, where she was to meet Laura.

She was there.

But Barbara was puzzled. Laura was standing with two men—a tall black man and a short, balding middle-aged man. Both were dressed conservatively. The black man was talking to Laura.

Laura turned and saw Barbara. She immediately broke away from the two men and went up to her.

"Who are they?" Barbara asked.

"That's David, and his lawyer."

Barbara had seen David booked, but he had been dressed so flashily that she had not made him now. Today he was dressed for the grand jury hearing.

Barbara looked at Laura. "What were you talking about?" She tried to hide her concern.

"He told me he turned over a new leaf, said he was sorry he did what he did, wanted bygones to be bygones. He also wanted to know where I was living, what I was doing."

Barbara had alternately been looking at the two men as Laura had spoken. But now she glanced sharply at Laura. "Did you tell him?"

"No way. I don't believe him. He's a gorilla. He'd love to get me alone. I know what he might do."

"Good girl," Barbara said, relieved. Laura was absolutely right. Barbara had set her up with a restaurant job

23

in Brooklyn, and she would be safe—as long as this pimp didn't find out.

"Wait here," she said.

Barbara walked up to the two men. The lawyer smiled as she came toward them. He was an oily little twerp. The pimp just watched her.

"Listen," she said, looking at the pimp. "I'm Police Officer Babalino. Don't try and con this girl. She knows you're a gorilla, and today we start the process which will put you away for a long time."

"Don't be so quick to judge," the lawyer said.

"Fuck you," Barbara said.

David the pimp looked at her. He had cold, black eyes. If he could have gotten away with it, he would have killed her right on the spot.

"Leave her alone," Barbara said, "or you'll be in even worse trouble."

She turned and went back to Laura, took her by the arm, and they went up the steps wordlessly. They got to the top and glanced back. The pimp was looking up at them.

"It took courage to do this, Laura. And you're helping yourself more than you probably even know."

They walked toward the door. Barbara felt the pimp's eyes on her back.

CHAPTER 5

While Grady was polishing his shoes in Queens, Detective First Grade Joe Lawless was on the NYPD firing range at Rodman's Neck on City Island. He was taking standard practice, firing at targets.

24

This range, or any range, no matter how realistic, was not like the real thing. At the range you shot under controlled conditions: the light was good, targets were 150 feet away and visible, you had plenty of time to squeeze off the rounds, and you were calm—or relatively so.

The average real shoot-out took two to three seconds, and it occurred in dim light and at very close range. Lawless had read somewhere that all but one of the 260 cops shot and killed since the NYPD was founded in 1854 had been shot from less than twenty-one feet. More than half of that number had been shot at less then ten feet.

But the range was better than nothing.

He had learned that on a sultry summer night some fifteen years earlier, when he was just three months out of the Academy and was riding a sector car with an old hairbag named Flanagan.

They were in the car when the call came through. The manager of the Olympia, a big table-service restaurant near Central Park South, had phoned in and said, as best the dispatcher could make out, that "there were trouble in ze bar."

Flanagan and Lawless were on the scene in a couple of minutes, fully expecting to find an altercation of some kind: restaurant owners, bar owners, hotel operators, and others were notorious for using cops as bouncers.

On entering the premises, which were dimly lit, Lawless was surprised to see that no one was sitting at any of the dining tables, and many of the tables had half-eaten meals on them, as if the people had suddenly just stood up and exited en masse.

Then, by the bar in the back, Lawless saw a lot of people clustered together. He had no idea what was going on.

Flanagan did. And his whispered words made Lawless's gut tighten.

"We're in a heist. Keep walking until I yell, then go down."

They took a few more steps and then Flanagan yelled, "Now!" and they went down, pulling their guns as they did, and then Flanagan was firing right next to Lawless's ear. Flanagan emptied his .38 before there was any return fire—just one shot. Then Lawless saw the perps, two blacks, running out the back, and he was about to go after them when he turned and looked at Flanagan.

He was on his back, his face the color of chalk, and Lawless knew he had been hit.

Lawless worked on him, gave him CPR, with his ears still ringing from the gunshots, unconscious of anybody or anything except this old life on the restaurant floor, and he kept it up until an EMS guy took over and jammed an oxygen mask over Flanagan and went to the hospital, and then he was dead.

Later, the shockers. Two.

First, Flanagan had emptied his .38. Six shots. They found all the slugs. Three in the wall adjacent to the bar, two in a column, one in the ceiling. Flanagan had missed every shot, and it was a wonder that he hadn't killed one of the diners.

And the other: Flanagan, wily old hairbag of an Irish cop, though required to shoot at the range twice a year, had been able to finesse his way out of it. He hadn't been on the range in *four years*.

Later, at the cemetery, Lawless had an image burned into his twenty-three-year-old brain that he would never forget. It was of Flanagan's wife, a heavyset gray-haired woman in black, flanked and supported by two of her sons, her face streaked with tears, and there in front of her in a flower-covered casket was Flanagan.

Lawless required the six men in his homicide squad, which included himself, to visit the range once a month. And he also suggested that they attend the business sessions of Sergeant Sam Turner, who read the roll before the morning tour. Turner gathered survival tips from police departments all over the country, things that cops used—or didn't use—to get out of armed confrontations alive—or dead. He didn't agree with everything Turner said, but most of it he did.

Lawless left the range about seven-thirty. He drove his own car, a battered 1964 white Impala, back and forth to the job. It was less conspicuous than an unmarked car, though he knew that if someone was alert they would eventually know it as his car.

As he drove along Fordham Road his eyes flicked this way and that, automatically looking for something amiss: someone acting suspicious, someone running, something just not right.

Spotting crime in progress, or about to be committed, could be a subtle thing. But Lawless's antennae were finely attuned. He had been in an anti-crime unit for six years, and the rest in homicide, the last year as head of the homicide unit at Fort Siberia.

He thought about the squad. Piccolo and Edmunton were on a drug hit, and so were Benson and Fassola. He and Grady were on a family killing.

Grady. He wondered if Grady was going to make it. Lawless intended to help him in every way he could, but things could get rough. Grady was walking a line.

If he had come just two months earlier he might have quit before he began. They had caught one of the worst homicides Lawless had ever seen.

It was of a little Puerto Rican girl. She was emaciated and looked about seven. She was eleven. They found her hanging by her father's belt from the back of the door. Daddy did it.

It was the book that was bad. One of those old-fashioned marbleized-covered schoolbooks. Every page, every line, was filled with a single sentence that he had made her write over and over again: "I will be a good girl . . . I will be a good girl . . . I will be a good girl . . ."

Bledsoe should have kept Grady inside. He had those good clerical skills, and he could have been a real asset.

But that wasn't Bledsoe. He was a burned-out, bitter guy, and he felt good when he could hurt you. Someday,

27

Lawless thought, they would find him down some alley, and the next stop would be the bone orchard.

Lawless stopped for a light at Fordham and Webster Avenue.

A shapely Puerto Rican girl passed in front of the car. She walked sensuously. Lawless watched her. She knew exactly what she had.

Lawless thought of Barbara Babalino. In the station she was known as "Towers of Babalino."

He had gone out with her twice, and she was more than a body. Much more.

Nothing much had happened on either date, and he knew that was by design—his, and maybe hers, too. She was not the kind of girl you had a simple affair with. Maybe someone else would, but not him. And that part of his life was sealed, shut off; he didn't need another involvement like the one he had had with Karen.

Still, he had enjoyed the two dates. But that was it. No more. Definitely.

He stopped at Fordham and Valentine Avenue and picked up a container of black coffee and a couple of donuts. Sometime during the day he would have a slice of pizza or something; or maybe when he got home, which was in the Pelham Bay section of the Bronx, he would make himself something. "The main killer of cops," a cop once said, "is their diet."

After their drinking, Lawless thought. At least that wasn't one of his vices. He thought of Grady.

He sipped the black coffee and drove down Tiebout into Death Valley. He wondered what the day would bring.

CHAPTER 6

Promptly at eight o'clock, forty-seven male and three female uniformed police officers assembled in the large, bile-green muster room on the second floor of the 53rd Precinct.

Sergeant Sam Turner read the roll, which he finished at 8:05, then went back and forth through the lines of cops, inspecting their dress.

They looked good, as well they might. Turner had been at the Five Three five years, four of them as roll-call man. In the first year or so he handed out a blizzard of Article 15's to the sloppy crews that were assembling in front of him. But gradually they got the idea, and it was a paradox that the cops of the Five Three were some of the sharpest in the city. A number emulated Turner's ways: he wore a uniform cut to fit his slim, tall form.

Turner didn't talk much, and he never smiled, it seemed. He was something of a mystery man. No one knew where he had come from, nor why he had chosen to stay in the Five Three. While many other cops would, as one cop said, "put their mamas on the street to get out of the Five Three," Turner did not.

Adding to the mystery was that he had a bad limp. Someone had once tried to find out what was wrong with the leg, and Turner had just sort of glared him off.

By the time Turner had finished with the inspection, some plainclothes cops, Benson, a homicide squad member, and Arnold Gertz had slipped into the room. Turner was a clearinghouse of information that might help on

29

other cases. Then, of course, there were his survival tips.

Standing in front of the group, he glanced at his clipboard, then looked toward Police Officers John O'Malley and Ephraim Delgado.

"Sector D, we have a report of an EDP in St. James Park. A man walking his dog heard loud yelling in Spanish, which he didn't know the origin of. But he saw a retriever-type dog running around like mad in the northeast corner of the park, under a tree. That's where the yelling was coming from. A Hispanic male was yelling and shaking the tree. The man didn't know what was going on, but he saw something drop from the tree.

"It was a squirrel. The EDP was shaking squirrels out of the tree for his dog."

The room erupted in laughter.

"The man said the guy shook three squirrels from the tree. The dog got one."

"Then," someone yelled, "the guy ate the dog."

More laughter, except from Turner.

"Robbery," Turner said when the laughter subsided, "is looking for a red Thunderbird, 1982, license number LAB 768. That's LAB 768."

A number of the officers jotted the number in their notebooks.

"Narcotics wants to know if anyone has seen a small Hispanic with bushy hair who wears aviator glasses."

There was silence.

"If you see such a person, call it in to Detective Caruso right away."

"Summonses," he continued, "are off. The captain wants an increase of ten percent by the end of the month. You should be able to do that easily," he said, "but it is strongly suggested that you pick your spots."

No one needed a translation. It was easy to get summonses in Fort Siberia. Most of the drivers didn't believe in such things as licenses, insurance, or inspections. Random checks—just stopping vehicles—would result in a raft of summonses. But it was not the same as giving out a summons in a normal precinct. You never knew what was going on inside the head of a guy who would drive without a license, no insurance, and no inspection. Push the wrong button and it's homicide time.

"Sector A, there's an Oreo team that's sticking up stations on West Fordham, down by the river. So far, both stickups have been in the afternoon."

It was funny. Turner was black, but he could say something like "Oreo team" and no one—or very few—would think of his blackness. It was not the way they thought about Turner.

Turner glanced to the back of the room. Arnold Gertz towered above the two uniformed officers flanking him.

"I was going to post this, Gertz, but as long as you're here—the captain wants to see you in his office as soon as possible.

"We have a survival tip today," Turner said without preamble, "courtesy of an officer in Cincinnati, who owes his life to it.

"He was involved in an armed confrontation with a perp in a street in downtown Cincinnati. He reports that he and the perp shot at the same time, and he felt himself shot—in the chest. He had missed the perp, and he figured he was dead because he was shot in the chest.

"But he had only gotten off two shots, and decided to squeeze off the rest. Maybe he wasn't dead.

"He did that, and the perp went down—he was dead. Later the officer learned that his wound was not in a vital area. His original inclination was to give up, but he had not.

"The tip is this: just because you're shot, don't assume you're dead. Squeeze the trigger until all your shots are fired."

Turner paused for a moment, turned, and walked away. The meeting was over.

A few minutes later, the men and women of the 53rd Precinct hit the street.

CHAPTER 7

Arnold Gertz went directly from the muster room to the men's room. He tried to urinate, but discovered that he couldn't. And he discovered too that he had started to sweat and give off an odor, something that had been happening since he was small whenever he got nervous.

What could Captain Bledsoe want?

Arnold's thoughts were jumbled, and he had difficulty thinking clearly. He wished Naomi were there. She would help.

All he could think was that it was probably bad. Captain Bledsoe never called him in for anything good.

Arnold stood in front of the urinal, trying to collect himself, until someone else came in. Then he glanced guiltily at the man and left.

Captain Bledsoe's office was on the first floor. Arnold went down well-worn metal stairs, then entered a large room filled with detective desks, plus those of civilian workers and some other personnel.

Bledsoe's office was in a corner of the room formed by the building walls and two partition walls with frosted glass on the top. Fletcher was directly outside at a desk.

As Arnold made his way across the room, he tried to appear nonchalant. Some of the desks were occupied, and a few people glanced at him as he went.

Arnold cleared his throat before he got to Fletcher. "The captain wants to see me, I think."

"Go right in," Fletcher said. He didn't look as if something was badly wrong.

"Yeah?"

"Sure."

Gertz tapped on the partially opened door and opened it. Captain Bledsoe was sitting behind his desk. His head was down, and when he brought it up Arnold saw he was scowling. But the sight of Arnold seemed to have a soothing effect. He smiled.

"Hey, Arnold," he said. "Thanks for coming in. Have a seat."

Arnold sat down adjacent to the desk. Maybe it wasn't bad.

"I've been watching you," Bledsoe said, "and you've been doing a good job."

Arnold smiled. It was something good. He hoped his odor wasn't reaching Bledsoe.

"I think," Bledsoe continued, "you're ready for bigger assignments."

"Yes, sir," Arnold said. His heart pounded.

"And last week something came in that I think is right for you."

Arnold nodded.

Bledsoe put on glasses and opened a manila file folder. He picked a color snapshot from it and handed it to Arnold.

"What's that, Arnold?"

"A goat."

Arnold was puzzled.

"It's called a nanny goat."

"Oh." It was making Arnold nervous.

"This goat—Grapes—was stolen last week from"— Bledsoe glanced down at the folder—"a Mr. Benjamin Jiminez." He pronounced the *J* hard, as in "Jimmy."

"I see," said Arnold.

"Jiminez is mad. And he's worried about the other goats he has being stolen."

"How many does he have?"

"Three more," Bledsoe said.

"Where are they?"

A slight smile immediately creased Bledsoe's face. "Two of them live in a pen outside the apartment house

33

where he's super, and the other one"—Bledsoe seemed to have trouble controlling something; his face got red—"lives *in* the apartment with him."

Arnold wanted to ask a very intelligent question. "Does . . . does he raise them?"

Bledsoe paused a moment before he spoke. "He gets milk from them and sells it. He also says they're his pets like you might have dogs or cats."

A broad smile had returned to Bledsoe's face. Arnold nodded. He did not know exactly what was expected of him.

"I want you," Bledsoe said, "to track down the thieves who took Grapes."

Grapes? Arnold thought. Oh, the goat.

"Yes, sir," Arnold said, feeling himself starting to swell inside. "I'll do it."

"Good," Bledsoe said. "Here's the complaint folder." He handed Arnold the file.

Arnold held the file reverently, as if it were an award. "I'll do the best I can."

"I know you will," Bledsoe said. "And there isn't a man in the station I'd rather have on this than you."

"Thank you, sir. Thank you."

Bledsoe stood up and extended his hand. Arnold shook it warmly, being careful not to hurt the captain. People sometimes complained that his grip hurt them.

"Good luck," Bledsoe said. "And keep me informed of how the case is progressing. If Jiminez calls, I'll tell him I have a top man on it."

Arnold could not speak. It was just like those days when he got his diploma in grammar school and high school, and the day Naomi said she would marry him. He felt very proud.

Arnold went out of the office and wove his way back across the large room. This time he felt good; he felt like any one of the detectives in the station house. He was Arnold Gertz, dick third grade, 53rd Precinct.

Just before he got to the door that led to the hall out of the building he heard laughter coming from the direc-

34

tion where he had been. He turned around. It seemed to be coming from Captain Bledsoe's office. Fletcher was not at his desk.

He kept walking. If he had a thought, he did not allow it to enter his consciousness.

CHAPTER 8

At eight-thirty, after a whirl around St. James Park to see if they could spot Squirrel Man, Police Officers John O'Malley and Ephraim Delgado parked their blue-and-white near Nick's Family Restaurant on Jerome Avenue and Kingsbridge Road. It was a ritual before every tour; you couldn't beat Nick for food—or rates.

Today Delgado stayed in the car and O'Malley went for the orders.

The restaurant, really a glorified luncheonette offering counter and table service, was pretty crowded, mostly blue-collar Hispanics and blacks.

Hostile eyes flicked toward O'Malley as he came in. Fuck you, spics and niggers, he thought, without staring back. Fuck you where your breathe.

Nick approached from his position at the grill. His disposition was in stark contrast to that of his patrons. A small, middle-aged, brownish man with thinning black hair, a prominent nose, and a cigarette perpetually poking from one corner of his mouth, he was smiling broadly, showing brownish teeth, as he always did.

"Hey, John," Nick said with a Greek accent. "How are you? Keeping you busy? What can I do for you."

"Ham and egg on a roll for me, scrambled and peppers on a roll for my Hispanic partner."

"Coffee?"

"A light-and-sweet and a black."

"You got it," Nick said, and turned and walked away.

A few minutes later Nick returned, handed him the orders, and waved off his offer to pay. Cops who ate at Nick's ate either for nothing, or for "full price" when someone was watching very closely. Then the cop would hand Nick a buck, or some other bill, Nick would ring up the correct amount, then hand the bill back to the cop as change.

"Thanks, Nick," O'Malley said, and left. He wondered how Nick could maintain his good humor with so many cops eating for nothing.

Nick watched O'Malley go through the door, then turned and headed back to the grill. As soon as he turned, his smile faded. All cop babies, he thought in Greek, should be born without legs.

"We got a squeal," Delgado said as O'Malley got back into the car.

"What?"

"A spade snatched a chain on Fordham and the Concourse. He's tall, thin, slight Afro, wearing a yellow shirt, purple pants, and white felony flyers."

"We'll never make him," O'Malley said, and dug into his sandwich. It was delicious. The smell of Delgado's sandwich was strong, but O'Malley had learned to hold his tongue. Delgado was a macho little fuck, and they would get into a beef. Anyway, he wasn't as bad as a nigger. O'Malley had ridden with a nigger, and they liked fuckin' hamburgers in the morning. It was enough to gag a maggot.

O'Malley's concern about the sandwich was cut short—neither of them got to finish their meal.

Delgado was halfway through his when he announced: "There he is. The spade."

Delgado was looking in the rear-view mirror. O'Malley grabbed it and manipulated it so he could see the other side of the street from where they were parked.

It was the spade bopping along. O'Malley wondered where the neon was.

"Take him on foot?" Delgado said.

"No way," O'Malley said. "He looks like fucking Edwin Moses."

They shoved their sandwiches in their bags, capped their coffees—a lesson O'Malley's crotch had learned the hard way—and put everything on the floor.

The spade, whose name was Wendell Taylor, had spotted them fairly far down the block, but he didn't want to arouse suspicion, so he had just kept walking along in their direction.

Then he saw them fuckin' with the rear-view mirror, and then he saw exhaust cough from the tailpipe.

Twenty-two years of street life had given him refined antennae: they were on to him.

There was no playactin' no mo'.

It was flyin' time.

From a dead start, though Edwin Moses would have beaten him, Wendell Taylor worked up to quite a speed, and his acceleration was aided by massive amounts of adrenaline pumped into him as he heard the wheels of the blue-and-white squealing through a U.

Then the siren went on, and Taylor turned on the afterburners.

He roared east on Kingsbridge. At Morris Avenue he turned right, running like hell toward St. James Park.

For a moment he considered going into the park—they couldn't follow with the car there. But sometimes you got plainclothes fuzz trying to sniff out drug deals—of which there were many—so he decided against it.

He had made a left and was running toward Creston when he heard the wheels screaming as the car turned into Morris. He was well ahead of it, but they would close the gap. He had to do something soon.

On Creston he saw it. A big gray abandoned building on the corner. He might have time to get into it before they spotted him. The basements of these buildings were like puzzles, and there was usually more than one way out.

Desperately, he crossed Creston, then up the wide courtyard of the once elegant building, then up another flight of stairs past assorted debris—bricks, railings—and finally up into a final set of stairs and through the open doors of the building itself.

He was no more than ten feet inside the doorway when he heard the blue-and-white go blasting by.

He was covered with sweat, breathing hard; his heart hammered in his ears.

He looked around. The light was dim, but he saw he was in the lobby of the building. It was high-ceilinged. There were broken mirrors on the wall; he looked and saw a jagged image of himself.

The floor was littered with broken masonry, tiles that had fallen off the walls, anything and everything. Intact tiles had graffiti on them.

He heard a little movement behind him and turned sharply. He saw a small rat disappear into a hole in the wall. Rats didn't bother Taylor; he had been living with them his entire life.

He knew he should go into the cellar. The fuzz might figure out what he had done and come back. It would be dirty and dark, but safe. And the deeper he went in, the safer.

He saw a doorway marked, in faded letter, STAIRS.

He went over, opened the door, and closed it behind him. Immediately he was in almost total darkness. He grabbed hold of a metal railing to guide himself down.

He went down two flights into the cellar, then he walked very slowly, his hand against a smooth, slightly damp wall to guide him. The whole place was super musty-smelling, as if it had been filled with water, then drained.

He kept his ears peeled. There was no sound coming from upstairs, and all he could hear was the sound of something dripping someplace and the sound of his breath-

38

ing and occasionally stepping on something. He had to be quiet.

Gradually his eyes became accustomed to the darkness, and after a while he could make out doors and doorways and walls in the dim light, made a little less dim occasionally by light coming in a dirty window.

He stopped and stood stock-still. Adrenaline flowed into him. Upstairs in the lobby he could hear talking. The motherfuckin' fuzz.

He stepped into an open doorway, concentrating on the sound from above. He was so absorbed, in fact, that it took him a moment to become aware of the smell. A thick, stomach-churning smell, like some sort of cheese.

His mind switched back upstairs as the voices seemed to get louder. They weren't leaving. Motherfuckers! Did he hear one say that maybe he went down into the cellar?

Wendell saw another doorway, this one leading from the room he was in: it was like a double room. They couldn't search everything. His heart pounded.

He moved through the doorway into the other room. The smell was even worse. Made him gag a little, but he had to endure it. Those motherfuckers were going to come down.

He crouched, and as he did his arm brushed against something cool and hard.

Wha' the fuck? he thought, and probed with his fingers, then grabbed the object. It was an arm.

Delgado knew he had balls, even more than O'Malley, who also had balls. It was Delgado's idea to go down into the cellar. It would be dirty and dark and a little spooky, but the spade could be there. He had vanished into thin air. It was worth a shot.

They were about to go down, Delgado leading the way, when they heard the yelp from the bowels of the building. Then, more noise: someone was coming toward the stairs fast.

In a moment, both had their guns drawn. They waited,

frozen in combat-shooting stances, guns pointing at the stairway's entrance, not knowing what to expect.

Wendell Taylor burst through the door. His eyes were like silver dollars.

"Wait," he said, putting out his hand. "There's a motherfucking body back there."

"What do you mean?" Delgado asked.

"A fucking dead person."

The cops nodded.

"Up against the wall," O'Malley said, "and spread 'em."

Taylor put his hands against the mirrored wall and spread his legs. O'Malley searched him while Delgado kept his gun leveled.

"Where's the chain," O'Malley said when he had finished his search.

"I ain't got no motherfuckin' chain."

"Watch your tongue, nigger," Delgado said, "or I'll break your face."

"I haven't got no chain." He didn't. He had thrown it away as he ran.

"Doesn't matter," O'Malley said. "We got the lady you snatched it from."

Taylor said nothing. He knew cops. He knew Delgado was itching to whack him.

"What's your name," O'Malley asked, "and where do you live?"

"Wendell Taylor. Three-fifteen Wadsworth."

"What are you doing up here, Wendell?"

"I took the wrong train."

"Okay. We'll have some detectives talk to you." O'Malley said, "Where's the body?"

"In one of those rooms."

Wordlessly, O'Malley took the cuffs off his belt and cuffed Taylor's hands behind his back.

"Lead the way." It was probably, O'Malley thought, some bum or hophead.

"I don't want to go back down there."

40

"Oh," Delgado said. "Little black boy afraid of the dark?"

Defiantly, Taylor headed toward the doorway, and stood there while Delgado went back to the radio car to get a flashlight. He returned and they started down.

Taylor led the way down the corridors he had traveled. Occasionally a pair of red eyes would appear, then scurry away. It was enough to give anyone gooseflesh.

Finally, Taylor didn't have to lead them anymore. The smell guided them. The smell of the putrefying body.

No one said a word as they went through the first doorway, then the second. There was no telling what the room had been used for. Now it was just a room without a door—with a body in it.

Delgado's flash found the body. Slowly he moved the light along it.

It was a dark-haired woman. She was on her stomach, nude. Something was stuffed in her mouth. She was tied in some exotic way with yellow cord.

She was pretty, despite the thing in her mouth, despite the dried blood that had come from her mouth and nose and despite her staring eyes.

Taylor was thinking what a nice body she had. Delgado was thinking about how the scene didn't bother him. O'Malley was thinking that she once had been a beautiful woman.

"We better get Lawless," O'Malley said.

CHAPTER 9

Before he left the station house, Arnold went into an empty office to look at the complaint file—and to call Naomi.

She was thrilled, and Arnold felt doubly proud. The plain fact was that they had not talked about his job in a long time.

He looked at the picture of the goat. Grapes looked like any goat, except for one thing he had noticed in Captain Bledsoe's office which he had said nothing about.

It had maroon eyes! It should be easy to find. He knew goats had sort of funny eyes—he remembered them from when he was young and his parents took him to baby animals farms—but they were not maroon!

Then, looking at the goat, he realized from a reflection on an object next to the goat that the picture had been taken inside. With a flashbulb. Anxiety gripped him. The goat didn't have maroon eyes. It was the reflection of the flashbulb!

God. He wasn't on the case ten minutes and he was making stupid mistakes. He started to think about the case that got him to the Five Three, but then stopped.

The anxiety remained. He felt like pumping iron, but there was no way he could do it.

There was a desk, but what would he say if someone came in when he had it lifted over his head? Besides, he might accidentally drive it through the ceiling, or drop it.

The best thing to do was to get on the case. He glanced at Jiminez's address and left.

On the street, he considered whether to take a cab or

car or public transportation. It was not an idle question. In Fort Siberia they would steal anything, including police cars. There were a few cases of recovered stolen cars parked outside the station being restolen. Now all cars had to be parked in a garage down the street whose owner was, they said, a former international terrorist.

He decided to take his car. Jiminez lived on 198th and Valentine, which was above Death Valley. It wasn't as bad. He kept a chain and lock in the trunk. When he parked he would lock the hood so they couldn't steal the battery, or the engine.

He headed toward the garage.

It was around nine o'clock when Arnold got to Jiminez's apartment house. He identified the place because it was one of the few houses on the block with a clear number sign. In fact, the entire house seemed to be in much better shape than the nearby apartment buildings and smaller houses.

He found a space directly in front of Jiminez's house, secured the hood, and looked up and down the block. No, up here was not bad. And it was still early in the morning.

He looked at the apartment house and his stomach fluttered. Though only five stories, it seemed to tower above him, a skyscraper, much larger than it really was. He thought of Naomi and how much she loved him and of the great Schwarzenegger pushing himself past the limits of endurance where his efforts tore his muscles. Arnold blinked—and was ready. He was Detective Third Grade Arnold Gertz. This was his chance—maybe his last chance.

He headed for the alleyway, where a small metal sign with an arrow said SUPER.

The narrow alley led to a wider alley, which ran between two buildings, Jiminez's and another, separated by a Cyclone fence topped with barbed wire.

The other alley was clogged with garbage, including a refrigerator, washer, auto parts, the trunk of a large tree, and assorted furniture, the centerpiece of which was a large sectional couch which looked like it had been ripped apart by wild animals. Everything was covered with a dark liquid that came from God knew where.

Jiminez's side of the alley was clean, just a stray piece of newspaper which had probably blown in.

The ground level door, also marked with a little sign that said SUPER, was freshly painted, and when Arnold pushed the bell he could hear it ring somewhere inside.

Arnold smiled at the man who opened the door. Arnold figured he was about sixty. Small, around five feet two, gray hair and piercing black eyes.

"Mr. Jiminez," Arnold said, pronouncing the *J* hard.

"Himinez," Jiminez said. "Himinez."

"Sorry. I'm Detective Gertz from the Fifty-third Precinct. I'm here to look into the loss of your goat."

The eyes got more piercing.

"Where the fuck you been, mon? Grapes stolen last week."

Arnold flushed with anger. His immediate reaction was to grab J. Himinez and throw him over the fence into the other alley. But he held his temper, and did not talk, because he could not talk.

Jiminez's brow furrowed.

"Where the fuck you guy? You guy quick to come we spit on sidewalk, but not when we got problem."

Arnold's thoughts were jumbled. He was trying to remember what the Patrol Guide said on how to handle this kind of thing. Certainly it didn't say throw the man over the fence.

Somehow, he was able to talk. "Mr. Jim—"

"Himinez!"

"Mr. Himinez, please don't . . . curse at me. I'm here to help if . . . I can. To get . . . Gr . . . Grapes back maybe."

Jiminez said nothing. His eyes seemed to soften.

"What . . . what happened?" Arnold asked.

Jiminez's eyes seemed to get extra shiny. He spoke softly. "Eight day ago. Junio nuevo, Monday," he said,

"Grapes . . ." He said the word more softly, like it was a woman he loved. "She take, maybe never come back."

Jiminez's eyes turned hard again. "I catch 'em, I kill 'em!"

"How . . . how did it happen?"

Jiminez stepped back and opened the door. "Watch you head. You a big guy."

Arnold followed Jiminez through the cellar. He had heard before how dirty cellars in Fort Siberia were. But this was freshly painted, clean; it even smelled good.

"You keep this place nice," Arnold said.

"I throw all the pigs out."

"Are you the landlord?"

"He do what I say or I leave."

Arnold trailed Jiminez into his apartment. They went down a hall in which were hung a number of religious pictures. There were a couple of rooms off the hall; Arnold glanced in as he passed. There were religious pictures on those walls too, and everything was neat and clean.

At the end of the hall, Jiminez turned left, Arnold following. As Arnold did he glanced to his right, through an archway into an open room. It was the living room. He was shocked. Standing in the middle of it, staring at him, was a black goat with a white streak down the center of its face.

The room to the left was the kitchen. It was filled with big pots, bottles, and odd-shaped devices that Arnold had never seen before.

A door from the kitchen led to the pen, which was hard-packed earth surrounded by a Cyclone fence topped with barbed wire. In one corner was a shack.

There was one goat, all white, in the pen. It had huge breasts that almost touched the ground, and it trotted toward Jiminez immediately; another goat, this one brown with white streaks on its back, came out of the shack. It also had huge breasts and went toward Jiminez.

He nuzzled both goats, and they *baa*ed in pleasure.

Jiminez turned his face up to Arnold. His light brown skin was flushed; he was smiling, showing gold teeth.

"This Maria," he said, touching the top of the head of the brown goat. "This one Blanca," he said, touching the head of the white one. "Iris inside. *Bonita,* no?"

Arnold nodded, but he didn't know what *bonita* meant.

"You get milk from them, huh?"

"They all milkers. I get five, six quarts a day from each."

"You drink all that milk?"

Jiminez looked at Arnold strangely. "Oh, no. I sell it around here."

"Oh," Arnold said, and remembered Captain Bledsoe had told him that.

"How did they steal Grapes?"

"I show you."

He led Arnold to the fence near the shack, then behind it. There was a big hole in the fence which was covered with new mesh.

"They come in late at night, take her."

"Did you see anything?"

"No. Nobody else see anything either. 'Round here everybody fuckin' blind."

"Do you have any idea who might have taken Grapes, or why?"

Jiminez paused. "Maybe devil worship. They do with goats." Jiminez's eyes looked downward. "They sacrifice goat."

Arnold was so sorry he had asked the question. "Oh," he said, "I'm sorry."

"Okay. Maybe not happen."

"What else could have happened?"

Jiminez's eyes looked downward again. Arnold was instantly sorry he had asked that question too.

Jiminez shrugged. But it was a sad shrug. "They could eat her."

"Oh. I'm sorry."

"In PR it's popular. Called Chevron."

What, Arnold thought, had a gas station to do with

goat meat? Then he realized it was the meat that was called Chevron.

Arnold nodded sagely. At this point he should be asking more questions, but nothing occurred to him. He looked at the goats for a moment and something occurred to him. He hesitated for a moment, then asked, "Mm, Mr. Jiminez. How much did Grapes weigh?"

"A hundred and seventy pounds. My biggest. She was pregnant."

He didn't like it, but he had to go on. "That, uh, would be a lot of meat. Too much for just a few people, wouldn't it?"

"They could sell to a restaurant or a bodega."

Arnold had a fantasy of how TV cops did it. They went to a few restaurants, there was a commercial, and a little while after the commercial ended they would find whatever they wanted to find, and at the end of the show trace it to the bad guys. That's all he had to do.

Then he remembered. He had seen it on *Hollywood Squares* or some other show. There were over twenty-five thousand restaurants in New York City. And then to that you'd have to add all the bodegas.

But no. Maybe he would just have to go within the Five Three. Then again, maybe they went outside the Five Three.

Maybe it was devil worship.

"Mr. Jiminez, do you know of any devil worshipers around here?"

"Hundreds all over city. Thousands. That popular in PR, too."

Arnold nodded and wrote in his notebook. Or, more precisely, drew something that looked like half of a three-ring pretzel.

What was he to do! Where was he to go? He had no idea.

He wrote the number of the Five Three on a page in the notebook, tore it out, and handed it to Jiminez.

"This is my number at the precinct," he said. "I'm going to get on this right away."

The line echoed in his mind. He had heard it on some cop show.

"You're watching your other goats, huh?"

"These guy come," Jiminez said, "they die."

CHAPTER 10

The room used by the Five Three homicide squad was located on the second floor, next to the muster room. It was a small, doorless place that contained a chalkboard and some battered green metal desks on which were—in a department that was one of the most computerized in the country—manual typewriters so old and decrepit that even Grady could only wrest about sixty words a minute from the best one. The room also commanded, through a big, dirty, multipaned window, a view of a brick wall.

Grady and Lawless were each at a desk doing paperwork when Sam Turner came in.

"Joe," he said, "Sector David just called in. They found the body of a woman in an abandoned house on 193rd and Creston. A bondage job."

"Do you know if Forensic and the ME were called?"

"I contacted them."

"Thanks, Sam." Lawless said. He turned to Grady. "Let's see what we got, okay?"

Grady had the feeling that Lawless would let him stay behind if he wanted to. He did, but he couldn't.

"Okay," Grady said, "I got to take a leak first."

"I'll get the car," Lawless said.

Grady went to the bathroom, which was empty. In one of the stalls he closed the door—it was the only stall door that worked—behind him and leaked the entire contents of his flask into himself. It was a tremendous belt, and would either totally anesthetize him or kill him from alcohol poisoning. Either way, he figured, was preferable to viewing this thing with only his breakfast screwdrivers in him.

Lawless was waiting in front of the precinct when Grady emerged.

"I'd like to get there fast," Lawless said. "People who aren't experienced can mess up a crime scene fast."

The trip to the scene took five minutes. A crowd had gathered, and there were a couple of blue-and-whites there.

There was no sign of the vehicles that transported Forensic or the ME. It would be a while, probably, before they arrived.

Lawless pinned his shield to the lapel of his jacket; Grady did the same. He wished the vodka would hurry and do its job.

They went up the stairs to the lobby. A couple of patrolmen were there. Lawless knew both of them.

"Hey, Eddie," Lawless said, shaking the hand of one of the men. "How you doin', Ray?" He shook his hand too.

"Good, Joe, fine."

"This is may partner, Leo Grady."

"How you doin', Leo," Eddie said. Ray merely waved hello.

"Do me a favor," Lawless said, glancing at first one man, then the other. "Don't let anybody down there who isn't from Forensic or the ME's office, okay?"

"You got it," the patrolman named Eddie said.

"Thanks," Lawless said. "Which way?"

"Down those stairs," Eddie said.

"By the way, how did Sector David find it?"

"They were in pursuit of a chain snatcher. He came down here to hide, but came running out when he discovered the body."

"Where's Sector David?"

"They took the collar back to the station."

Grady followed Lawless to the door. He felt a little dizzy, then a little dissociated from things. The vodka was starting to work.

They went down the stairs. Someone had put a Coleman lamp in the corridor, so seeing wasn't a problem, but the flickering light gave the cellar the appearance of a cave. Later, Lawless thought, they would bring a generator and lamps and light the place up like daylight.

Occasionally, when they came to a jog in the corridor, Lawless would call out and the answer would guide him in the direction to take.

Grady started to feel better. The walking seemed to be distributing the vodka faster. He started to get the feeling he wanted: he was aware of what was going on, but not really affected by it.

Once, Lawless looked at him, but did not speak. Grady could almost read his mind: How are you doing?

As with Delgado and O'Malley, the odor guided them over the last part of the journey. Grady had never smelled anything like it in his life. He could not describe it.

Two patrolmen were standing outside the entrance to the rooms. Lawless did not know them. He introduced himself and Grady and then went inside, and stood outside the entrance to the room where the body was. Grady hung back in the first room.

Someone had put a Coleman lamp in the room, and Lawless could see the body fairly well.

The woman, nude, was on her stomach, lying on a sheet. Her body was bent back so she looked like a bow, and she was tied . . . *elaborately* was the word that came to Lawless's mind. At first glance, all the ropes seemed to be interconnected. And her hands were taped or something.

He went up to the body. The smell was truly intense.

The woman's face, turned toward the door, had caked blood coming out of her nose and mouth, which was stuffed with some sort of cloth. Her eyes were open, riddled with petechial hemorrhages.

50

But nothing could hide the fact that she had been very pretty, and very well built.

He looked closely at the ropes. Or cord. He felt it. Nylon, he guessed, and braided.

Everything was interconnected—and taut. Her hands were tied behind her back at the wrists, and her elbows were also tied together. There were ropes extending from the elbow cord to the ankles, the legs were spread wide and bent at the knees.

The key, Lawless figured out, was the cord that went from the elbow cord and was looped twice around the neck. The effect was that someone could enter her vaginally or anally and if she moved even a millimeter that's how much pressure would be put on the elbow cord, which was really, then, a ligature.

He looked closely at her hands. Each was taped the same way. Thick, wide tape had been wrapped around all her fingers and around the wrist. She could not move.

Lawless was on the doorway side of the woman. He walked around to the other side. There were no bruises or marks of any sort he could see. He squatted, touched her upper arm. Cool and hard. She was in full rigor, but there was no putrefaction on the body that showed. There was extensive lividity.

He would have to wait for the medical examiner to turn over the body. He was not authorized to do it. He didn't want to move it anyway, not until Forensic had gone over the scene a bit. When he was a golden boy, on his way up in the department two years before, his CO had told him that that was one of his strengths as an investigator: he knew his limits; he didn't try to do it all.

He walked over to the corner of the room, on the right side as you came in the doorway. There was a pile of clothing. Faded blue dungarees, a yellow tank top, sandals, no brassiere. No panties. Then he realized where the panties were. In her mouth.

He looked closely at the clothing. It had been cut. Since it was jumbled, it was hard to tell exactly how. It would be something to determine later.

Grady had come into the room at just the time Lawless went over to examine the clothing. The vodka had prepared him, and he stood looking at the girl, the wall of vodka separating her, him, and his feelings.

He should, he thought, be having a very bad reaction. What he was looking at was horrendous, horrible, disgusting—any bad words you wanted to use—and what was more, Jean and Jennifer couldn't be much older than this girl. Yet nothing registered emotionally.

He stayed a couple of minutes, and then went outside with Lawless.

About ten minutes after Lawless and Grady came on the scene, a team from Forensic arrived and went about the business of gathering and tagging evidence.

The assistant ME, Victor J. Onairuts, M.D., arrived shortly thereafter. Lawless was glad to see him. Unlike many medical examiners, he was free of pretension, free of the need to present his profession as super-scientific. "Only Quincy is right all the time," Onairuts once said. In the final analysis, he knew that facts about a dead person could be open to very wide interpretation.

On the other hand, Lawless knew, when Onairuts said something was so, you could take it to court and not have to worry about a defense counsel tearing it apart.

While he examined the body, Lawless had a word with the head of the Forensic team.

"Was her clothing cut?" he asked.

"It looks to me like he tied her up, then cut her clothing off her body."

Lawless watched Onairuts conduct his examination. Grady did too. People, Lawless thought, surprise you all the time.

Onairuts examined the back, then, with help, turned the body over and examined the front. Lawless could not see any marks or bruises of any kind.

Finally, Onairuts was finished.

Lawless waited until they were outside the room. "Do you know when she died?"

"No," Victor J. Onairuts said.

"Do you know how?"

"I'd say asphyxia, but I want to wait until I open her up."

"When?"

"Tomorrow morning."

"Was she assaulted?"

"Anally, at least."

"Thanks, Doc."

No ID had been found on the girl. That would be the first order of business.

Lawless, Grady at his side, spent ten minutes going through the rest of the cellar. There were some more rooms, all either without doors or with open doors, but there didn't seem to be anything related to the girl's murder, at least at first glance, and that is what this amounted to.

Near the rear of the cellar they found a door that led to an alley, it seemed. When he returned to the crime scene, Lawless alerted one of the Forensic people to dust it for prints.

They waited until the body, ropes intact, was lifted onto a litter and covered up—it was too big, tied, for a body bag—and then loaded onto the wagon from the morgue.

They watched the wagon pull away, then Lawless said, "Let's go back to the station. We'll get more done there." That was fine, Grady thought as they got into the car. He had another bottle of booze stashed at the station, though he doubted very much that what he was feeling now would wear off quickly.

So, he thought, he had survived the kind of horrible scene that he had imagined he would have to face in Fort Siberia.

That was good. With vodka, he could do anything.

Then the interior of the car became very quiet. Tears formed in his eyes and rolled down his cheeks. He looked out the window. Lawless said nothing, and neither did Grady.

CHAPTER 11

When they got back to the station house, Lawless got some coffee and lit a cigarette. He sat down at one of the desks and looked through the big grimy window at the brick wall.

He had sent Grady to check with Missing Persons whether anyone answering the girl's description had been reported.

Lawless wondered how Grady was going to make it through the summer—booze or no booze. If it would do any good, Lawless would talk with Bledsoe. But it wouldn't do any good.

Still, Grady was still there—booze or no booze. He hadn't quit yet, and people surprised you all the time. Maybe he would make it.

Lawless thought of the deceased. Who was she? He might get the ID through Forensic. They would send her prints to the FBI. If she had a sheet, they would get a make on her right away.

He didn't want to take the dental chart route. That would take a lot of manpower and a lot of time, neither of which he had enough of.

He didn't want to canvass the neighborhood with the girl's picture. That too would take time and people. Besides, the populace was very badly anti-cop. Most people in the precinct hated cops, and the feeling was mutual.

Still, depending on how the case developed, they would have to talk to some or a lot of the people in the neighborhood. Maybe there were squatters in the building. Maybe it was a shooting gallery—lots of junkies used abandoned buildings to shoot up.

He dragged deeply on the cigarette, let the smoke out.

He pictured the girl in the cellar, pupils fixed, petechial hemorrhages, the way she was tied.

He had seen people tied something like that. But not as elaborately or intricately. You'd get it with gays; you'd get it with people who would tie themselves up for kicks and die in the process.

But this one had a personality all its own. It was malevolent. Move a millimeter, choke that much.

He saw the hands. Fingers taped together, the tape extended around the wrists.

It reminded Lawless of the way ballplayers taped their fingers and hands—football players, boxers—except it wasn't. Ballplayers left the thumb free. Here, all the fingers were taped. No, this was different.

Maybe, he thought, it was a serial killer. He had once gone to a seminar given on that by the FBI. Bizarreness was the key there, and usually they found something wedged in the vagina. They would have to wait until the post came down.

Bizarre. Bizarre to a normal person, but something with a very special meaning to a killer. The tying, the tape. The question was: What did they mean?

By the time he got back to the station with Lawless, Grady was feeling the full effect of the vodka, and ready for just about anything. It occurred to him that he didn't need to worry about Fort Siberia anymore. Just stay drunk. He could stay drunk twenty-four hours a day, seven days a week (less the time he slept) and everything would be swell.

When Lawless told him to contact Missing Persons he declined to verbally answer, merely nodding his head. It was hard, ho-ho, to verbally respond when you had a hogshead full of vodka in you.

Grady first went to see Sam Turner. Turner told him

that there had been no missing persons reported in the precinct over the last few days or even couple of weeks.

"I'll have to call downtown," Grady said, conscious of carefully pronouncing his words

"Use any of the offices you want," Turner told him. Grady thought he could even have gone into Bledsoe's office and Turner would not have objected. Sometimes when you were a little soused you saw things much clearer than when you were sober. Turner, Grady figured, didn't like Bledsoe. It occurred to Grady that Bledsoe probably didn't like Bledsoe.

He found a room with a door and ceiling, as opposed to one of the ceilingless cubicles that gave one a sense of privacy but wasn't private.

He called Missing Persons five times before it occurred to him that they probably had the phone off the hook. He had seen lots of clerks, particularly ones who always received complaints, do the same thing. He had done it himself when he didn't want to be pestered.

But he had a way around it. He called the general switchboard at headquarters.

"Police Department," the operator said as if she were the one who was drinking.

"This is Deputy Inspector McGrath," Grady said in a pompous, officious, annoyed tone. "Are you having trouble with the phones in Missing Persons? I can't get through."

The mush went out of the voice. "Sorry, sir. Just a minute, please."

Ten seconds later Missing Persons was found.

"Missing Persons, Sergeant O'Neill," the crisp voice with a Brooklyn flavor said. "May I help you?"

"This is Deputy Inspector McGrath, Sergeant, of the Five Three. You've helped already by answering the phone."

"Yes, sir."

"We're trying to get a make on a female, age eighteen to twenty-five whose body was discovered here. Dark

56

hair, dark eyes, five-three, a hundred and twenty-five pounds, wearing jeans and a yellow tank top."

"I'll check, sir. Please hold."

Grady could picture what the sergeant was doing. All his career he had made it a point to familiarize himself with new systems, especially the computer, whose significance he had seen fifteen years earlier.

The sergeant would be punching her description and precinct of origin into the terminal. In seconds, perhaps a minute, he would have a make or—or no make.

Grady, concerned with some things that mattered to no one in the world except the individual clerk mentality, timed the sergeant. He was back on the line in exactly thirty-three seconds.

"Yes, sir," he said. "We got a description of a missing like that."

"When and where?"

"Well, this girl was reported missing June fifteenth, eleven P.M. Name of Mary Baumann, 2567 Grand Concourse. But . . . but while everything is the same—her father, Richard, who reported her missing, says she was wearing a yellow tank top and blue dungarees—there is a major discrepancy between her and the girl you're looking for."

"What's that?"

"Age. This one's only thirteen."

A few minutes later, Grady was in the squad room. Lawless was at one of the desks.

"I double-checked," Grady said. "The description is the same."

"It has to be her," Lawless said.

He did some work with an address locator.

"2567 Grand Concourse," he said, "is right around the corner from where she was found. That nails it even more. Let's try to find out."

CHAPTER 12

Grady went to the bathroom—this time to actually go to the bathroom. While he was gone, Lawless dialed the number left by Mr. Richard Baumann.

It rang twice, and a small female voice answered. "Hello?"

"Mrs. Baumann?"

"Yes."

"This is Joe Lawless. I'm with the 53rd Precinct."

"Did you find Mary?" Mrs. Baumann cut in.

"No," Lawless said, "but I was wondering if we could come up and get some more information about her."

"Richard—he's my husband—will be coming home for lunch in a little while. Maybe you can come up then."

"When will that be?"

"A half hour."

"Fine."

Grady returned to the squad room a couple of minutes after Lawless finished talking with Mrs. Baumann. Lawless told him what had transpired.

"You're, uh, not going to tell her we probably found her daughter?"

"Not right away," Lawless said. "If we do, she—they—might shut down on us. You can't learn anything then."

Grady smiled. He still had a snootful of vodka. "I'm not tough enough for this job," he said. "It's—"

"You get used to it," Lawless said.

"Yeah, but how long does it take you to get used to it?"

"It doesn't happen overnight," Lawless said.

They left for Baumann's ten minutes later.

It was a short trip to the apartment the Baumann's lived in, a big three-wing red brick affair one block off Kingsbridge Road. It was in good condition—superb, compared to most of the buildings in the precinct.

Lawless rang the bell. They were buzzed in and rode the elevator to the fifth floor. On the way up, Grady realized he needed a little nip.

The Baumann apartment was a few doors from the elevator. Mrs. Baumann was standing in the partially opened door. Lawless showed his badge and identified himself and Grady.

She was matronly, plain, probably mid-forties. She had light hair and eyes and, Lawless thought, was maybe not the mother of the girl in the cellar. But he doubted that.

She led them into the apartment, through a short hall into the living room. It was neat, clean, nicely but not expensively furnished. Typical middle-class, not unlike the environment Lawless was from.

"Please sit down," she said. "Richard isn't home yet. He should be here any minute. Would you like something? Coffee?" She was very nervous. There was something pathetic about her.

"No thanks," Lawless said.

Grady shook his head no. What he wanted was in his flask.

Lawless and Grady sat down on a couch. Mrs. Baumann sat opposite them in an upholstered chair. Her hands were clasped together on her lap.

"Do you have any idea," Mrs. Baumann asked, "where Mary might be?"

"No," Lawless lied. "Maybe you can answer a few questions to help us."

"I . . . I don't know. I'll try."

"What did Mary do on the day she became missing?" Lawless asked.

"She just went to school and then to St. James Park. She wasn't supposed to go there."

"Why not?"

"Her father told her. It's such a terrible place. Just terrible. Do you know about it?"

Lawless nodded. "Was she with anybody?"

"Yes. Richard found out. George LaRocca, Betty Johnson, and Michael Reilly."

"Were they the last ones to see her?"

"George LaRocca was. He told Richard that he walked Mary home."

"I don't understand," Lawless said.

"George told Richard that he walked Mary all the way to the corner and that the last time he saw her she was heading right to the house. What could have happened to her?" Mrs. Baumann was blinking rapidly. She was close to tears.

"Do you have the addresses of her friends?" Lawless asked softly.

"I'll get them."

Mrs. Baumann went out of the room and returned shortly, slightly out of breath. "This is her address book. It's how Richard located where she'd been. He called them all."

She handed Lawless a small pink book with a flower design on it.

He leafed through it. "May I hold this for a while?"

"Yes."

"Do you have any pictures of Mary?" Lawless asked.

"Yes, but most of them are when she was young. The last few years both Richard and I have worked, and we haven't gone out on many family outings together."

"I'd like to see them, if you don't mind," Lawless said.

Mrs. Baumann went out of the room again and brought back an album of pictures. Lawless leafed slowly through the pages. Grady looked on.

They were mostly family shots at the zoo, an animal farm, street scenes; there were a few of Mrs. Baumann

60

and of a tall, angular man whom Lawless took to be Mr. Baumann.

"Is this your husband?"

"Yes."

Most of the pictures were of a little girl who looked maybe six or seven. She was dark-haired and dark-eyed. She bore no resemblance to her father.

There were no pictures of the little girl beyond the age of nine or ten. In the last few pictures he could see the beginnings of a womanly figure. There was no question in his mind that Mary Baumann was the girl in the cellar. At one point he heard Grady make a sighing noise that only he could hear. Grady was sure too.

"Thank you," Lawless said, his face calm. "On second thought, I think I will have some coffee."

Mrs. Baumann nodded and got up. "I wonder where Richard is," she said. She started to leave the room.

"Also," Lawless said, standing up, "I wonder if we could have a look at Mary's room."

"Oh. Yes, I guess so. It's in here."

She led them to the room, then left to make coffee.

Lawless went into the room, Grady following, and immediately over to a dresser. On top of it was a brush and a small box. He looked at the brush. The bristles were entangled with dark hair. He put it down and opened the box.

It was filled with lipstick and many other different kinds of makeup. A lot of makeup, he thought, for a thirteen-year-old girl. But he cautioned himself: this was a different generation. Now you could catch ten-year-olds making it on the roof, at least in Siberia.

He closed the box and opened the closet door. On the back was a full-length mirror. Inside was a large array of clothing and shoes, including a number of pairs of flashy high-heel shoes.

He closed the closet door, walked over to a window, looked out. There was a view to the Concourse. He looked down at the sill outside. It was plain brick, but speckled with black spots. Cigarettes had been stubbed out on it.

He released the catch and opened the window slowly and quietly.

He picked a toothpick off it. A roach holder. In a corner of the sill he touched some flakes.

He turned his head slightly toward Grady. "Marijuana," he said softly.

He slipped the material into his jacket pocket and closed the window.

There was a small desk adjacent to the window. He opened and closed drawers. They held stuff you might expect in any teenage girl's desk: some fan magazines, a battered paperback on a rock star, some tiny stuffed animals, old schoolbooks, stationery, an errant tube of lipstick.

He went to the doorway, listened for Mrs. Baumann. He heard water running in the kitchen.

He dropped down on his belly and looked under the bed. Nothing. He went to the other side and gently lifted the mattress. Nothing was under it.

Lawless went to the door and closed it softly. "Stand against it," he whispered. Grady stood with his back against the door.

Then Grady got it. Quickly and quietly, Lawless proceeded to open each of the drawers of the dresser, which Mrs. Baumann could see if she were coming down the hall and the door wasn't closed.

He pressed down the clothing in each open drawer to see if there was anything underneath.

In the middle drawer there was some brightly colored cloth. Two pieces. He picked them up. A bikini bathing suit. The bra was large.

In the bottom drawer, which was almost empty, there was an open box of sanitary napkins.

He pressed the napkins down, felt something. He lifted them up. He picked out a tin of condoms, opened it: three of the six were missing.

Grady was startled. What would a thirteen-year-old

62

girl be doing with condoms? The answer was all too obvious.

Lawless closed the tin and put it in his pocket. He put the box of napkins back and closed the drawer.

"Let's go outside," Lawless said.

That was fine with Grady. He felt clammy.

Mrs. Baumann came into the living room a minute after Lawless and Grady. Grady realized that it had only seemed like a long time in the girl's room—it had actually been just a few minutes.

"Did you find anything?"

"No," Lawless said.

"Oh. The coffee will be ready soon."

They made small talk about the good condition the building was in. Then she went for the coffee.

Just as she came into the living room with it, the sound of a key could be heard in the front door.

"That's Richard," Mrs. Baumann said. She seemed relieved.

It was Baumann. Lawless could tell from the album pictures.

He had aged considerably. He had lost some of his sandy blond hair, which was streaked with gray, and the lines on his face were much deeper. Lawless made him for mid-fifties, maybe older.

He was dressed in workman's clothes and smelled of paint. He didn't explain why he was late, and she didn't ask.

"This is Detective Lawless," she said, "and this is Detective Grady. They're here about Mary."

"Did you find anything yet?" Baumann said. He looked first at Lawless, then at Grady, then back to Lawless. He had flat, lifeless gray eyes.

"No," Lawless said. "We thought maybe you could help."

"I'll try." He sat down on a straight-backed chair.

"The night she didn't come home. What happened?" Lawless asked.

"She was supposed to be home for supper at six o'clock. She didn't show up."

"You were concerned?"

"Not really," Baumann said. "Not at first. She had done this before. She's a discipline problem."

"How so?" Lawless asked.

"Well, at school she sometimes plays hooky. Doesn't study. Sort of rebellious. She defies me and my wife a lot."

"Do you know why?"

"Her friends," Baumann said. "She got in with the wrong group of people. A bunch of bad people."

"When did you get concerned?"

"Not until nine-thirty or ten o'clock. That was late even for her."

Mrs. Baumann had been busying herself with serving the coffee. Lawless sipped his. Grady forced some down.

"What'd you do then?" Lawless asked.

"I got hold of her address book and started calling her friends. I located them—"

"I told the detectives about them," Mrs. Baumann said.

"That's all right," Lawless said. "It's okay to repeat things."

"I found out," Baumann continued, "that she had been at the park with George LaRocca, Michael Reilly, and Betty Johnson. George LaRocca walked her home, dropped her off at the corner, and left."

"What time was that?"

"About nine o'clock."

"Did anyone notice anything strange in the park? Anyone different hanging around."

"I didn't ask."

"How about Mary?" Lawless said. "How was she acting during the day?"

"I don't know. I didn't really see her. I'm a painter, and by the time she gets up, I'm gone."

"I work too," Mrs. Baumann said. "At night in a hospital. By the time I get home, she's gone."

Grady looked at them. What was life coming to? he thought. What mattered? Then he felt guilty. He realized with a gripping sensation in his stomach that their daughter was dead.

"Do you know anyone who would want to harm Mary?" Lawless asked.

The Baumann's shook their heads.

"And you have no idea why she wouldn't show up at home?"

They shook their heads again.

"Do you have any other children?" Lawless asked.

"No," Mrs. Baumann said. Grady looked down at the rug. It was killing him.

Lawless hesitated. There was no easy way to do what he was about to do.

"Uh, this morning . . ." Lawless said.

"Excuse me," Grady cut in. "May I use your bathroom?"

"Sure," Baumann said. Grady went out of the room quickly.

"This morning," Lawless said softly, "we found the body of a young woman not too far from here. A murder victim. She bears a close resemblance to your daughter. I didn't want to tell you until I was fairly certain it was her."

The blood drained out of Mrs. Baumann's face.

"Where?" Baumann said.

"On Creston. The abandoned building on 193rd."

"But it could be any girl, right?" Mrs. Baumann said. "Not just Mary." Her lip was turning down. She was on the edge.

"What do you want us to do?" Baumann asked.

"Take a look," Lawless said.

At his own insistence, Baumann traveled alone with Mrs. Baumann in their own car, following Lawless and Grady in the radio car.

Lawless drove directly to the Five Three. Grady waited in the car.

65

The person he wanted to see—Barbara Babalino—was in. And she agreed to accompany him to Bellevue, where the body was. Anna Baumann, he thought, might need someone supporting her in case she started coming apart. For some reason, he had a visceral reaction to Richard Baumann: if his wife did start to go, he just sensed Baumann wouldn't be much help.

They drove down to Bellevue in fifteen minutes and went directly to the viewing window on the lowest level of the hospital. As bad luck would have it, the TV monitor, which was normally used, was being serviced.

The couple waited nervously in front of the window, which had a mechanical shade inside. Despite a fresh infusion of vodka in the Baumann bathroom, Grady was very nervous. Lawless looked on blankly.

The shade rose, and Mrs. Baumann's hand jerked to her mouth. "Oh, God," she said.

Her husband looked on, only his jaw muscles working.

"Is that your daughter, Mary Baumann?" Lawless asked for legal reasons.

Mr. Baumann nodded, and closed his eyes briefly. Mrs. Baumann started to cry softly. Grady felt like crying too. Christ, he needed another drink.

Mr. Baumann remained motionless. Barbara stepped close to Mrs. Baumann and touched her arm.

"I'm sorry," Lawless said.

"How did she die?" Baumann asked mechanically.

"Asphyxia, we think," Lawless said.

Neither of the Baumanns responded. The silence was broken only by Mrs. Baumann's soft sobbing.

After they left the viewing area, Mr. Baumann made arrangements with Lawless about the remains. Lawless told them he would drive them home in their own car, but Baumann declined. He said they would be okay.

Lawless and Grady and Barbara accompanied them to their car and watched them drive away, swallowed by the traffic of Second Avenue.

Grady glanced at Lawless as they all walked down the block. Christ, he was a hard man. Hard as nails. Grady felt that Lawless could go through this stuff and not really be affected by it that much.

Lawless did not notice Grady's glance. He was thinking about the girl's staring brown eyes, hemorrhaged, pupils fixed and dilated. Eyes that beseeched someone to care.

CHAPTER 13

On Friday, Lawless let Grady go home early. He simply had taken too much amperage that week.

Late Friday afternoon he received the post from Dr. Onairuts. It confirmed something that Lawless had perceived at the Baumanns'. Mary Baumann was on the wild side. The autopsy reported that there was a "well-healed hymenoidal scar." There was no telling when she had first had sex.

As the details registered, it also occurred to Lawless that he was involved in one of the most sadistic murders ever.

In the first place, Onairuts said that the girl had been dead ten to twelve hours when found. That meant that, assuming the killer snatched her at around nine o'clock Monday night, June 15, he would have had her—alive—the night of the fifteenth, and all day the sixteenth before she died.

In his opinion, she had indeed died of "asphyxia" caused by a combination of the panties stuffed in her mouth and her own efforts to pull away from what was being done to her, plus panic, which makes one hyperventilate.

"Tending to confirm asphyxia," Onairuts said, "the

cartilagenous framework of the larynx and hyoid bone are intact." Translated, that meant pressure was steady rather than sudden, which would have caused fracturing.

Onairuts found "many sperm heads and intact sperm and strong acid phosphatase activity" in her anus and vagina, and acid phosphatase in her mouth. The man had sodomized and raped her repeatedly, and when she tried to pull away, she strangled.

The killer—or likely the killer—had left something on the body. Onairuts found a single pubic hair on the anus. It was blond.

As evidence went, Lawless knew, pubic hairs weren't worth much in court. A pubic hair wasn't a fingerprint. But if they ever got a strong suspect, a pubic hair that could be matched to him would give Lawless strong incentive to find other evidence that could work in court.

After he completed his second reading of the report, Lawless took from a desk the envelope that contained the photos Forensic had taken at the scene, and which had been delivered earlier in the day.

He took the pictures out. They were eight-by-ten color glossies, eighty-four of them, taken from every conceivable angle of Mary Baumann prior to autopsy, the cord still in place.

He lit a cigarette and went through them twice, slowly, not forming any ideas, waiting for something to come to him.

When he was through, he got up, went over to the window, and looked out through a pale image of himself at the brick wall.

He remembered, from when he had been a young cop and first starting out in homicide so many years ago, a streetwise sergeant who had that certain suspicious look that most homicide detectives get after a while. It asked, Who have you done lately?

"Homicide," the sergeant had said, "is the only crime where the complainant is dead. But if you listen closely you can hear the body talking. Remember that."

Lawless inhaled deeply, let the smoke out.

What was the body saying to him?

First, that the killer was a psycho. A sadist. The girl had suffered agony.

Second, that sex had nothing to do with the killing. He knew cops who would think him weird for saying that, but he had been on too many rape homicides not to know its truth. The rapist was getting off on pain, control, and degradation of the woman. Coming in her was almost incidental.

What were the ropes telling him? The way she was tied. Anything special? The knots looked ordinary, and they had found that the rope was ordinary—polypropylene, usually used around pools because it floats.

The hands. What did they say? Why taped?

He thought about it, but nothing came to him. At one point, he thought, he would talk to O'Hara, a psychologist from the FBI who had helped him in the past.

Over the weekend he would start talking to her friends, the people who had last seen her alive. He also wanted to check out the building, the neighborhood: Had anyone seen anything?

On Monday he would be getting some help from downtown, the main reason being that the story had been in the newspapers. That's the way headquarters was. If the newspapers got it, the case would get the manpower. If it didn't, it would not.

But Lawless knew that the help would be temporary— maybe a week or two at most. He would have to lay things out so he could get the most out of it, because soon he would be on his own with his squad. And the hot months were almost here. Then it would be on to new business—lots of it.

He knew also that this was a case that would never really go in the drawer.

CHAPTER 14

A week and a half after he caught the Jiminez squeal, Arnold Gertz sat down for supper in his home. Naomi, mixing a salad at a counter in the kitchen, stole glances at him to confirm what she had been feeling since he came in. He was depressed; she was sure of it. She had known Arnold for twelve years, ten as his wife, and could pick up his mood with the precision of a seismograph.

She stalled around with her own supper until the twins had finished and galloped off to the basement. Then she sat down. "Everything okay, Arnold?"

Arnold slowly twirled his fork in a clump of sauerkraut on his plate. "Everything's fine," he said.

Naomi cut off a piece of hot dog, speared it, and put it in her mouth. She chewed a little, then lowered her eyes to the plate. "How's the case going?" she said.

Arnold shifted a thousandth of an inch and blinked. It registered 7.2 on Naomi's Richter scale.

"Not much to go on," he said after a while. "Kind of hard."

Naomi read the pain clearly. He was hurting.

"What's happening?" she asked softly.

Slowly, he explained his activities on the case over the last ten days.

He had, he said, first gone to the recap sheets. There were no similar crimes during the last six months.

Then he had been able—though the dispatcher had laughed—to get a description of the goat, Grapes, out on the "alarm board," where they normally only describe missing cars.

70

He had also questioned some informants, who also thought it funny.

And finally, today was the sixth day of canvassing restaurants and bodegas in the Bronx to see if any of them had goat meat for sale. All he had met with was a lot of resistance.

To sum up, he wasn't getting anywhere.

"Well," Naomi said after he had finished, "that is difficult. But you can't expect yourself to solve it in just a little while."

"I have to submit reports on it every other day. I think if I don't make progress soon, Captain Bledsoe will take me off the case."

Arnold cut off a piece of one of the four hot dogs on his plate and chewed it. When he was in good spirits he would take a hot dog at a time.

Naomi watched him for a moment, then went back to her own plate.

She was the original Jewish mother, but that's the way she liked it. She wished she could help him, but she didn't really know anything about police work, except what Arnold talked about and what she saw on TV, which Arnold said wasn't true to life.

After supper, instead of playing with the twins as he usually did, Arnold went into the darkened living room and sat down on the couch and watched TV. Watched but did not understand. He did not want to think about being taken off the case, yet he did. He wished he could think of some solution.

He thought back to the day Jiminez told him about the goats, about the thefts, about . . . he could come up with nothing.

Tonight, Naomi left the dishes in the sink and joined him on the couch. She snuggled up to him. She stared at the screen. People were laughing every so often, there was applause—but she wasn't concentrating either.

She wanted to help Arnold. She needed to help him. She concentrated with all her heart and soul. And immediately she had an idea. "Honey," she said, "didn't you say a lot of goats had been stolen on Long Island?"

"Yes. Huntington."

"Maybe the detectives or whatever would have some ideas. I mean since they've dealt with it already."

Arnold said nothing, but he felt a little spurt of excitement. After a short while he said evenly, "It's worth a try."

He didn't tell her that he thought it a great idea. He didn't need to. Naomi knew what he thought. Her seismograph was fully operational.

CHAPTER 15

On a rainy Monday morning in the first week of July, Barbara Babalino, on a day tour, doing busywork—male chauvinist pig work—inside the station, received a call from Joel Gold, an assistant district attorney in Bronx County.

"Good news," he said, "the grand jury returned a true bill on that pimp walker. Class C felony."

"Excellent," Barbara said. "When are they going to rearraign?"

"Tomorrow."

She thought about Laura. "Do you think they'll raise the bail?"

"I'm asking for no bail," Gold said. "This guy's got a sheet which includes assault, assault with a deadly weapon, promoting prostitution, some drug arrests, and attempted murder. Those are the highlights."

"What do you think the judge will do?"

"If we get McElroy—who's supposed to be sitting—no

problem. If we get Andrews or someone else, I don't know. But I'm going to point out that we feel strongly that if he can make bail it will endanger our chief witness against him—our only witness."

"I'll keep my fingers crossed."

"I'll call you as soon as I know."

"Thanks, Joel."

An hour and a half after she had received word of the indictment, Barbara, now in plainclothes and driving an unmarked car, pulled into a parking spot on DeKalb Avenue in Brooklyn. She had taken great pains to insure she wasn't followed. She knew very well that if she was, and Walker found Laura . . . it was not something she wanted to dwell on.

Her destination was two blocks straight ahead on DeKalb, but though it was raining, she walked around the block in a sort of circuitous route, approaching her destination—Howie's Always Tasty Delicatessen—from the other direction.

The street was empty due to the rain, so it was easy to spot anyone behind her. She was not being followed.

There were only a few customers in Howie's. He did some breakfast business in the form of Danish and coffee, but afternoons and evenings were much better.

Laura, dressed in her waitress uniform, was working behind the deli-style counter when Barbara came in. Laura's face lit up when she saw her.

She came out and Barbara gave her a little hug.

"You look good," Barbara said. "How are you doing?"

Laura gave her an impish smile. "Fine," she said. "Though the tips aren't as good."

Barbara laughed. "Have time for coffee?"

Laura nodded. "I'll get it."

Barbara took a seat in a booth near the window. She was not thrilled with the plate-glass window that fronted the store, but as safe areas went, she was quite pleased with it. It was in a quiet residential area, where Walker or his cohorts were not likely to accidentally stumble in.

Laura had gotten a room close to the restaurant, and the restaurant usually had in it Howie Leinoff, a friend from her old neighborhood who was very streetwise.

Laura brought two coffees over and sat down opposite Barbara. Barbara balked at telling her the news, and engaged in small talk about the job and pay and the neighborhood for a few minutes before getting into it. Finally, she did.

"Walker was indicted."

"Good," said Laura. "I hope they execute him."

"It's a Class C felony, what he did to you. He could get fifteen years."

"He deserves more than that," Laura said. She took a pack of cigarettes from her uniform pocket, offered one to Barbara, who refused, and lit up.

"We're going to find out tomorrow," Barbara said, "if he's going to get bail. This DA is going to request no bail."

"Do you think he'll get it?"

"I don't know. There's a good chance."

"I think he could make any bail. He makes a lot of money with his stable. And he had friends."

The streets had toughened Laura, and Barbara just knew, without getting into details, that she had probably survived experiences that would have broken many people. But she was human. She had to be more afraid now than ever. Now there was going to be a trial. Now Walker would intensify his efforts to find her.

Barbara reached across the table and touched Laura's hand. "Would you feel better away from New York? In another state?"

Laura did not answer right away. Before she did, Barbara looked at her in a strange new way. She seemed so much younger and more vulnerable than ever before.

"No," she said. "I'd rather be near you."

Barbara touched her face. Laura swallowed.

"Okay," Barbara said.

Before she left, she told Laura she would contact her as soon as they found out about Walker's bail.

Howie also showed up. She thanked him again for helping Laura. Howie said that she was working out fine.

It had stopped raining by the time she emerged from the delicatessen, and there were a few people on the street. She walked to her car, and for a minute or so had a little paranoid seizure: she thought someone—a middle-aged white guy—was following her. She fantasized that he was a friend of Walker's.

The sheer ridiculousness of it hit her by the time she got in the car, but a little ripple of fear remained. She hoped like hell that Walker would not get bail.

CHAPTER 16

Around seven-forty-five the next morning, Arnold called the Suffolk County Police Headquarters in Yaphank, Long Island. He was told he would have to call back at eight-thirty.

He did. He was then bucked to a series of five people before he got through to the 13th Precinct in Huntington and Police Officer Raymond Sanders, who had, he was told, done the major investigative work on the case.

Arnold identified himself, then said, "I'm looking into the theft of a goat here—the precinct here. And I had heard that you guys had—or you—had done a lot of investigating into a series of goat thefts, and I thought you might be able to help me."

"Why?" Sanders asked. There was an edge in his voice. It was the second word he had uttered all morning (the first was "Yeah" when he answered the phone).

"Well, uh, you handled the case, didn't you?"

There was a silence, but it wasn't empty. Arnold sensed something. Then Sanders spoke.

"I thought you NYPD dudes were the finest. Why you need us country boys?"

Arnold felt hurt, then anger. He said nothing for a moment.

"I . . . I just called for advice. To me police are police all over." It was a little white lie, but he needed Sanders.

"Okay," Sanders said after a while, his voice softer. "We did have some goat thefts. What's the MO?"

Arnold explained, and was honest: he was getting nowhere on the case.

"Well, I don't know if this will help," Sanders said, "but we had eleven goat thefts over eighteen months. The first few, everyone laughed at—who gives a fuck about a goat, you know—but it got serious. All kinds of shit came down—we got all kinds of shit from goody-goody groups.

"We turned out the troops," Sanders continued, "and after a while I saw a pattern."

Arnold felt a little excited.

"In every case except one," Sanders said, "the goats were stolen for the meat."

"What was the one case?"

"Some assholes in Northport stole a goat for a devil ceremony."

Arnold asked a question he was really proud of: "How did you know the goats were stolen for the meat?"

"Weight. The eleven goats were stolen from five farms in the Huntington area. And in every single case, they took the heaviest goat, the one most ripe for becoming steak. Except Northport. Those punks took a skinny goat.

"What's more," Sanders said, "we figured there was no way that whoever was copping the goats could eat all the meat. They had to be selling it somewhere."

Arnold thought that he had figured this out. He was anxious to know how the Suffolk Police approached the problem.

76

"For a while," Sanders said, "we hit restaurants and bodegas around here, but that didn't work, and then we realized that no matter how many guys we had on the job doing busywork, the chance of finding an outlet was almost shit. Not only spics eat goat meat, you know. It's tough, but if you cook it right they say it's delicious, like lamb. You could find it on some millionaire's plate in Southhampton.

"Anyway, we decided to sit on the farms. We got a feeling that whoever was doing this would be back. Because they had come back even after the publicity started. They had balls.

"So one night they did come back, two spics with yellow sheets as long as your arm, and we collared them. They went to the joint for a quite a while."

Arnold was trying to see how any of this could help. Maybe it could, but he couldn't see it.

Sanders broke through his thoughts.

"How big was your goat?"

Arnold tried to remember. He thought Grapes . . . no, Jiminez didn't tell him how big she was . . . yes, he did: "She was the biggest."

"How big are the others?" Sanders asked.

"Big."

"Good. Then they'll probably be back to try get 'em."

"You think so?" Arnold asked. "Why would they be back? Was that part of the pattern or something?"

"If they're like ours, they'll be back."

"Uh, why?" Arnold asked.

"They were addicts," Sanders answered.

The conversation with Sanders gave Arnold hope. Because he knew something about addicts. It was, in fact, why he had made Detective Third Grade.

The incident had occurred about eighteen months earlier. He was in the Six Three, in uniform.

On the occasion, though, he was in plainclothes, on his way home in his car, passing through a side street in Queens.

As he passed in front of an apartment house on a quiet, tree-lined street, he noticed two guys who just didn't seem right. One was a muscular black guy, the other a skinny white guy. They were standing outside an alley, looking around, and just after he went by they disappeared into the alley.

Arnold stopped the car, made a U, and came back. He went down the alley, then into a cellar, going as quietly as he could.

He wasn't too far into the cellar when he heard a metallic sound and then realized what it was. There was a sign to a laundry room. They might be in there trying to get the money out.

It was exactly what they were doing.

Arnold loomed in the doorway, showed his tin, and the black guy, his hands full of coins, became docile. But the white guy didn't. He pulled a blade and went at Arnold, who immediately broke both his arms.

Within a week he had the gold badge. And he learned that this Oreo team had been hitting washing machines and dryers in apartment buildings in the area for months. They had hit the one where they were caught four times previously.

In so doing, they had taken a big chance. But they didn't care. It was the way, one detective explained to Arnold, addicts were. Once they found a gravy train, they rode it until further notice.

Arnold decided to stake out the Jiminez pen. There was, of course, no guarantee that the perps would be back. Or that they were addicts even. But Arnold had high hopes, and the daily report he would write in, the DD 5, would look good.

CHAPTER 17

"Just one announcement today," Sergeant Sam Turner said to the assemblage of cops after the roll call the day following Barbara's visit to Laura.

"Sector Raymond and adjacent sectors, be alert for possible unrest. Nothing may happen, but you never know with these people. Last night there was a birthday party for a man named José Oliver at El DeLuxo Social Club on 174th Street and Anthony Avenue. A fight started over a woman, and shooting started. Four people were killed, including the guy whose birthday it was."

Laughter erupted.

"It would appear," Turner continued, "that they all killed each other. But the homicide squad doesn't know yet, and there might be some revenge plans about."

Turner paused. He scanned the room full of cops.

"The survival tip today was not in the body of knowledge possessed by a female police officer in Philadelphia. You may have read about it.

"She tried to do something that is one of the most difficult things for a man, and even more difficult for a woman, and should only be attempted as a last resort, when no other backup officers are present: she tried to cuff a perp alone. As you may know, the perp got her gun and shot her in the head."

You could cut the silence with a knife.

"The department has a special booklet on how to cuff a perp when you're alone, but it is suggested that you not only read the booklet but practice it with someone playing a perp who wants to get your gun."

He looked a moment more, then limped off.

CHAPTER 18

The day David Walker was arraigned, Judge Frank McElroy had come down with a stomach virus, so Judge Walter Schaufler sat in his place.

Though Assistant DA Gold pleaded, the judge, well known for his liberal leanings, set bail at $100,000. David Walker was on the street within three hours.

The lawyer told him it would be four to five months before the trial, maybe longer. Walker looked at that as time. Time to find that nothin'-ass bitch. And when he did, she wouldn't say nothin' to nobody.

He also figured there was no time like the present. He put the word out that he would pay one large one for her whereabouts.

After a week, nothing had come back, so he decided it would be best if he got into active looking for her. If she got away with it, other bitches would try the same thing.

Also, he might be able to kill two birds with one stone. So far he hadn't gotten a new bitch for his stable, and every day that went by he was losing bread.

He decided to visit joints where there were lots of bitches and where he could rap with the players: maybe she was trying to get into a new stable, though a player would have to be a real chump to take on a bitch who looked like her.

On a Friday night, at around eleven o'clock, he started to pop into the bars in the West Forties in Manhattan. He would sip a little Chivas, rap with the players, inquire as to Laura's whereabouts.

He stayed only a short time in each of the bars, and by two A.M. he had visited seven. It was enough. His own bitches would be comin' in around three, and he would have to be there for the collecting.

He would follow the usual routine which was to wait at Spangles, a topless bar on Webster and Fordham where lots of pimps and their hos gathered.

His Eldorado was parked in a garage on 43rd Street and Ninth Avenue, and as he walked down 42nd Street, he looked at the store windows for something that might suit his fancy.

Then he saw the bookstore. He had an idea—he had made a few scores with it. The newspapers and magazines carried personal ads, and a half-dozen times he had answered them and had turned out a couple of the bitches.

He entered the brightly lit store, which was typical of the Times Square area of New York. It had no back room. The back room was all up front. There were racks and racks of magazines of just about every sexual interaction known to man and woman except bestiality. Publishers didn't mess with this, because the magazines could then not pass Canadian customs, and Canada was a good hunk of the bottom line.

There were current magazines, old magazines, sex newspapers that went back six months. Many of the magazines were in plastic sleeves (so, one cop who patrolled the area said, "the cum could be wiped off easily"). Though it was after two o'clock, the store was crowded, the clientele a mixed bag from Times Square offal to Westchester businessmen. Nobody talked to one another. They just communicated silently with the magazines.

A small, aggressive-looking Hispanic in a guard's uniform complete with nightstick and sidearm stood at the doorway and watched the proceedings.

Walker leafed through a couple of newspapers and wrote down a couple of box numbers. Many of the contacts would be hookers, and he didn't want to tie into one of those, but sometimes he did get a young bitch with relatively little experience, or none. Walker liked to get 'em when they were young. Then he could teach his way.

He drifted over to a large table on which were perhaps fifty stacks of old sex magazines, from *Playboy* to *Punish Me*.

Sometimes there were personals in the magazines, too.

He looked through three or four of the magazines, and then he spotted one called *Big Ones*, with a cover line that caught his eye: "I Was A Part-Time Pimp."

He read a few paragraphs and saw it was talking shit. No way was the dude in the life.

He leafed through the rest of the magazine, stopping to look at pictures of the bitches. He had better-lookin' bitches in his stable.

But he lingered over an eight-page layout of a blond bitch. She was fine-lookin'. In his stable he could almost guarantee she'd pull a grand a night.

Walker moved on through the rest of the magazine, checked out a few more personals, then tossed it down and left, walking east along 42nd Street toward the garage.

He was some fifty yards from the store when he slowed down and stopped. He turned and looked back toward the store, then started walking back rapidly.

CHAPTER 19

On Monday night, a few days after David Walker's arraignment and release, Barbara Babalino lay in bed in her basement apartment on West 72nd Street and thought about Laura. She thought about her a lot. It was now one A.M., and she had been trying to get to sleep since around eleven.

She had called Laura as soon as she found out the bad news. Laura said she would do whatever Barbara wanted her to do. Barbara wanted her to stay put, and she said she was going to. Barbara hoped it was the right thing. She thought about locating Laura out of state, but decided against it.

In fairness, she had also told Leinoff of the development. "You worry too much," he told Barbara. "This guy will never find Laura."

To help insure that, she had lied to everyone about Laura's whereabouts, including—and maybe most of all—Bledsoe. He had a big mouth, and since he didn't care about anyone, he might mention it to the wrong person.

It bothered her, but Barbara also lied to the assistant DA, Joel Gold. She told him—and Bledsoe and her own squad commander—that Laura had gone out of state, and was staying at her aunt's house in Minneapolis.

Barbara did not like lying to colleagues—at least the good ones. But she had seen people get killed because other people talked. It wasn't that people were vicious or stupid, just unaware and careless.

She tried to think of other things, to get her mind off worrying about Laura.

Next Sunday, she thought, she was going to have dinner with her mother, who still lived at the same place in Brooklyn where Barbara had been raised. She only wished Daddy were still alive, but he had died about five years ago. At least he had lived to see her graduate from the Academy. That meant a lot to her—and to him.

Barbara enjoyed the visits to her mother's. She was the only child who still lived in the New York area—an older brother was an engineer who lived in San Francisco, and a younger sister was married and lived in Chicago—so her mother made a big deal of her visiting.

Barbara smiled in the darkness. She figured if she lived to be a hundred, her mother would treat her like a little girl. But that was okay. That was love. She had seen enough of what happened to people without love, particularly in Fort Siberia.

Just yesterday, she thought, a woman had killed herself and a young baby on Creston Avenue. Barbara had seen the "apartment" she had lived in for two years—alone. If she hadn't seen apartments just like it before, it would have defied belief.

The phone rang softly and startled her. She was a cop, and normally you could expect phone calls in the middle of the night, particularly if you were one of the few females in a precinct, but her nerves were on edge.

She picked up the phone, which was on a night table.

"Hello."

"This the poleece lady?" The voice was male, black, sullen.

"What police lady?"

"Bubbalino."

"Yes."

"This is Walker. I want you to meet me, bitch."

"Watch your tongue, cockroach."

"Listen to me, bitch, I say. I want you to meet me about the case. The case against me."

"There's nothing to talk about. You beat a girl half to death, and you're going to prison, where you belong."

"I say: Listen to me. You meet me in a bar, Spangles, up on Webster and Fordham at nine o'clock tomorrow night."

"I'm not going anywhere, except to your trial."

"Don't you want to see the pictures? The pictures I got of you in *Big Ones*, bitch."

Barbara hung up the phone, and she knew immediately, completely, clearly, and coldly, what Walker was going to do: Trade the pictures of her in the magazine for Laura's address. No, Laura's life.

She sat up, flicked on the light.

She had nothing to worry about, right? Consuela Fernandez, another female police officer, had posed in the nude, and the court had ultimately sided with her. If, Barbara thought, she could take being dragged through the media, then she would be fine.

She inhaled sharply.

Not quite.

Right after the hullabaloo about Fernandez erupted, the Department had required everyone to sign a statement—a Statement of Denial of Moral Turpitude, it was officially called—that they had done nothing that could ultimately adversely reflect on the Department. The key provision was not the one about pre-employment morality; it was lying. Lying on that statement, it had been made clear, could result in dismissal.

Barbara opened her eyes. She remembered thinking about what to do, debating it. Working herself into a froth.

She had signed it.

She thought of Walker—his hard, cold eyes.

Her stomach tightened.

He had something on her.

Abruptly she thought of her mother. It might embarrass her a little, but . . . no it wouldn't. Her mother wouldn't care.

Barbara got off the bed and started to pace slowly.

She had thought, hoped, that she had put it all behind her. Put it all in a little room in her mind, closed the door, locked it, and thrown away the key.

Deep down, though, she had always known that maybe one day the door would open.

She closed her eyes, stopped. It wasn't only the posing in the nude, the terrible embarrassment of posing, and of both the "publisher" and the "photographer" trying to screw her—and, she sensed, even the makeup lady.

It was that Jeff, her beautiful Jeff, was also inside that room, and inside it too, were all their dreams.

She sat on the bed, and the door opened. Tears rolled down her cheeks.

But all the dreams had died, and Jeff had died with them. Twenty years old, gone. Jesus, she had loved him since he was seven.

Oh God, she should have been stronger. Stronger for both of them. If only she hadn't gone along with him. If only she had drawn a line and not let him cross, he might be alive.

"Don't blame yourself," a psychologist had said. "You were both very young. It takes a lifetime to learn the simplest things, and even a lifetime isn't enough for some people. You're eighteen. That's hardly a lifetime."

The words were right, and time passed, but the only thing that had helped was locking it away.

And being a cop, a police officer. That had helped too. A lot. When she had been in the audience on graduation day, listening to the police commissioner and the mayor tell her that she could make a difference in the world, she had told herself she still could.

She had made a difference, hadn't she? She would make a difference, wouldn't she?

Right now she was the difference for Laura Hutchens. She had been the difference for other people, too.

But if she was exposed, if it came out, she would be gone. And she wouldn't make a difference to anybody anymore. She would just be seen as a whore and a liar.

She could not see a way out. She could not give up Laura, and she hated the end of her career, and what it meant.

She didn't know what she could do.

CHAPTER 20

The next day at around nine o'clock, Barbara Babalino sat on a banquette of a crowded, smoky diner on Southern Boulevard in the East Bronx, waiting for Joe Lawless.

She did not feel like the coffee in front of her; she did not feel like anything. This was going to be tough in more ways than one.

She had decided to call Lawless sometime in the wee hours of the morning. She needed to talk it over with someone, and she also had come up with an idea that would, perhaps, have Walker facing another charge. She would make sure he went down with her.

But it was going to be tough telling Lawless about it—and what she had done. Still, somehow, she felt that she could, though he had never given her any explicit indication that he would understand. It was just something she sensed.

Since her arrival at Fort Siberia six months earlier, he had asked her out twice, and she had gone out with him both times. He was a good-looking man, though perhaps a little old for her at thirty-seven. But he was polite and soft-spoken.

Both times he had bought her dinner and they had gone to movies they both wanted to see. Both times he had taken her home, but there had been no attempts to get in—anywhere.

She had found herself getting a little interested in him, and had asked what she hoped were a few discreet questions around the station house of other female employees.

She had put together a little biography of him based on scraps of information she had come up with.

He was unmarried—divorced—and did not, as far as she knew, go out with anyone. He lived over in the Pelham Bay section of the Bronx, not too far from where the police firing range was. No one knew exactly why he was at the Five Three; one of the women said he had gotten into a beef with someone at headquarters over one of his men.

He was described as "dedicated" and "hard-driving," and Barbara had once playfully—and deviously—asked one of the men in his squad what kind of boss he was.

"The best," was the answer, plain and simple.

In fact, Barbara had found the two dates a little boring. All Lawless seemed to talk about was police work. Past cases, cases going on. Or he listened—he was a very good listener—to her talk about her favorite things: the lack of justice in the world, the disadvantaged, the obligation that everyone had to each other.

Maybe, she thought, she was a little boring too.

In sum, she had nothing to go on that would indicate he would help, or even could help. It was only something she sensed.

She had managed to take a sip of the coffee and had just put the cup back in the saucer when she saw him come through the door. Quite surprisingly, the sight of him made her feel calm. She knew—*knew*—he was going to help her.

"How are you, Barbara?" Lawless said, slipping into the seat opposite her.

"I've been better," she said, suddenly a little nervous again. "How's the case going?"

"Which one?"

"Baumann."

"Plodding along."

The waitress came over.

Lawless ordered coffee. "Do you want anything else?" he asked.

"I can't even get through this," Barbara said, glancing at the now cold coffee.

"Okay," he said when the waitress left. "What's the problem?"

She looked straight into his powder-blue eyes. "I'm going to be blackmailed," she said softly, "by a pimp."

Lawless said nothing.

"This all started," Barbara said, " a few months ago, when I got involved with a prostitute named Laura Hutchens. . . ."

She explained what had happened to Laura, the indictment, the safe area—she told Lawless precisely where Laura was—and as she recounted it, she realized she was putting off the inevitable. She summed up the last part of the story, then got to the bomb.

"Nine years ago," she said, "I posed in the nude for a girlie magazine . . . and . . . and I lied on a moral turpitude form we were all required to sign after the Fernandez case. I did it to get some money for my husband."

She paused, then continued. "I'd rather not give you the name of the magazine. No, I'll give you the name. It was *Big Ones*. Anyway, this pimp has apparently gotten hold of a copy. Last night he called me and told me he wants to see me."

"Why did your husband need money?"

"Because . . ." Barbara said, and found herself filling up. "Could we talk outside?"

"Sure."

Lawless dropped some money on the table and they left. They walked away from the diner, down the street, past some ravaged buildings.

"Because," she said, "he had become a drug addict. And one time we were living in a roach-infested apartment that wasn't like in Siberia but was bad enough, and we didn't have any money for days, and he begged me, and I had been stopped on the street by a photograper and given a card. The result was a hundred twenty-five dollars—seventy-five of it went for horse."

"How did he get into heroin?"

"God knows. Smoke a little marijuana, pop a few pills. You know the syndrome." She paused, then continued. "He was a solid guy once. In the Peace Corps. We even had plans to work in Appalachia. I honest to God don't know, though, how or why it happened. It just happened."

"Where is he now?"

"He's dead."

"What happened?"

"He got some bad stuff. Maybe he was just too delicate for this world. I don't know."

Tears suddenly streamed down her face.

"What a fucking world, huh, Joe Lawless?"

Lawless put his arms around her. She sensed stiffness, but it was better than nothing. Much better.

After a while they walked over to what was once

technically known as a park. Now, though, in mid-July, none of the grassy areas had grass, almost all the slats were gone from the concrete-based benches, and all the playground equipment had been removed except the monkey bars, which actually had been bent into a parallelogram shape.

They sat down delicately on a bench with two consecutive slats. Lawless lit a cigarette and offered Barbara one, which she refused.

"You said you had an idea, Barbara," Lawless said. He inhaled deeply.

"Yes, I thought I could wear a wire to my meeting with this pimp. Then we could get him for a Class C and attempted blackmail. I want to put him away for a long, long time. I know I'm going down the old tube, but he's got to pay the price."

"Why do you think your career's going down the tube?"

"The circumstances are a lot like when Consuela Fernandez was fired. Except worse, because I lied about it."

"That's not why she was fired."

"Why, then?"

"She embarrassed the brass. It was a vindictive act."

"She had a trial and everything."

"You mean the departmental hearing? That's not a trial. That's a kangaroo court. You get one hearing officer who's employed by the commissioner, right? He does what the PC wants, pure and simple. You know what the conviction rate of this 'court' is?"

Barbara shook her head.

"About ninety-nine percent. Compare that to a regular court."

Barbara nodded, but she was a little confused.

"I don't understand, Joe. How can you ask why I think my career's going down the tube if you know all this? You think maybe because my case is different, because I had a better reason to pose?"

"No," Lawless said. "That certainly could be a factor, but it depends on the political currents down at headquarters at the time—remember, they don't care about anybody but themselves—but I doubt you'd do well. What I was thinking of was talking to the pimp.''

Barbara looked at Lawless, her face expressionless. She was incredulous. ''Why would he do anything? He's a vicious guy. Tough, street guy. He almost killed Laura.''

''I can talk with him, tell him that if he doesn't do anything he'll be better off. If he does, we'll hassle him.''

''You think that will be enough? He's looking at seven-and-a-half to fifteen.''

''I'd like to try. It would mean you'll have to give up the blackmail thing.''

''Sure.''

''An extra charge is not enough to sacrifice your career for,'' Lawless said, dropping his cigarette on the earth and grinding it out. ''Anyway,'' he said, looking at her, ''we can't afford to lose police officers like you.''

Barbara felt the urge to kiss him, but held back. There was that thin, invisible wall. ''When will you speak with him?''

''When are you supposed to meet him?''

''Tonight, Spangles Bar on Webster and Fordham at nine o'clock.''

''I know it. I'll go in your place.''

''Do you want me to go with you?''

''No, that's all right.''

They stood up.

''I don't know what to say, Joe.''

He shook her hand and smiled. ''See you later.''

He turned and left. He had only touched her hand. But she had felt a different physiological reaction elsewhere.

CHAPTER 21

Sabrina Cole, David Walker's bottom woman, sat at the kitchen table of the Webster apartment Walker kept for his hos. She was sipping straight bourbon. A little dribbled from the corner of her mouth. Her eyes misted.

Sabrina had been drinking since around noon, after Walker had left to deck out his new ho, a little piece of white trash that he had just caught yesterday.

Sabrina was drunk, and she knew that when Walker got back he was going to beat her, maybe bad. He didn't want his hos doing anything that would interfere with their ability to turn tricks.

Yeah, she thought, the motherfucker was going to beat her, but she was going to kill him.

She wiped an eye clear of a tear, took a sip of the bourbon. How many times, she thought, had he talked shit to her?

"Oh yeah, baby," he told her. "You my special lady. I pay no mind to those hos. I don't care nothin' 'bout them. You my bottom lady."

She sipped the bourbon.

Four years. That's how long she had been on the stroll for him.

It took a long time, but she had figured out the numbers just today. She figured she turned six or seven tricks a night, at around $40 each. $1,680 a week, say 340 days a year. In four years, it came to around $381,000, all of which she had given him.

She drained the glass and refilled it.

She had been through a lot for him. In prison, in the

hospital, seven abortions, had helped him catch so many other ladies, and twice she had almost been wasted by freaks.

"You my lady," he said, over and over. "You my lady. Got it saved up for you. Goin' set you up good when your strolling days are over."

She didn't mind the little lies he told her. That she was the finest-lookin' lady in his stable, that she was the only one made him cum when he chippy, that he absolutely did not know what he would do without her.

This she could take. It was the big lie that got her. Because it told her once and for all that 'he was a motherfucker.

For a long time she had asked him just how much he had put away for her, and he kept putting her off.

Today, when he left, she searched for the bankbook, and found it.

He had started putting money in it four years ago. Never put much in, never took much out. The balance was $98.50.

It was the big lie.

What could she do? She was almost thirty, and she had been on the street since she was twelve—more than eighteen years. She was not the looker she once was. She had trouble keeping her weight down, and Spandex could do only so much. She sagged a little.

She was scared. That motherfucker didn't care. Someday he would just throw her away. She had seen it done. Just two weeks ago. A girl named Twinkie. She got too old. David just threw her out. Sabrina heard she had died.

Her eyelids dipped. He would be home soon. She would have to get off the booze now to be able to do something.

She capped the bourbon, then woozily walked to the kitchen cabinets and put it away. She rinsed the glass and put it away.

She listened for the sound of the front door opening.

Nothing. She opened the cutlery drawer, took out the ice pick, and closed the drawer.

She walked slowly into the living room, ice pick in hand, and sat down on the couch. She slipped the ice pick between cushions.

She blinked slowly.

Across from the couch were two paintings, in beautiful Day-Glo colors on black velvet, that she had given him, one of a tiger, the other a leopard—he really liked the leopard one. She had saved up from money he had given her to buy them special.

Tears formed. Motherfucker, she thought. Come on home.

Then she waited, listening for the scratch of his key in the door.

Fifteen minutes later, she fell asleep.

Sabrina awoke. Her neck hurt. She realized, as she opened her eyes, that she had been sleeping in a bad position.

Blearily, she became aware that someone was looming above her, looking down. It was David. His eyes were hard. The new ho stood behind him.

"You been boozin'," he said.

Fear cut through the booze. She was aware of the ice pick. If she tried to stick him and missed, he would waste her.

"I had a few drinks, honey," she said, her mouth feeling like it was full of mush.

David reached down, grabbed her by the hair with his left hand, and pulled her up off the couch. He slammed her face so hard with an open right hand she saw stars. Then he slammed her again and let her drop to the floor in a heap. He stood above her and stripped off a thick leather belt.

"Oh, baby, please, no!"

"I like my hos straight," he said, his voice lowering. "Dig?"

Then he was at her with the belt, his arm flailing wildly. She screamed in pain. The other ho looked on in terror.

94

CHAPTER 22

Hard-driving rock music hammered through the closed doors of Spangles Nite Club on Fordham and Webster Avenue in the Bronx. Outside, a small, animated Hispanic in a spangled tuxedo exhorted passersby to come inside into the air-conditioned club for music, drinks, and topless dancing—"the most beautiful girls in the Bronx."

The streets were as alive as inside the club. It was a hot night, getting hotter, and people had started to pour out of their apartment houses at around six P.M., seeking relief from the heat—and the grinding, humdrum pettiness of their lives. They played dominoes under street lamps, drank Colt 45 and wine and whiskey, smoked grass, popped pills, snorted coke, mainlined, made love on rooftops and in alleyways, and jabbered and listened to the driving repetitiveness of their music, a cacophony of piano, cowbells, and trumpets.

Later, when the booze and pills and whatever took effect, there was sure to be violence, and someone—maybe more than one person—would be hurt badly, maybe killed. Then the package would be complete: classic Fort Siberia.

The pimps who gathered in Spangles parked their cars—Cadillacs and Porsches and BMWs—as close to the front entrance as possible and paid a Puerto Rican kid twenty bucks to watch them.

On the parapet of the one-story building were colored Par lights, which highlighted the club and helped the kid watch the cars better. Around this orbit of light was relative darkness.

Lawless came out of the darkness. He looked like a tourist out to have a good time. He was dressed in slacks and loafers and had on a colorful short-sleeve shirt worn loose over his belt line.

He had ridden an unair-conditioned bus down Fordham, then made the short walk to the club. He was a little sweaty. He went past the barker and into the club. It felt like a refrigerator.

Music pumped. It was so loud he could feel it vibrating in his lungs. To his right, on a platform, a topless girl gyrated wildly to the music. Many eyes watched her.

Straight ahead was a dance floor. Through the crowd he saw an L-shaped bar along the walls in back, though it was not simple to see in the light, which was a sort of murky red. Clustered along the bar were garishly dressed pimps and prostitutes.

He waited a moment, getting a fix. In the back was an exit door. There were more pimps sitting at tables.

He started to move through the crowd toward the bar. Just as he did, the music abruptly stopped and a deejay with a Spanish accent said they'd be back in five.

Lawless scanned the faces of the pimps. He had pulled Walker's mug shots, but all the pimps wore hats and such flashy clothing they tended to look alike.

Then he saw him. Near the middle of one leg of the bar, facing the crowd with what looked like a joint in one hand and a drink in the other.

He was dressed, Lawless thought, like a Mexican rhinestone cowboy, complete with leather pants, boots, a two-tone western-style shirt, and a sombrero. He was tall and wiry with lots of jewelry on his fingers. Flanking him, sitting on stools and facing the bar, were two hookers, one white and the other black.

Walker was just looking, not talking. There was no way to tell who at the bar might be his friend. Lawless assumed everyone.

Lawless went up and stood in front of him. Walker was a little taller.

96

"Are you the pimp," Lawless said, "waiting for Barbara Babalino?"

"Who you talkin' to, honky motherfucker?"

"You. I'm Lawless from the Five Three. I'm here in her place."

"I ain't talkin' to no messenger boy," he said, and sipped his drink.

"Whatever," Lawless said. "Don't use the magazine against her. If you do, I'll have you killed."

"What the fuck you talkin' 'bout?"

"If you use the magazine against her—or if you make it public—the next day I'll make a call to a dick I know in a midwestern city. He will fly in in the morning, put two in your head, and be back home having dinner with his family while your coon cadaver is on a gurney in Bellevue being opened up with a Black and Decker."

Walker managed half a smile, a hunch of his shoulders that said, "Bullshit," but Lawless read his eyes. They believed.

Lawless turned and made his way through and around the crowd. Walker watched him go. He drained the drink and took a deep hit on the joint. His insides were awry.

One of the hookers flanking Walker was Sabrina Cole. Her face was expressionless, but she had heard it all. That white boy had made that nigger into a punk.

She sucked on her cigarette—carefully: she had to. Her lips were swollen, and there were cuts on the inside of her mouth, damage from the beating Walker had given her.

She had seen the magazine. He had been laughing about the cop lady. Sabrina only wished Walker would use it. He would be wasted. That's exactly what the motherfucker deserved.

Joe Lawless had to walk three blocks before he found a phone that worked. In Fort Siberia, there weren't many left.

He dialed Barbara Babalino's number.

She picked up after the first ring.

"Joe Lawless, Barbara. I talked to Walker. Everything's going to be fine. He's not going to use the magazine."

"No?"

"He doesn't want any hassle."

There was a little silence.

"Thank you, Joe . . . I . . ."

"No thanks necessary. Like I said, you're a good cop. And we need every good cop we have."

Barbara could hardly talk. "Thank you."

"You're welcome."

CHAPTER 23

Fifteen minutes after Lawless called her, Barbara got the idea. It was something her mother used to do for people who had done her a favor, who she especially liked, or just to give the family a treat. It was to make "Lasagna Knocka You Socks Off."

Happily, she started to prepare it, and as she did she remembered being in the kitchen with her mother. She must have been twelve or thirteen, and the room was filled with the wonderful aroma of the dish. Her mother told her how it came to be.

"You know, Barb," her mother had said, "everyone thinks that Julius Caesar was murdered by members of the Senate because of political reasons. But that wasn't it at all. 'Lasanga Knocka You Socks Off' is why. He wouldn't share the recipe with them."

Barbara grinned, remembering how funny she thought that was.

It was a complicated recipe, but she knew it by heart. The Babalinos had found many people to be thankful to, and many people to like, and they were a family that demanded its quota of treats.

It was years since she had prepared it. In fact, the last time she had made it was during her days with Jeff. Maybe that was why she hadn't made it in such a long time. It reminded her of him. Although it was also a fact that it contained about half a million calories per forkful, and—she laughed to herself—she didn't want to be carrying her breasts around in a wheelbarrow!

As she cut up some vegetables—a cucumber, of course! —she wondered if he was going to think her too forward. Probably. So what! It was the way she felt. She smiled. "Lead with your heart, Barbara," her mother had told her. "You'll get hurt sometimes, but you'll recover quickly."

That's what she was doing. Leading with it, because her heart told her that she was starting to feel something for Lawless.

She was grateful, but this definitely went beyond grateful.

One day she was in despair, about to see everything go down the tube, and the next he had just come out of nowhere to help her. No big deal. He was just there.

Maybe it was his strength she was relating to. She had loved Jeff very much, but there were so many times when she secretly had longed for him to be stronger, times when she had felt so weak herself.

Maybe it was his physical attractiveness. Battered good looks, tight, wiry body with such nice buns. Yeah, she had certainly noticed his body, and thinking about it now made her nipples feel a little sensitive against the fabric of her brassiere.

But there was something else. She sensed something deep about him, something that went beyond his poker face and his wry smile and those beautiful soft-yet-somehow-hard eyes.

Maybe it was everything. She didn't know. She just

99

knew that by his single act, Lawless had released things in Barbara that she had not even known were there.

She wondered if he had feelings toward her. She hoped so, but he was so withdrawn. Not aloof, just held-back. Why he was like that, she didn't know. Whatever, it was in diametric opposition to her.

Certainly she was not madly in love with him. Maybe it was just a physical thing. That wouldn't be too bad. It had been over a year since she had had sex with anyone. Wouldn't the boys at the office be shocked, she thought.

An hour and a half after she started preparing the dinner, Barbara called Lawless. He should be in, she thought. He was working days—then again, he was working that murder. Maybe he wasn't in. Maybe there was a girl there. Maybe . . .

"Hello."

It was Lawless.

"Hi, Joe. Barbara. I was just thinking of a way to particularly pay you back for your help and I came up with it."

"How's that?"

"I'm cooking a meal for you. It's called 'Lasagna Knocka You Socks Off.' All you have to do is show up tomorrow night at seven o'clock."

"I can't," Lawless said. "I'm on the Baumann squeal."

"How about the day after?"

"I'll still be busy."

It was time, Barbara thought, to back off. Baloney.

"I already made it. It won't keep forever. Please come," she said, and thought, Lead with your heart.

There was a deafening pause.

"You're tough," Lawless said. "Should I bring anything?"

Barbara was elated. "A big appetite. Seven o'clock."

She hung up and looked at the phone. She felt things moving, shifting inside herself. She had not felt like that about a man since Jeff.

CHAPTER 24

Most New York City cops have built up a thick skin when it comes to shocking experiences, and therefore don't react to most cases they come upon. Or, if they do, the reaction is internal and a mask is presented to the world.

Joe Lawless was better at not reacting than most cops not only because of the development of a skin over the years but because of a natural reticence to show any feelings. Thousands of maggots at work—noisily—on a cadaver? No problem. Listen to a contract killer relate—while he eats a salami-and-onion sandwich—how he cut his girlfriend's throat "ear to ear like a deer"? No problem. Watch an autopsy on a baby? All right.

But when Barbara Babalino opened the door when he showed for dinner the next night, the mask dropped. He blinked. He was stunned. On the two dates she had dressed rather conservatively, and around the station she wore the female version of the bag men wore. He had never seen her like this.

She was awesome. An apron partially covered a tight-fitting low-cut white dress which clearly showed why her nickname was "Towers of Babalino." Her lustrous black hair was piled up on her head, and her makeup accentuated dark lovely eyes.

She smiled warmly and said hello softly and stepped deeper into the apartment so Lawless could pass inside. All he could manage was a nod and a plastic smile as he went past her.

He went down a short hall, registering the fact that

there was a small kitchen off the hall to his left, a bath to his right. There was a strong smell of Italian cooking.

The hall terminated in a living room. Against the right wall was a couch and glass-topped coffee table; on the wall were bookcases. The far wall had windows and a door with windows in it which looked out on what seemed to be a small garden; against this wall was a set-up dinner table. Against the left wall was a large platform bed.

He went into the living room. Barbara came up beside him and looked up at him. Her eyes did things to his stomach, but he had been able to regain his poker face.

"What'll it be? I have red wine, beer, scotch, rye—well, you name it."

"Red wine's good."

"Coming up," Barbara said.

She left, and despite trying not to, he watched her go. It was worth it.

While he waited, Lawless checked out the bookcase. There were some novels and popular nonfiction books, but most were tomes on psychology, sociology, and police work—just the kind of thing he would expect from a good cop like Barbara. To her it was part of becoming a better cop.

She returned with a pair of glasses and the wine. She had removed the apron, and her physical presence was even more impacting.

She handed Lawless a glass, then filled it and her own. She put the bottle down on the coffee table.

Her eyes glistened, and for a moment Lawless thought she was crying. Maybe she was.

She raised her glass. "To Joe Lawless, who saved me."

Lawless was touched, but all he did was smile a little. "Like I said, you're a good cop, Barbara. You deserve it."

She came over and kissed him lightly on the lips. "Thank you," she said.

He looked at her and nodded. He hoped he could

retain his cool. Her lips were incredibly soft, and it had been a long time since he had been kissed like that.

"The lasagna should be ready in fifteen minutes or so. Why don't we booze it up for a while?"

Barbara sat at one end of the couch, which was not that long, and Lawless sat at the other.

He was, she thought, shy, reserved . . . no, even more than that: he was afraid of her. Yes, she had not really seen that before, maybe because around the precinct he had a reputation for fearlessness.

But she was well aware that a relationship between a man and woman could be a whole different thing. She was a little afraid herself.

"How's the Baumann case coming?"

"Still routine. Talking to friends, relatives, school administrators, teachers, etcetera."

"Any leads?"

"The murdered girl could lead us somewhere. It turns out she was promiscuous from a very early age—we've nailed down eleven. She was into marijuana, pills—no heroin or coke as far as we can tell. She was rebellious and got into a lot of trouble when she was in school. She was suspended twice."

"Do the parents know anything?"

"Not really. We know more than them. We found out they've both been working since she was about eight. She's more or less been on her own. I mean, she would come home to an empty house, make her own supper sometimes, that kind of thing."

"How terrible," Barbara said.

"Yeah," Lawless said. "I find a lot of kids who get in trouble raised like that. Then the parents wonder why they get in trouble."

"Her father's cold," Barbara said. "I was glad I came that day."

"Maybe," he said, "he was just trying to hold himself together."

Barbara said nothing, but she didn't agree. Once, just before the viewing shade went up, her eyes had met

Baumann's. His eyes were lifeless; gray had struck her as such a good color for them.

Barbara refilled their glasses.

"We're also pursuing a rope angle," he said.

"Yes, I remember someone saying she was tied up."

"Elaborately," Lawless said. "But the guy who did it had to learn it from somewhere. We're trying to find out where. And," he added, "there are the hands. All the fingers were taped together—we're trying to find out what it all means."

"How so?"

Lawless explained how Mary Baumann was bound. Barbara listened attentively, but part of her was being distracted by the way he looked. He wore a tight-fitting polo shirt and tight denim pants, and when he moved his arms the muscles worked under the skin. At one point she felt her nostrils almost flare.

"Also," he said, "we found a blond pubic hair on the girl—not hers. All we need is a suspect to match it to."

"I know you'll get him," Barbara said. "I have a feeling you're very determined."

"We'll see."

"Hungry?"

Lawless nodded. Indeed he was. Today his diet had varied. Instead of a couple of donuts and a cup of coffee he had had coffee and a buttered roll. And a slice of pizza—washed down with coffee, at around two.

"I'll get the stuff."

"Need any help?"

"I'll holler if I do."

Lawless watched her go. Her sensuality was starting to affect him, overpower him. Maybe, he thought, I should cool it on the wine. So he promptly poured himself a refill.

A few minutes later Barbara emerged from the kitchen with a steaming tray of lasagna.

Lawless stood up as she put it down on the table. It looked and smelled delicious.

"I guess I could use your help," she said. Her eyes went directly into his stomach.

Between the two of them they brought things from the kitchen—antipasto and bread and vegetables and salads and more wine . . . and more. When they were finished there was barely enough room for a lone candle. Barbara lit it.

They sat down at the opposite ends of the table and dug in. After five minutes, time for the lasagna to cool enough so Lawless could get a good taste of it, Barbara asked, "How is it?" She was not smiling. She had any good cook's concern for her creation.

Lawless said, deadpan: "Knocka you socks off."

Barbara laughed.

They ate mostly in silence. It was delicious, Lawless thought, the best meal he had had in ten years.

"Great," he said a couple of times. He continued to drink the wine. Barbara occasionally glanced at him eating. She loved the sight of it.

"Are you a native New Yorker?" Barbara asked at one point. "You sound like it."

"I was born and raised in Brooklyn."

"No kidding. I'm from Brighton Beach. You know, the Irish Riviera. Where are you from?"

"Where I'm from is gone. They call it Bedford-Stuyvesant now."

"Oh, that's sad."

"*Sic transit gloria mundi.*"

"Thus pass all the glories of this world."

"You got it."

While the coffee was brewing, Barbara got down to some serious questioning. She didn't want it to sound like an interrogation, but she wanted to know him in a personal, deep way, the way she wanted to know everyone who mattered in her life.

"Have you always wanted to be a cop?" she asked.

"It runs in the family. My father walked a beat for thirty-six years."

"No kidding! Is he still alive?"

Lawless shook his head.

"Both my parents are dead."

"Oh, I'm sorry."

Lawless said nothing.

"What," Barbara asked, "was your mother like?"

"Nice," Lawless said, sipping the wine, "really nice."

"How about your father?"

"Hard. I guess you might say he had the personality of a coal miner. Never complain, just keep going, never give up, determined. He was a very good cop, I'd say. Reserved, too. Very reserved."

Barbara would have loved to pursue that, but she let it drop. To push it, she sensed, would have been a mistake. "Were you in the war and all?"

"Vietnam. Three years."

"That's a long time."

Lawless had been looking out through one of the windows when she mentioned Vietnam. He looked at her. She had never seen his eyes softer. For a hair-raising moment, she thought she was looking into the eyes of Jeff when he was young.

"You learn too much about the limits—or the lack of limits—of human deceit. And you take your graduate studies in the Police Department."

"You think so?"

Lawless nodded. "It's not that anybody's bad. It's just that one thing leads to another when someone is trying to save his pension. Things get lost—things that matter most get lost along the way."

"Like what?"

"Basic things. Integrity, loyalty, why you got into the job in the first place. The only thing that matters is money coming in the mail every month when you get older. You live for tomorrow, not today. Don't you see that?"

"I guess I do," Barbara said. "It just seems kind of nutty to me that the same cop who will walk with relative cool down a dark alley where a perp with a knife is

106

waiting will tremble when the PC or any brass calls him in."

Lawless said nothing.

"How did you get transferred to Fort Siberia?" Barbara asked.

"I had a fistfight."

"That's all?"

Lawless smiled a little. The wine was loosening him up.

"It was with the assistant chief of Manhattan North."

Barbara giggled. "Oh? What over?"

Lawless took a sip of the wine. "He flopped a member of my squad back to uniform for a spiteful reason."

"It was lucky he didn't flop you."

"Lucky for who?" Lawless said. "How about you?" he asked. "How did you become a cop?"

"After Jeff I had a number of jobs. I got into social work, but I just felt I wasn't contributing that much. So I decided to take the police exam."

"How long you been on the job?"

"Five years."

"How'd you get to the Five Three?"

A look of distaste passed across her face. "My CO tried to put the make on me—twice. The second time I slapped him in the face—and was immediately transferred."

"Did you fight it?"

Barbara shook her head. "It would have been to the death. And he had a family and all."

"You should have. He's no good. He'll do it to somebody else."

Barbara couldn't deny it. But she was not sorry for what she did.

"Can I enlist your aid," she said, "in clearing dishes?"

"Sure."

He helped her clear them; he liked the feeling of working with her.

Barbara then served strawberry shortcake—which she had made from scratch—and coffee.

They ate in silence, and as they did, something disturbing occurred to Lawless. He started to remember those first days when he had met Karen, and the aching need he had for her. It was a part of him that had been closed for years. It was why he didn't want to come. He should not have come.

He finished the last of his coffee and set the cup in the saucer. He glanced at his watch. It was close to nine, dark.

"I'd better be going soon," he said. "I have an eight-to-four."

It grabbed Barbara in the stomach. She was deeply disappointed, and made no attempt to hide it.

"Can't you stay a while longer? Have a drink. Live a little."

He hesitated a moment. The wine was starting to really nail him. But one more wouldn't hurt him, and he was traveling by subway.

"Okay," he said.

"More wine?"

"Okay."

He watched her leave the room—he wondered about the wisdom of his staying.

She returned with a new bottle and two glasses. There was a funny playful look in her eyes, he thought. Or was there? His mind wasn't at peak efficiency.

She filled the glasses. She took a small sip, then got up and went over to the stereo near the bookcases.

"You like Sinatra?" she asked.

Lawless nodded. He sipped the wine. His stomach was moving a little.

She put on "Strangers in the Night," the volume low.

Barbara went over to the windows. In turn, she pulled each of the blinds.

"This place is like a goldfish bowl at night," she said.

Lawless felt his stomach tightening.

She went to the bathroom, and returned a couple of minutes later. He swallowed. She had let her hair down.

108

He had never seen her with her hair down, in the precinct or on the two dates he had been on with her.

It was luxurious, and softly waved; it went halfway down her back. It gave her a wild beauty that almost made her seem like a different woman. Two words came to mind: "Jesus Christ."

She went to the table but did not sit. Instead, she took off first one high heel, then the other, trained her beautiful eyes on Lawless, grabbed his hand, and pulled him up.

"Let's dance," she said softly.

A moment later they were on the polished wood floor, dancing slowly, the soft, mellow sound of Sinatra enveloping them.

She danced very close, her arms wrapped around his body. A couple of times his thigh went between her legs and she made no effort to pull back; in fact, she pressed harder.

There was no way, he thought, she could not feel the increased beating of his heart.

And she was, he knew, coming on very strong. He had known from the moment she gave him a playful look that she was trying to seduce him.

He fought it, trying to relax, but halfway through the song he started to realize he was getting hard—and then her thigh brushed against his penis—and stayed there.

He should leave, he thought, get out now. He did not want any involvement, he did not . . .

She stopped moving and took his face in her hands, pulled it gently down to her, and kissed him.

Her tongue was inside his mouth, and he felt her breasts, harder it seemed, her thighs. He felt himself growing harder and bigger and he slid his hands along her back and then out, following the sharp curve of her behind. He grabbed hold of her there and felt his resistance totally crumble.

They were near a wall switch. She reached over and flicked it off. The room went into darkness except for the flickering candle.

Her hands were on him, and he felt himself being unzipped and unbuttoned, and he helped her undress him.

They moved over to the bed, and he sat down on it and leaned back and she pulled off his pants, then his underwear. He was totally erect, quivering with desire.

She remained standing and peeled off her dress, slipped out of her panties, then unhooked and removed her bra. Lawless could feel his heart hammering inside him.

She stood for a moment in the soft, flickering light, as if to prolong it just a little more, then she was down on the bed next to him and without any warning her mouth was all over him, licking and sucking at him loudly.

As she did, without taking her mouth off him, she slowly positioned herself until her thighs straddled his face.

It occurred to Lawless, through a wave of rising pleasure and lust, that Karen had never sucked him, or he Karen. He was thinking that as Barbara lowered herself onto his face and he did not resist, then he was at her with his mouth in a frenzy.

A few minutes later he was on top of her, inside her, kissing her, probing gently with his hands, their bodies moving in unison.

There was no verbal communication, but their bodies understood, and they held back as long as they could, and then it happened, wonderfully and shudderingly, and at that moment Lawless felt something he had not felt with anyone else in his life except Karen; he and Barbara were one, and he did not know where her body began and his left off.

Later, he cradled her head in his arm.

"I'm pretty good, I think, at hiding my fear of you," she said. "But I see yours. Why are you afraid of me?"

There was no instinct to lie. Not now, not at this moment. He simply told her. "I don't want to get involved. You're the type of woman I could get involved with."

"Why not?"

110

"Ten years ago," Lawless said, "I got married. It didn't last—and it left me in shreds."

Lawless hardly recognized the words he had uttered, the honesty. It was something he had buried in ice such a long time ago.

"What happened?" Barbara said. "If it's not too painful to talk about."

"Her name was Karen," Lawless said. "I met her while I was taking some criminalistics courses at John Jay. We went out for about a year and then got married. The marriage lasted nine months.

"In the beginning," he continued, starting to feel those feelings of so long ago, "she thought it very romantic and exciting that I was a cop. And I sure liked her. Very dedicated—she taught exceptional children."

He paused now, remembering it all fully.

"I guess," he said softly, "in our own way we were going to help change the world, or maybe just make it a better place. She would help those who couldn't help themselves, and so, in a way, would I.

"I guess I should have known better. I had been to Vietnam. I knew how things could get turned around, but . . .

"Anyway," he went on, "I made plainclothes shortly after we married, and I worked very long hours. And there were all these unwelcome surprises, and quite a few missed dinners. You know how it is."

Barbara nodded.

"We had some arguments—she said she couldn't stand being a cop's wife, and I told her that it was the way it would always be. I didn't want to give her any baloney.

"She just burned out—became like a lot of cops' wives—and one day she told me she was leaving. I didn't know what to say. To say I'd change or the job would change would be a lie. So she left.

"The problem was I still loved her."

The statement hung in the flickering light, and Barbara knew Lawless was remembering what it was like.

She lifted herself up on one elbow and kissed him on the mouth, then snuggled back in his arm.

"You're right, Barbara," Lawless said. "I'm spooked by you. Because for the first time in years I remembered"—and he said it softly so she almost didn't hear it—"what it was like to be in love. And to lose it."

"Joe," Barbara said, "you're not alone. I'm afraid too. I remember love too, and you know what it must have been like to see someone you love become addicted, and to lose him. But I have to let my feelings go, follow them wherever they take me. And you have to, too."

"Why's that?"

"If you don't, you'll regret it. I know that deep in my heart. Everybody gets burned, but the big sorrows in life come when you don't take a chance, and you always regret what might have been. It's what might have been that causes most of the sorrow in the world."

"You're right," Lawless said.

And then he thought of the years after Karen. There was a girl here or there that he felt drawn to a little, but he never tried to make anything happen. He just, he thought, would rather take his walks down dark alleys.

But as much as he avoided involvement, there had always been a part of him that said: someday he would take another chance.

Someday.

If not now, when?

He turned his head and kissed Barbara gently on the mouth.

CHAPTER 25

The plain manila envelope was addressed in printing that was barely readable. Michael Murphy, the police officer in charge of the mailroom who saw it first, was surprised it even got there. It was addressed, he finally figured out:

POLEECE
INTURNAL AFFEARS
23RD & PINEE STRE. ST.
BROOKLYN, NY

Murphy logged it in at Monday morning, 10:11 hours, July 23.

Since there was no individual's name on the package, Murphy didn't know who to route it too. So he carefully slit it open and withdrew the contents. His pupils dilated with interest.

It was a girlie magazine called *Big Ones*. There was a slutty-looking spic on the cover with huge tits and a come-hither look. The cover line promised a number of filthy stories which he would have liked to get a peek at, but it was not the place to be caught glomming a girlie magazine.

There was a slip of paper stapled to the front cover. It said: "See p. 72."

Murphy opened the magazine to page 72. On it was a nude blond with very big tits. She was sitting on her haunches leering out. Above her was the title: "Blonds Have More Buns."

There was something scrawled across the tits in felt-tip marker that he simply couldn't read, try as he might.

He leafed through the following pages. On page 73 she was joined by another blond, and on that and the other pages they were doing dirty things to each other. The first blond had dark hair but had dyed it, because Murphy noted that her pubic hair was black. She was very good-looking.

Murphy went back to page 72, studied the writing, and finally made it out—and his pulse spurted. It said, "This a cop. Bubbalino. 53 pct. Ck it out."

Murphy replaced the magazine in the envelope and went out of the mailroom and down the hall to the office of his immediate supervisor, Sergeant Dick Mulligan.

Murphy tapped on the open door and went inside. Mulligan, a neatly dressed man in his fifties, in plainclothes, sat behind a plain gray metal desk in the small neat room, only a few papers on the desk.

Murphy handed him the envelope.

"This just came in the mail, Sergeant," Murphy said. "I thought you should see it right away."

Mulligan took the magazine out of the envelope.

There were no lines on his rather handsome face, except one, a single crease that ran from the tip of his nose to his full, gray hairline and which became visible when he became disturbed. Now the crease showed as he looked at the cover, page 72, and the following pages, and, as Murphy had, strained to read the writing across the blond's breasts.

"It says," Murphy said: "This a cop. Bubbalino. Fifty-third Precinct. Check it out."

"Thanks, Murph," Mulligan said, the crease suddenly as deep as it could get.

Murphy nodded seriously, but inside he glowed. He liked to get on Mulligan's good side whenever he could.

The crease remained after Murphy left. Mulligan lifted the receiver of his phone and punched out an interoffice number. It rang in the reception area of an office upstairs. It was the office of Deputy Commissioner Ralph

LaPalma, who was chief of the Internal Affairs Division and all FIDU units, undercover operatives within precincts whose job it was to monitor and report on any malfeasance by police officers.

"Commissioner LaPalma's office," his male secretary answered.

"This is Sergeant Mulligan. I have to see the commissioner right away."

"He's all tied up for the day, Sergeant."

"We may have another Fernandez affair."

"Hold on."

A short while later, LaPalma came on the line.

"What have you got, Sergeant?"

"Sir, we received an envelope—it was mailed—containing one of those girlie magazines, like Fernandez was in. Someone has written in it that one of the female models posing nude is a police officer. It's quite gross."

"Bring it up, please."

A few minutes later Mulligan was ushered into the office of Deputy Commissioner LaPalma.

If Mulligan's office was neat, LaPalma's was sterile, a plain beige room containing a metal desk on which sat framed pictures of his family, an American flag, and a letter opener. That was it. One wall was filled with law volumes. The joke was that he kept the hearts he had broken in a storage warehouse in Queens.

Mulligan felt a little gripping sensation in his belly as he went into the office and LaPalma looked at him with dark, intense eyes. Mulligan had nothing to hide—far from it—but he was still a little afraid, at the same time looking up to LaPalma as someone who epitomized what a police officer should be.

Mulligan, at LaPalma's behest, sat down next to LaPalma's desk. Mulligan handed him the envelope and the magazine.

LaPalma looked at the envelope as Mulligan translated the printing.

He examined both sides but made no comment. Then he looked at the magazine, leafing through it very slowly.

When he came to the multiple spreads featuring the purported police officer, there was no discernible change in expression. LaPalma might have been looking at actuarial statistics.

When he finished, he looked for and found the indicia, the small type that contained facts on the publishers, date of publication, and the like.

"This magazine's nine years old," he said.

Mulligan nodded. He had forgotten to look for the date.

LaPalma handed the magazine back to Mulligan.

"Make sufficient copies of all relevant pages, and return the magazine to me."

"Yes, sir."

"I'll get back to you," LaPalma said, "as soon as we decide what to do."

Mulligan left the office, and LaPalma got up and stood in front of the multipaned window behind his desk.

The IAD headquarters was in Brooklyn Heights, a neighborhood dominated by clean, well-kept brownstones huddled together on a series of hilly streets close to the historic Brooklyn Bridge. It was a clear day, and he could see the skyline of Manhattan.

LaPalma saw his role as a fact gatherer. He assembled evidence in as methodical and careful a fashion as he could, and then presented it to others to evaluate whether disciplinary action was required.

But he also saw himself as a surgeon, cutting out any cancer in the Department before it metastasized and affected other areas. To keep the Department as pure and clean of corruption, malfeasance, and what he called a "carcinomic moral climate" as possible. He knew that nothing—absolutely nothing—would ever interfere with that.

Sometimes it had been difficult. Grown men had stood in this very office and cried like babies for mercy, in anger, or when asking that he look the other way at certain facts. And he knew that sometimes—an astonishingly large number of times—police officers had taken

116

their lives because of investigations by his unit. And he knew, also, that most police officers reserved for the IAD their most virulent epithets.

No matter, the greater good of the Department would be vigorously pursued and preserved.

The information furnished would be examined, and other information developed, like any case. But special precautions would be taken. Unlike in some cases, the PC and the mayor would be kept fully informed. The Fernandez investigation and trial had been a journalistic three-ring circus, embarrassing to both men. The PC had been angry, the mayor, a man of bottomless ego, livid. And for his part, LaPalma saw it as very disruptive and, if not dealt with swiftly and decisively, a factor which would foster that carcinomic moral climate.

He went back, leaned over his desk, and lifted the receiver. "Get me an appointment with the commissioner, please."

"Yes, sir."

"And get me Ledbetter and Green."

CHAPTER 26

Arnold Gertz was dreaming about the Mr. Universe championship. It was sometime in the seventies, and all the movements were in slow motion.

He was standing on a brightly lit stage facing a large crowd. He was dressed only in shorts, and his body was shiny with oil. To his left was a huge black guy with finely chiseled muscles—it looked like Pouret—and to his right was a legend: the one and only Arnold Schwarzenegger. It was an honor just to be so close to him, but

Arnold realized he was in a *contest* against him, and they were waiting for the judges' decision on who would be the next Mr. Universe.

The third runner-up was announced: the black guy—Pouret.

And then the second runner-up was announced and Arnold Gertz's heart took flight: it was Schwarzenegger. Arnold Gertz was the new Mr. Universe!

The crowd went wild, applauding and yelling, and Arnold realized that he had fulfilled the dream of a lifetime; he felt hot tears come to his eyes, and then he turned and the great Schwarzenegger, perhaps the greatest bodybuilder of the century, extended his hand, his handsome Germanic face wreathed with a broad smile.

Arnold reached, grasped it, pumped, and watched Schwarzenegger's mouth move to say something.

But something was wrong. No words came out. Just an animal sound: *Baa . . . Baaa . . . Baaa . . .*

Arnold awoke. He was covered with sweat. His eyes were wet with tears.

He realized where he was. He was hiding in an abandoned, gutted building in the rubble-strewn lot in back of Jiminez's goat pen.

Arnold checked his watch, which had luminous numbers: 5:12. He looked up and scanned. Buildings were silhouetted blackly against the dark sky.

All was quiet except for the driving sound of disco and the incessant cacophony of cowbells, trumpets, piano. In the summer it went on twenty-four hours a day; on Friday and Saturday nights everyone played their music at once. It was a madhouse.

Arnold was perhaps twenty-five yards from the pen. He looked at it. He could see Blanca. Where was Maria? Had to be in the shed. A little flutter in his belly.

He looked along the fence. The hole that Jiminez had repaired was there. Good.

Arnold's eyes went farther along the fence. The barbed wire was intact there. Good.

Arnold stopped breathing. There was another hole.

He was tempted to start running, but he fought the urge. He fought to think.

They would have to transport the goat in a vehicle. They couldn't walk. It was a long way over a rubble-strewn lot to the street if they came his way.

Schwarzenegger! *Baaa! . . . Baaa!* It had to be recently.

Oh, God, he still had time. They had to have taken the goat to the street in front of Jiminez's building. Had to. Please.

Then he was out of the building, running across the rubble like a madman, not caring if he fell, then past the goat pen, down into the alley. He roared up it, then through the passageway to the street.

He looked one way, then another.

God, empty. The Puerto Rican music jangled, the disco beat drove.

Then, far down the street, he saw it. A car pulling out. A big boat. A sixties vehicle. It had to be. It was his only shot.

His own radio car was parked directly outside the passageway so he could watch it from his stakeout spot. As long as he didn't fall asleep!

Remaining calm, he looked at the hood chain—it was there. He unfastened it. He opened the door easily, got in, turned the key, and the car coughed to life. Within seconds he was moving down Valentine, toward 198th Street.

He made a decision—a bold one, he knew: to just keep the car under surveillance, see what it did, where it went, make no attempt to apprehend. Anyway, he didn't know if the car actually had the goat, or how many perps there were.

He slipped the safety on his belt holster, took out his .38, and laid it on the seat beside him.

At 198th Street the car, which he saw was a red '59 or '60 big-finned Cadillac, went through the red light, no big deal in the Five Three: hardly anybody paid attention to lights.

119

Arnold strained to see the plate number. He couldn't—there was no plate.

The big car moved slowly down Valentine. Arnold nursed the accelerator, closing the gap to about twenty yards. He strained his eyes, trying to see into the dark interior of the car, but he couldn't.

Then he heard a noise, like the sound of a race car, and saw a souped-up car roaring up Valentine toward them.

It blasted by, and it was the break he needed. For a millisecond the headlights of the souped-up car illuminated the interior of the subject vehicle and Arnold saw three heads: two bushy human heads in front and, between them, in clear profile, the long head of Maria, the goat.

His heart leaped with joy. He was going to get those bastards!

Arnold hoped he was doing the right thing. Maybe he should just apprehend. No. If he followed, he might catch more people

He hung back.

The car slowly crossed 196th Street and then, halfway across, it suddenly lurched forward and a made a sharp, squealing right.

The move caught Arnold by surprise. But he jammed the accelerator to the floor and made a fishtailing right.

There was a red light at the Grand Concourse. The Cadillac went through without slowing. Arnold followed, not slowing either, his peripheral vision making him wince as he roared through the light.

The Cadillac squealed left on the Concourse. Arnold snatched the mike off the radio as he followed and opened up the frequency that connected him to Central Communications.

"Central K. This is Charley Five-Three."

"Central K. Go ahead, Charley Five-Three."

"I have a red Cadillac, 1959 or '60. In pursuit on the Grand Concourse, going south near 195th Street."

"Okay, Charley 53. K."

In a few minutes, Arnold knew, the entire area would be flooded with blue-and-whites.

The Cadillac was doing about seventy, but Arnold was gaining. The radio car had an engine under the hood that would let it catch anything that couldn't fly.

The lights were green all the way. Then, at 192nd Street, they changed to red, and Arnold grimaced as the Cadillac ran the light and just barely missed a cab which had moved into the intersection. He manhandled his own car to get around it, and caught a glimpse of the driver's terrified face.

The Cadillac went out of sight as it dipped down into the viaduct that went under Fordham Road, but Arnold spotted it a moment later.

At 188th, the top of the underpass, Arnold saw it start to make a left—and disaster loomed. Heading north at high speed was a huge truck.

Arnold forced himself to keep his eyes open as the truck's air horn blasted and air brakes screamed, but the madmen in the Cadillac paid no attention, continuing to drive, and Arnold waited for the rending crash, but it didn't come—the Cadillac got past the front of the truck by just a few feet, extending the left into a U-turn that brought it up on the sidewalk.

Arnold followed, roaring behind the truck, which had stopped, and bounding up onto the sidewalk, driving along it, past parked cars on his left and storefronts on his right.

The Cadillac had gone across Fordham Road, and it pulled to a stop on the far side of the street.

Unlike the other avenues, there was some traffic on Fordham, and Arnold couldn't get across right away.

Then he saw the back rear door of the Cadillac open. A small, bushy-haired man led the goat out of it, and down into a nearby subway entrance.

Oh, Jesus!

Then the Cadillac was off, roaring north.

Arnold got across Fordham. There was only one thing he could do.

"Charley Five-Three to Central K," he barked into the mike.

"Central K."

"Charley Five-Three. That Cadillac, red, is heading north on the Concourse. I'm going in foot pursuit of another perp."

"Okay, Charley Five-Three. We got it."

Arnold parked where the Cadillac had been and ran down into the subway. It should be easy, he thought, to catch him. He couldn't move fast with a goat on a leash.

He took the stairway down two steps at a time and was in the subway in a few seconds.

There was no one in sight. His heart pounded.

To his right was a token booth, closed, and a caged turnstile that required a token to operate. He had none.

To his left was a long tunnel.

He started to trot down the tunnel. To his right, dividing the tunnel, was a floor-to-ceiling fence of iron bars. Every now and then there was a stairway which led to platforms below.

Where were they?

In the distance he heard a click, a clack. A train was coming. It sounded like it was on his side, which would be downtown.

He trotted a little faster, and when he came to a stairway he stopped and looked down through the bars to see if he could spot them.

Nothing anywhere.

The train got louder. He felt a tickle of panic. He fought it.

At the end of the tunnel was a wide-open area with many turnstile banks and entrances and exits. The 188th Street entrance to the Fordham station. There was a token booth that was open.

He went up the cage. The black token seller's eyes widened.

"Did you see a guy with a goat?" Arnold asked.

The teller shook his head. He looked at Arnold as if he were nuts.

Now the train was coming into the station.

Arnold fought to think.

There were many exits from the subway here, but the token seller couldn't see them.

Sweat trickled down, and the roar of the train seemed to mock him.

Arnold hadn't seen them, but he'd been in the subway only seconds after they entered it.

He must have had a token, gone in at the turnstile back at Fordham.

Right?

Arnold bolted for the turnstile, and then he realized that the train was in. The train doors would be open, and they would be closing. . . .

He took the stairs as if they didn't exist, totally demented.

Be open! Be open!

They were open, and Arnold was in luck—there was a pair just opposite the foot of the stairs. He jumped into the car just as the doors were closing.

The train lurched and started to move. He was committed. They had to be on the train.

He looked to his right. He was on the first car. Through the window he could see the train lights probing the tunnel.

To his left, other cars.

He started to walk. There were only a few people on the train. They kept their heads down, avoiding eye contact.

He patted his pocket. He had slipped his .38 into it before he left the radio car.

He went rockily through each of the cars, opening a series of sliding doors with windows.

On each car there were people. A few glanced briefly at him, then looked away. Only a Bowery-type drunk eyed him quizzically.

As each car proved empty, Arnold started to feel similarly empty in the stomach. A sense of despair, and gloom. Let them be on the train. Please.

He was, he knew, running out of train. He had maybe two, three cars to go.

The train started to slow down. It would be pulling into the next station, 183rd Street.

He should have followed the car. He would have had help, they would have tracked down the other perp. But he wanted to save Maria and get the perp. He should have.

A bushy head, framed in the window of the sliding door a car away, faced him, then disappeared instantly.

The perp!

Adrenaline poured into his body. He entered the next car, the one before where the perp was, which looked like the last car.

He took his .38 out of his pocket. A woman screamed; people shied away. He thought of Naomi and the twins. He had to forget them now. This was his job. He was a cop.

What he had to remember, if it came to that, was what he had learned about how to stay alive.

The train made a sound like thousands of knives and forks being dropped on the tracks. It was braking.

He was oblivious to the screams behind, the worried faces looking his way, some shying away as he came into the car low and fast.

The goat was tied to a pole in the middle of the car. There was no sign of the perp.

Arnold's eyes flicked this way and that, his .38 raised, waiting. One woman who had seen him was swooning, near fainting. His heart was going like a trip-hammer.

The train stopped completely.

The doors slid open. Where was he?

Then, down near the end of the car, movement, and suddenly Arnold saw the perp race through the doors. Arnold was up in an instant. The perp was racing across the station.

Arnold was on the platform.

He dropped into combat-shooting position, raised the gun—"*Halt! police!*"

124

The perp did not halt. He ran like hell.

Arnold only had him sighted for a second, then he lost him. Maria!

He jumped back onto the train. He had to get her off.

He untied her, and started to lead her . . .

The doors closed. The train started to move.

He left the goat unattended for a moment and ran down to the end of the car, broke the glass, and pulled the emergency switch. The car came to a sharp stop that knocked him half off balance.

Then, a new scream. A woman, down at the other end of the car. Continuous. Then other cries. Arnold ran back.

Maria had crapped over everything and everyone in range.

Feeling like he was nuts—having people on the train regard him as such—Arnold brought the goat back to the Fordham Road station via an uptown D train.

The sun had come up when he emerged from the station.

A pair of blue-and-whites were at his car, and his stomach dropped when he saw it. It was up on blocks. All four wheels were gone, and the hood was up.

"What happened?" he asked one of the uniformed cops.

"A gang of punks got the tires and battery."

"Did you get them?"

"No."

"Do you know if they collared a guy in a Cadillac?"

"He abandoned the car around Van Cortlandt Park. It was stolen. He got away, as far as I know."

Arnold walked from Fordham Road to 198th Street to Jiminez's house. All the way he told himself that he had saved the goat. But the perps had gotten away, and look what had happened to his car.

Jiminez was beside himself with gratitude, and for a while this made Arnold feel good. But he knew how Captain Bledsoe would view it, and as he got on the bus heading south toward the station he did not want to think about it.

CHAPTER 27

Arnold Gertz got back to the station house about seven o'clock. He could have gone home, because he was actually on a four-to-twelve tour—the wee-hours stake-out was on his own—but he did not want to. He wanted to write his report and find out what Captain Bledsoe thought. He did not want to go home with anything hanging over his head.

He wrote the DD 5 in longhand, and tried to keep it as brief as possible. Long sentences were treacherous for him. Once he started one he never seemed to be able to finish it.

As he wrote, he got a very strange feeling. It was not as if he were writing a report, but a confession. He became more and more convinced that he had acted wrongly. But there was always the outside hope that Captain Bledsoe would see he had done the right thing. He did get the goat back.

But he shouldn't have fallen asleep in the first place, right? He cut off his thoughts.

He put the report on Fletcher's desk at around a quarter to eight, and clipped to it a note which said he would be in the "dormitory" room taking a nap if Captain Bledsoe wanted to see him.

As he headed for the room, he was tempted to call Naomi. But he wanted to wait. He didn't know if he would have something good or bad to tell her.

There was no one else in the sour-smelling room that the cops of the Five Three used as an all-purpose flop-house, from catching catnaps between official duties to

126

lying unconscious after a session at a local watering hole.

Arnold stripped to his shorts, carefully hung his clothes up, and lay down on the cot. The room was warm, but he got under the covers anyway.

He thought he would not fall asleep. Bledsoe would be in, according to the large-faced electric clock above the doorway, in ten minutes. He would call him in right away.

He kept watching the clock. He was sure he would not sleep.

He thought he was dreaming, because a dark, shadowy figure loomed above him. His eyes focused. He inhaled sharply. He wasn't dreaming. It was Fletcher.

"Captain wants to see you," Fletcher said, and left. He seemed annoyed.

He sat up and glanced at the clock. It was five after nine. He had slept over an hour. He had a little spurt of hope. Captain Bledsoe came in at eight o'clock. Maybe he didn't regard it as bad, or else he would have called him in earlier. Maybe.

Arnold tried to act casual as he approached Fletcher's desk, but he felt nervousness building. No one seemed to be looking at him, but when he was halfway across the room Fletcher glanced up and looked at him. Fletcher still seemed just as annoyed.

"Go in," Fletcher said when he got to the desk.

The door to Bledsoe's office was open. Arnold went in.

Bledsoe had his head down. He glanced up. He shook his head. "Hey, Arnold, what happened?"

He was angry; Arnold could smell it. All he wanted to do was calm Bledsoe down. "It was just bad luck, sir."

Bledsoe pointed at him with a forefinger. "Hey, Arnold. Good cops make their own luck. How come you followed that perp on foot?"

"I want to, uh, get him. I wanted to save the goat, Maria."

"Fuck the goat!" Bledsoe exploded, his voice creating an instant lowering of sound outside the door. "Fuck the goat!" It got even quieter. "Your first obligation is to make a collar. You had backup coming. You could have nailed the perp in the car easy."

"I . . . I . . . I figured I . . . I could do both."

"You figured wrong, didn't you!"

Arnold swallowed. He was afraid to talk. He would start stuttering uncontrollably.

"Did you know," Bledsoe said mockingly, "that I just got a call from the *Daily News* wanting to know all the details of the goat caper?"

Arnold shook his head.

"Did you know that they got a picture of your fucking radio car on blocks?"

Arnold looked at him. He felt himself starting to fill up a little.

"Well, they did. And we're hoping they don't publish it. And we're hoping that they won't find out all the details of the goat caper—particularly the goat shitting all over the subway train!"

Arnold was silent. His thought processes had shut down. Now he was just a large target, a victim. He couldn't argue back, couldn't think of anything. Now he was six years old. Now he was standing in front of his father, a big galoot.

"I'm taking you off the case," Bledsoe said evenly, and Arnold felt something drop inside him. He had to talk.

"Please, sir . . . I'll . . . I'll . . . I'll do . . . do . . ." He heard laughter from somewhere. "I'll do better. I'm sure . . . sure . . . sure . . . of it."

"The problem is, Arnold, I'm not sure of it. Fletcher will give you your new assignments."

Bledsoe lowered his eyes. It was over. Arnold stood a moment, then left.

He did not stop at Fletcher's desk. Not now. He could talk no more. He walked across the squad room. It was very quiet. He felt thousands of eyes on him.

On the way out of the building a couple of cops said

hello to him and he just looked at them and nodded and kept going.

He was on the street. It was another sunny day. Fort Siberia was going to be hot.

He turned left, walking south, deeper into Death Valley.

There was no one in the world who could help him, no one who could make him feel better now. Not even Naomi. He was alone. He knew that this was the end for him. He knew where he was. He was in Fort Siberia, the bottom of the barrel, the highest-crime precinct in the city. If you couldn't get something to investigate there, if you couldn't do the right thing there, you couldn't do it anywhere.

But then, wasn't that what everyone had been telling him since he was small? That he couldn't do anything? Wasn't it?

He did not know where he was going, yet he did. He was heading into the worst part of Fort Siberia, the deepest part of Death Valley. It was early morning, and he knew that the danger of attack or a problem was small. He wanted badly, very badly, to get in the middle of something where he could take his gun out.

Nothing happened. He was eyed by a few people on the way as he walked, but they seemed to know instinctively that this huge man was even more dangerous than his size obviously made him. He was not a cat you fucked with now.

He walked to the southern end of Fort Siberia—Sector John—and the Cross Bronx Expressway. He grasped the fat rail and looked down. Cars hissed rapidly east and west, heading for Jersey or the Island.

He put his chin on his chest, and tears dropped on the railing, and then he was crying hard, as he had at so many other times in his life.

CHAPTER 28

Arnold went home in the early afternoon. He told Naomi only that things didn't work out, that he was tired and maybe they could talk about it later. Then he went to bed and slept through until supper.

She made him his favorite dish—chicken soup—but he ate it halfheartedly, and then after dinner he told her what had happened. That he had tried to do the right thing, but that Bledsoe had seen it as very bad indeed, and that he was off the case.

Naomi went through the motions. She was good at that. As small as she was, she was almost disproportionately tough, and she told Arnold that it seemed to her that Bledsoe seemed like someone who didn't know what he was doing, and that Arnold would feel better soon, and that certainly it was not his last case at the station. Just wait and see.

And then, later, in the bathroom, the water running, she let the tears come, racking her small body. Her man was hurting, and there was nothing she could do about it, and she started to think of all the hurts he had had in his life, and it was almost unbearably sorrowful for her.

But she knew—she knew—it would go away. Time. Time would heal it. And telling herself that now did exactly no good whatsoever.

Then, later, they sat on the couch, and she sat close to him, and she racked her mind, but there were no answers this time. Nothing at all.

They were midway through watching the early news—

Arnold grateful that the escapade had not hit TV, at least—when the phone rang.

Naomi went into the kitchen to answer. What else could happen, she thought, on this day?

A short while later she returned.

"It's someone from the precinct," she said. "Joe Lawless? You know him?" She just hoped—with a name like-that—it was not someone into cruel pranks.

"He's head of the homicide squad," Arnold said, getting up.

"Oh," Naomi said.

Arnold had no idea what Lawless wanted. He had met him once or twice and had seen him around the precinct, but that was it. He knew he had a reputation as a very good detective, and he knew he did not get along with Captain Bledsoe.

"Hello," Arnold said.

"How are you, Arnold. I heard about your misfortune with Bledsoe."

Arnold was silent.

"He was wrong in what he did, Arnold. Like he's wrong on just about everything he does. That was a good piece of police work you did."

"You think so?"

"Definitely. Your job is to protect the public and their property. That man's goat is alive because of you. If you went the other way, after the perp in the car, you might have caught him—and by the time you got the other one the goat could be dead."

"I wish I could of thought to say things like that."

"It wouldn't matter," Lawless said. "All he cared about was that the bad publicity embarrassed him."

"Oh."

"He's a bitter, burned-out guy. No one will ever satisfy him."

"You don't think he should have taken me off the case, then?"

When Arnold had taken the call in the kitchen, he had

walked deeper into its dark recesses. Now he came to the doorway. Naomi was moving slowly toward him.

"No," Lawless said, "but he probably won't put you back on it."

"I know where he'll put me," Arnold said.

"What he does doesn't matter," Lawless said. "Put yourself back on the case."

"What do you mean?"

"Work on it in your off hours. He'll probably put you on days. Work nights."

"How? I don't know where to start."

"You might try the stakeout again."

"They won't come back, will they?"

"I don't know," Lawless said. "They might."

"You think so?"

"Maybe. It would be clever, don't you think? Addicts get clever. They're in the business of surviving."

"I could try."

"That's right," Lawless said. "Give it everything you can. And if you decide you can't crack it, then take a walk from it. Don't let him push you."

Arnold was bouyed. He put his arm around Naomi, who had come up and was standing next to him. He had done the right thing. Lawless had said it.

"I will try," Arnold said. "I'll try again."

"Good luck," Lawless said. "If I can help in any way . . . we work in the same place."

"Thank you."

Arnold hung up and hugged Naomi gently. "He said I did the right thing."

"I told you that," Naomi said. "He's just telling you what I knew."

Arnold kissed her gently, and then they walked toward the bedroom.

And she thought: A kiss for you, Mr. Lawless, wherever you are.

CHAPTER 29

Lawless made the call to Arnold Gertz from the homicide squad room. He hoped it would help. But Arnold was a simple, insecure guy, and he didn't know. Only time would tell.

Lawless was tired. It had been a long day.

Early that morning he had been called to investigate the death of a male black in a transient hotel off Fordham Road. It was likely a suicide. The guy had been found at the bottom of an air shaft that extended from the top floor to the first, with his head smashed through the ceiling of a common bathroom used by the inhabitants. His head had been sticking out of the ceiling for two days and it had not been reported—probably not even noticed.

In early afternoon he had been summoned to look at a suicide. No question about that one. The guy had lain down on his bedroom floor, laid a brand-new shotgun up the middle of his body into his mouth, and pulled the trigger.

Grady was on the Baumann squeal, so Piccolo and Edmunton had accompanied him on this one. Piccolo had commented, "Geez. Look at him. He looks like a rose. Just like a rose."

Lawless had to agree with Grady. Piccolo was crazy, or partly crazy. But he was a good cop, and in some situations was invaluable.

Both homicide and suicide were keeping pace with last year. Before the year was out there were bound to be a couple of specials—family jobs. A mother would take out herself and her kids. And a husband would do himself, then his kids. Or vice versa.

No, nothing was bound to be. You could never tell what you'd get in police work.

His mind drifted back. Sometimes his father, normally a very quiet man, would have a few belts and become talkative. Lawless remembered him once telling him of the experience he had had with jumpers.

"I spent thirty-six years on the job—twenty of them in a radio car," he had said, "and during all those years I only had two jumpers—but *both* on the *same* day. One in the morning, the other in the afternoon."

Most of Lawless's day had been spent reading the DD 5's of the detective task force that had come in over the last couple of weeks to work on the Baumann case.

Collectively, they had talked to over two hundred people: students, school officials, counselors, neighbors, the girl's doctor, dentist, relatives, her parents again— everyone who touched her life.

And lots of people who didn't: addicts, informants, people in the area, a few people who were in the park the day she disappeared and thought they noticed her.

It had all yielded nothing, and the extra detectives were starting to be reassigned. If anything happened on the case, it would be his squad who would do it.

He had hoped that the tape would yield something, but it hadn't. He still had no idea why the killer had taped all her fingers. It wasn't anything functional. It just meant something to him.

Grady was working on the way the girl was tied, but so far had not come up with anything.

Lawless was pleased with the way Grady was working that angle. He was methodical and thorough, and his DD 5's were a joy to read, in terms of both the logical quality of the writing, and the typing.

Forensic had confirmed that the clothes had been cut off the girl. In other words she had been tied, then the clothes cut off with scissors. He drew no special significance from that.

The sheet had been tracked. It was very ordinary, easily obtainable at a thousand different places. Untraceable.

Lawless had been through the building twice in daylight.

He discovered there were no squatters, and few addicts, though a few used the lobby as a shooting gallery from time to time.

He had gone over every room he could on the first two floors. He could not go higher, because there were no stairs.

The cellar, of course, interested him the most.

It was a labyrinth, a maze of halls and rooms, many empty, others filled with debris.

Except for the room where Mary Baumann had died. That had been swept clean, readied for her. Prepared.

It had all been carefully planned, but how was it carried out?

Lawless had thought about it, and had a theory. It was a theory he could only test in the darkness, at the same time, as near as he could figure, as the killer had pulled it off.

He checked his watch: 8:45. About now.

He left the station house and took a gypsy cab to the Concourse, where the LaRocca boy had last seen Mary Baumann alive. He had dropped her off on the corner.

Lawless started to walk down the street toward her house.

He looked around as he did. Was an abduction possible? he thought. Could she have been snatched right off the street?

There were people leaning against the cars, a group of men playing dominoes under the corner streetlight, and as he walked he was eyed. There weren't too many blond-haired white dudes in Fort Siberia at night.

Mary Baumann would have been eyed too. Eyed because she was built like Sophia Loren. No way could she have been snatched off the street without someone noticing.

He turned into her building. There was no one in the

courtyard. He went into the entrance to her wing, on the far left.

The lobby was empty. He stood there, listening. Aside from the music from the street, he could hear laughter through the closed door of one of the apartments, which was out of sight down a hall, then jabbering in Spanish, then more laughter. The hall smelled of Spanish cooking, mixed with non-Spanish-cooking smells.

Straight ahead was the elevator.

He lit a cigarette, checked his watch, and waited.

Nothing happened for three-and-a-half minutes. Then a couple came in the front door, eyed him nervously as they waited for the elevator, and then were gone, into it.

The arrow above the doors indicated the elevator had taken them to the fourth floor.

If this, Lawless thought, was typical of the activity in this lobby the night she was snatched, then the killer would have had plenty of time. Indeed, he could have staked it out before and known he had lots of time.

The lobby was large. He could have been waiting in one of the halls and come out when Mary Baumann showed up. But that was unlikely. He would have had to know exactly when she was coming. And there was always the risk of someone surprising him.

It was far more likely that he had followed her into the lobby, and then into the elevator.

He pushed the button and waited as the elevator returned to lobby level. The doors slid open. He stepped on and pressed the button that said "B." The doors closed, and the elevator went down toward the basement.

The killer, he thought, would have made his move once he was in the elevator. He could have pulled a knife or a gun. The girl would have been very scared.

The door opened and Lawless stepped out. The doors closed behind him.

The cellar was empty and dimly lit. It was a maze of rooms and halls, he figured, just like the abandoned building.

He walked down a long corridor, the light getting

136

worse as he did, but he knew what he was heading for. He had seen his destination in daylight.

He came to it. A rear door.

He opened it, stepped outside, closed it.

He was in a narrow alley, flanked on one side by the building and on the other by a concrete wall; on the other side, he knew, was an empty lot. It was very dark, no light at all except from the moon.

He went up the alley, stopped at the entrance, peeked out. The street was empty. The only building on the other side was the abandoned one.

He made it across the street, to an alley behind the building, in about seven to eight seconds. The killer, girl in tow, could easily have done the same. Here, in the darkness, even if someone spotted them, it would have been assumed that they were two lovers, or addicts, or thieves, or whatever. Not a murderer and his victim.

He walked along next to the building, hidden from sight by a high fence flanking another lot.

He came to a rear door. Forensic had not been able to tell if it had been jimmied, but it was open when he first found it. It was this way, he thought, that the killer had gotten in.

He opened the door, went inside, and closed the door softly behind him. It occurred to him that he didn't know why he did it softly. No one was there. It was just something he did.

Just a few steps inside it was so black he couldn't see his hand six inches in front of his face. It was much darker than in daylight.

A noise. He stopped, motionless. Scurrying. Rats or mice.

He walked very slowly. He had a flashlight with him but did not use it. There were some windows in the cellar. The killer would not have risked a light.

He stopped. A thought. Maybe the girl went willingly. But why? It didn't make sense.

He started again.

She must have been terrified, he thought. At the very

137

least, she knew she was going to be raped. She must have been crying, hyperventilating, maybe screaming for someone to help her, probably begging.

Lawless stopped. His intuition, all those years as a homicide cop, spoke to him: the killer would be enjoying it.

When Lawless got to the entrance of the double room his eyes had become accustomed to the darkness, but once he stepped inside the room adjacent to the one where the girl had died he was in total blackness again. He stopped. A weird thought: What if the killer were in the other room? No way. But killers did strange things.

Be there.

He stood in the doorway and slowly played the light across the room. It was so clean, so different from the other rooms. Prepared.

An execution chamber.

They had come down on the elevator; up the alley; across the street, briefly exposed; then to another alley and into the cellar. Simple.

Simple—and clever. But someone had to be familiar with the cellar to find his way in the darkness to this room, a perfect place to do her.

How? Either he would have had to run through the building in the daylight—addicts probably did that—

Or . . . or he knew the building before it was abandoned. When it was occupied. Maybe he had lived here.

That could be just about anybody. It was not the kind of thing Lawless could track down, not with his squad. But it was something to file, and maybe it would help him at another time.

He turned to go, and it occurred to him that he had been a detective for longer than Mary Baumann had lived.

Lawless took the subway downtown. On the way he wrenched his mind from thoughts of the Baumann case. When he was doing new business, he had found himself thinking about it. That could be bad. You got so close you couldn't see anything.

It would be pretty easy to lift his mind away. He just thought that in a half hour or so he would be in Barbara Babalino's apartment, as he had been every night for the last week or so, and they would be eating her great food, or talking—just as delicious—or making love.

It was, he thought, so different from the life he had been leading over the last ten years.

It had been ten years of TV dinners and TV and listening to old fifties records, which he liked very much, and an occasional night out with some of the guys on the job, and an occasional roll in the hay with someone from one place or another.

But nothing had ever really been that satisfying since Karen. Just a routine existence, with the only real satisfaction coming from what he did on the job.

Job satisfaction was deep. He never talked about it with anybody, but just doing it right made him feel very good. It was something he had learned when he was very young from his father on one of the rare occasions when they had something like those father-son talks that only exist in movies and books.

"Always do the right thing," his father had said, "the thing that you can live with. Make a line for yourself, boy, where the right thing is on one side and the wrong thing is on the other. Never cross it. If you do, you may not be able to get back to the right side."

His father had never told him what it would take to stay on that side of the line. But he showed him, and Lawless realized that one day when it was close to the end of his father's life. He was dying of cancer, and spending his last days in his bedroom, and Lawless, who had been on the force a year, came into the room to talk with him, to say he didn't know what.

"How are you feeling, Pop?"

"I'm okay."

And Lawless looked at him: that tough old gnarled face

139

all sunken in, his body gone to bone, tubes sticking out of him. He had to be in great pain.

And just looking at him, the light from the window shining on his face, it came to Lawless what he had showed him. About integrity, and courage, and living with a sense of responsibility, and all the old virtues that somehow seemed to be getting lost as life rushed on: to do the right thing.

It was, Lawless thought, like a gift. A heritage that his father would leave behind, that would live inside him and enable him to make something good of his own life.

And he put his arms around his father and whispered to him, "I love you, Pop."

And his father lifted an old skinny arm and put it around him, and Lawless, twenty-four years old, wept, and so did his father, and his father said, "I love you too, Joe. You've grown into a fine man."

Two days later, he was gone.

Remembering now, Lawless's throat thickened.

Why did he think of all this? He had not thought about that incident in years.

Why? He did not really know.

He thought of Barbara.

He wondered what she'd have for a snack tonight. Last night she had brought in some deli food.

He wondered what they'd talk about. He enjoyed talking with her very much. They didn't agree on everything—no way—and she was a tenacious arguer. Full of spice and life. He just enjoyed watching her get worked up about things.

He wondered about what she was wearing. Last night she was wearing jeans and a striped polo shirt. He had licked his lips without any attempt to hide it, and she had laughed heartily.

Lawless could hardly wait to see her.

He got to her apartment about eleven o'clock. She opened the door a crack, chain still on. She peered through.

"Yes?"

"Hi. How are you?"

"Who are you?" Barbara said, her eyes playful.

"Joe Lawless. I'm a cop with the Five Three."

"Show me."

Lawless showed his badge.

"What would you like?"

"To talk with you."

"Okay."

Barbara opened the door and Lawless went in. The apartment was dark, except for a dim night light in the living room.

Barbara closed the door behind him. He had glanced at her as he came in. She was wearing something sheer. He could smell her perfume.

He turned and looked at her. Her hair was down. Wild. Her breasts seemed immense. It was as if he were seeing her for the first time. Lawless's stomach tightened, and he felt himself engorging.

She came up to him, put her arms around his neck, and probed the inside of his mouth with her tongue.

She withdrew. He felt a little breathless. She pulled his head down and whispered in his ear, "I'm horny."

"Me too," Lawless said.

They didn't bother to strip the covers off the bed. They did it on top of the bed, and with a controlled fury that kept the goal always in mind: maximum pleasure for each partner.

An hour later, both their bodies sweaty and their bodily and head hair damp from their various interactions, they lay side by side, spent.

"Why do I get the feeling," Lawless said after a while, "that we both should be arrested?"

It made Barbara explode with laughter. Then: "You ain't seen nothing, Lawless," she said. "I'm going to commit felonies on your body you never dreamed about."

Lawless found her hand in the darkness. He picked it up and gently kissed it.

CHAPTER 30

Leo Grady was miffed. The last thing he wanted to do on this boiling hot day in late July was talk to a pervert.

Grady was on the Sixth Avenue subway, traveling downtown in an unair-conditioned car to meet with Ernest Brown, president of a society of, as Lawless had described it, "self-proclaimed sadists and masochists," called "My Way, Inc."

It was unpalatable, but it might be helpful, as nothing so far had been. Brown was an expert on how people tie each other up.

Why do they do it? Grady had asked Lawless.

"It's bondage. They get a sexual thrill out of it."

Ugh, Grady thought. It made you want to go back and view a nice homicide. But not quite.

Lawless, who had never explained his relationship to Brown, or how he knew him, had set the meeting up. Grady was due at Brown's studio—he was a commercial photographer by trade—at two o'clock.

Sweating freely in his usual suit, shirt, and tie, Grady dabbed himself with a handkerchief.

Over the past few weeks he had become something of an expert himself on braided polypropylene and tying. Maybe the world's leading authority.

He had pored over books in the 42nd Street library, talked to rope and cord manufacturers, visited hardware and marine supply stores, talked to sailors and merchant seamen—and one cowboy.

On the poly, as they called it in the trade, he knew such data as its safe working load, breaking strength, resistance to rot, mildew, sunlight, handling, oil and gas, heat, and abrasion, its durability, the sizes it came in (the size used to tie Mary Baumann was 3/16-inch #4), and much more.

Its outstanding characteristic, of course, was that it floats. So somebody involved with a pool might have access to it. But it was just an isolated fact—nothing, as it were, to tie on to.

Grady figured he knew enough about knots to sign on as a merchant seaman. And yet it was a simple square knot, commonly used by ordinary people as well as professionals, that had been used.

It was the system that was complicated. And no one had ever heard of that.

But somewhere, someone had to know something.

The train stopped at 34th Street and Grady exited. He carried with him five color photos of Mary Baumann, her face airbrushed out, making the pictures seem even more macabre. They showed, from various angles, how she was tied. If he thought it possibly productive he would show them to people. And every time experience the same flutters. At home, he kept them in a box in a hall closet, his mind banishing them. But not really. He though of her as a thirteen-year-old girl—never mind that she had been a bad girl—and all he could really remember was what his own daughters had been like at that age, or around that age: so *young*. Younger than springtime. In that awkward land of fear and hope and enthusiasm between childhood and adulthood. The last thing a little girl of thirteen thought about was being murdered.

Every day he stopped at St. Aloysius and said a prayer that her soul was in Heaven.

Blessedly, the street, though boiling hot, was cooler than the subway. But by the time he reached the address, on 29th Street off Sixth, now Avenue of the Americas, his suit was soaked through in spots.

Ernest Brown Studios, the directory downstairs said, was on the second floor.

143

Steeling himself for the encounter, Grady rode the elevator to the second floor. The elevator doors opened directly out into Brown's studio.

Steeling had been in order. Sitting behind a desk, behind which was a wall covered with eight-by-ten black-and-white photos, mostly portraits of model types, was a pretty, dark-haired woman who got up and approached Grady as soon as he stepped out of the elevator. He felt his face turn hot and crimson. The top of her dress was a see-through veillike material, and her small breasts were in full view. Grady's eyes flicked guiltily off them to her face, then her neck. Aiee! She was wearing a tiny silver padlock!

"Can I help you-all," she said with all the enthusiasm of a zombie. She had a slight Southern accent.

"I'm Officer Grady. I'm here to see Mr. Brown."

"Master Brown is in here," she said. "Please follow me."

Did she, Grady thought as he followed her, say "master" instead of "mister"?

Grady followed her down a short hall at the end of which she somewhat tentatively entered a large room. Arrayed around it were light boxes and all kinds of developing equipment; contacts sheets and numerous photos were pinned to walls. Bent over one of the light boxes, examining negatives, was a shaven-headed black man.

"Master Brown," the girl said, "this is Police Officer Grady."

Brown turned his head. He smiled. Light glittered off his gold-rimmed spectacles. There was no telling how old he was.

"Be with you in a minute, Officer."

Mother of God, Grady thought, a black pervert. And there was something unnatural about his relationship with the girl.

Brown wore designer jeans and a flowery shirt. He had a lot of jewelry around his neck and on his fingers.

Grady looked at the pictures on the wall. The vast

144

majority, like those in the reception area, were of handsome young men and pretty young women; the rest were artsy kinds of modern things. Grady wondered what perversions Brown practiced with the women.

After a minute or so, Brown flicked off the light box and came up to Grady. They shook hands.

"Sorry for the delay," he said. "I think we'd do better in my office."

Grady followed Brown down a hallway that terminated in a large room. Grady half expected to see torture devices. Instead he saw a lot of lights on stands, big rolls of photographic paper, aluminum umbrellas, and all kinds of other photographic stuff. There was not a torture device in sight.

There were a couple of doorways off the main room. Brown led him into one.

He sat down behind a desk and beckoned Grady to sit down. He did.

"Beer, Officer?" Brown asked.

It was a good idea, Grady thought. He was nervous and had not taken any infusion of vodka in quite a while. Too hot.

"Okay," he said.

Brown picked up a phone, tapped a button twice. He listened a moment then said peremptorily, "Two beers," and hung up.

Brown smiled brightly, his eyes playful, his teeth very white against very dark skin.

"The service around here," he said, "is superb."

Grady smiled weakly for a moment, then got it and felt like not smiling. The girl was some sort of slave. A Southern white slave for a black master. Ugh.

"Are those the pictures?" Brown said, glancing at the envelope Grady had.

Grady nodded and handed them to Brown. Just before he did, the woman came into the room with a tray on which were two sixteen-ounce Budweisers. They were open. She put one in front of Brown, the other in front of Grady. She went away. Brown didn't even look at her.

Grady took a long pull from the can. It was cold, and very good. Brown took a sip and opened the envelope. Grady took another pull.

Brown spread the pictures out across his desk, left to right. Grady watched him.

Brown's forehead furrowed. Grady cared about nothing. He just wanted Brown to help.

Grady watched for a glimmer of something. There was just a look of distaste—and puzzlement.

Finally, the furrowed forehead relaxed somewhat. "Oh," Brown said. "I see. He takes her from behind. If she moves, she chokes." He paused. "Sick."

Grady's heart sank. "No ideas where the method may have come from, what it is?"

"Not really," Brown said. "I've seen people tied something like this, but not with the poly around the neck—except in the case of suicides." Brown shook his head, looked at Grady. "We play games. This is the work of a psycho."

Grady nodded. Tell me about it, he thought. "What about the hands?"

"Sorry," Brown said. "I have personally never seen anything like that either. Nothing's mobile."

"Right."

Grady took a long swig on his beer. He was almost finished with it.

"Another?" Brown said.

"No thanks."

Brown looked at the photos again. "If I can, I'll make copies of these photos and show them to some other people."

"Okay," Grady said.

Brown made copies of the photos, then returned them in the envelope to Grady. He walked him to the elevator. The woman was nowhere in sight.

"Sorry I couldn't help, Officer," Brown said as he

pressed the button. "But we may yet come up with something."

"I appreciate the help."

Then Grady was gone. He would go home, take a shower, have a few, and go to bed.

CHAPTER 31

It was August 1. Sergeant Turner completed his roll call at 8:10 and looked out at the assemblage of cops massed in front of him. They looked wilted already. By seven o'clock the mercury had climbed to 73. It would top 100 today, no problem.

He glanced at his clipboard.

"Last night all the plumbing was removed from all five floors of 1908 Walton. If you hear anything, Sector George, please contact Dave Raymond in S&L.

"Sector David, last night there were two dogs killed by an archer. One at 175th and Anthony, the other three blocks away—178th and Anthony. It was done with competition-quality equipment, apparently from rooftops. Look up every now and then.

"Detectives in anti-crime would appreciate any information on a black male named James Johnston, nicknamed 'Squid.' "

Turner put his clipboard by his side.

"From time to time, as those of you who have been around here awhile know, there is an attempt here to improve the quality of DD 5 writing. An example for the necessity of that was supplied in a DD 5 filed yesterday by an officer who shall remain nameless."

Turner leafed through the clipboard.

"The report reads, in part, that a perpetrator was observed coming down the stairs. Coming is spelled 'c-u-m-m-i-n-g.' In other words, the DD 5 says, in effect, that the perpetrator was having an orgasm going down the stairs."

There was raucous laughter.

"Since the perp was only arrested for burglary, we can assume that the officer meant to spell 'coming' a different way. If he meant it the way he spelled it, then there should have been an additional charge filed against him."

More laughter. Turner put the clipboard back down by his side.

"Since it is particularly hot today, it is suggested that all officers be well aware of some of the survival techniques detailed here over the months.

"Be particularly alert on non-felony traffic stops. As I have mentioned before, some thirteen percent of all officers killed each year have it occur while stopping motorists.

"Also, be acutely aware when answering a call to a family disturbance. Do not—absolutely do not—get involved without backup."

And with that, Turner limped out of the room, and the men and women of the Five Three hit the street again.

CHAPTER 32

On August 1 Barbara Babalino was, as usual, on a day tour. Around ten o'clock, while she was in the middle of typing up a burglary complaint, Fletcher came up to her desk.

"Captain wants to see you, Babalino," he said sourly.

She knew Fletcher didn't like her, and the feeling was mutual. He—a married man—had once asked her out, and she had turned him down flat with no sugar coating on the rejection at all. She viewed him as an oily survivor, the perfect complement to Captain Bledsoe, the oil king.

Bledsoe rarely if ever called her into his office, perhaps because he knew how she felt about him. So she was mildly concerned. What could it be?

"Close the door," Bledsoe said as she went into his office. She did. There were two guys sitting at one side of the office. They were both in their thirties and squeaky-clean-looking. Suits, white shirts, conservative ties, clean-shaven, with close haircuts.

Barbara sensed Bledsoe was perturbed.

"This is Sergeant Ledbetter and Sergeant Green from Internal Affairs, Babalino. They want to ask you some questions, and tape it."

Barbara felt the blood drain from her face. It could only be about one thing.

One of the IAD men reached across and activated the recorder, which was on the edge of Bledsoe's desk.

Bledsoe and the other IAD man looked at Barbara. The man who activated the recorder looked at it.

"This is Sergeant Frank Green, conducting interrogation of Police Officer Barbara Babalino, Tax Registry Number 786543, Fifty-third Precinct, August first, 1985, 11:05 A.M. Present are myself, Captain Warren G. Bledsoe, Sergeant Nicholas Ledbetter, and Officer Babalino."

Barbara's stomach was hollow. Now all the men were looking at her.

Sergeant Green asked her some preliminary questions about her name, rank, and the like, and then asked the question that confirmed what it was about.

"Were you ever a model?"

Barbara was about to answer. Her natural instinct was to be open, direct. But she recalled what Lawless had said—or at least the warning implied—that day she had

149

told him about Walker's attempt to blackmail her. Namely, true justice is not necessarily a thing you get when the Department goes after you.

"Do I have to answer?"

"No," Bledsoe said. "You don't. But if you don't you go under immediate suspension."

Bledsoe had hit her in what she called her Sicilian part. She wanted to tell Bledsoe "Fuck you" and walk out. But she didn't. She said, "I'd rather not answer any questions."

Ledbetter, who had been watching Barbara very carefully, without seeming to do so, spoke up. He was half smiling. He had hazel eyes. There was no warmth in them.

"Barbara," Ledbetter said, "this isn't a trial. This is just some questions to see where we go from here. There's nothing to hide here."

He reached down into a slim briefcase leaning against the chair, unzipped it, and took out a magazine.

"We received a communication that you posed in this magazine. We want to find out whether you did, and if you did, why, and the circumstances surrounding it. It's all open and aboveboard."

"I still don't want to talk," she said.

"You're making a mistake," Ledbetter said.

"That's the way it is."

The smile left Ledbetter's face.

Bledsoe glared at her.

"You know the routine," he said. "You're under suspension forthwith."

Barbara got up and went out of Bledsoe's office. She had to get to an outside phone. She had to get to Joe.

CHAPTER 33

About a half hour before Barbara Babalino entered Bledsoe's office, Joe Lawless entered the small, cozy office of Dr. O'Hara O'Hara high up in a building overlooking Foley Square in Manhattan. O'Hara had once explained to Lawless that his parents' philosophy was "If you're Irish, flaunt it." A psychologist, he was technically an employee of the FBI.

O'Hara did not look like the popular image of a psychologist. He looked, Lawless thought, like a career employee with the New York City Transit Authority. He was small, ruddy-faced, cherubic, with a bald dome and thatches of white hair. His clothes were rumpled.

But he had, Lawless thought, an uncanny understanding of the homicidal mind. In fact, on one previous occasion O'Hara had been so accurate that it struck Lawless briefly that "O" must have been involved in the crime. If anyone could tell Lawless something useful about the Baumann killer, it was O'Hara.

O'Hara motioned Lawless to a seat, then poured both of them coffee from a pot taken from a hot plate in the corner. He put the pot back in place, put the coffee in front of Lawless, then sat down behind the desk. A window behind O'Hara showed nothing but blue sky.

Lawless sipped the coffee, then lit a cigarette.

"You look good," O'Hara said. "Put on a few pounds?"

"Maybe. I feel good."

"Anything special happen?"

"A girl."

"That'll do it every time," he said, smiling. "Can make you lose weight, too," he added with a smile.

O'Hara's smile lingered for another moment, then faded as he glanced down at a thick sheaf of material on his desk. It was reports, photos, copies of everything of an evidentiary nature that Lawless had on the Baumann case.

O'Hara looked up. "It's right up there with the worst I've ever seen," he said.

Lawless nodded. "What do you think?" he asked.

"He's psychotic, of course—filled with rage. Do you know how angry you have to be to work on someone like this for twenty-four hours?"

"Is that why he killed her?"

"In a way, yes," O'Hara said. "He killed her to relieve the pressure. From the rage. It was building for a long time."

"You want to run that by again?"

"You know Ken Bianchi, the Hillside Strangler?"

Lawless nodded.

"A classic psychopath, in many ways. When he was a young boy in Rochester he took a tremendous amount of abuse from his mommy. So what did he do about it? Nothing. He swallowed the abuse, and buried the rage he felt at mommy. Why? Because if he expressed it he would come into confrontation with her—which terrified him. It was terrifying because a young child feels so dependent on his mother."

O'Hara sipped his coffee.

"The problem," he said, "is that those feelings grow and fester over the years. Sometimes the psychotic can keep them in check, but sometimes he—or she—can't. They have to relieve the pressure. In the case of Bianchi and your guy, the only relief was homicide."

"Why the girl?"

"The rage was simply transferred to her. Displaced. That's what psychotics—and neurotics—do. It's safer. Bianchi, in killing all those girls, was killing a symbol."

Lawless persisted. "But why Mary Baumann? Why not another girl?"

"Good question," O'Hara said. "To answer: The victim—the symbol—must have some qualities, mannerisms, looks, similarities, to the actual person he wants to kill. Just a few things are necessary. Don't forget, the psychotic wants to create a scenario within which he can act. That feeling must be discharged."

"So Mary Baumann reminded him of someone for some reason?"

"That's right."

"Why do you think he taped her hands, tied her like that? Why not shoot her or something?"

"I get a sense of control and domination," O'Hara said. "A sense that the killer was trying to control and dominate someone. Why, I don't know. But the taped hands do indicate this—so do the cords.

"And," he added, "the sex is part of it all. We go back to the rage. The act fits the feeling. It's the rape syndrome, where power and pain are more important than sexual pleasure—or are the reason for it, carried to the ultimate."

Lawless put his cigarette out in an ashtray on the desk. He looked at O'Hara. "He's going to do it again, isn't he?"

O'Hara nodded. "Yeah," he said, "because the problem is still intact. The rage is dissipated temporarily. It's not anything like so-called rational murder for greed, jealously, love, etcetera, where one act finishes it. This never ends. The rage will build, and he'll have to handle it."

"With who?"

"Probably someone like Mary Baumann."

"Any idea about how old he is?"

"Usually they're in their twenties," O'Hara said, "but they could be older."

"What can I look for?"

"I'd say anyone who's been into bondage. It would have been a way of coping with the feelings. He might have done a number on someone but didn't go all the way. In fact, I don't think he's killed before."

Lawless lit another cigarette.

"You smoke too much."

"You drink too much coffee," Lawless said.

There was a little silence. A tiny 727 passed in silhouette in the blue rectangle behind O'Hara.

"When?" Lawless asked.

"I don't know," O'Hara said. "They usually kill in clusters; Bianchi did."

"Can I stop him?" Lawless asked.

"Only," O'Hara said, "if you catch him."

Lawless left O'Hara's office and waited by a bank of elevators.

He had not expected answers to anything, and O'Hara had not provided any. But he had gotten a better sense of who he was dealing with, and there was no telling when a random piece of information could be helpful. The more you knew, the better off you were. It was that simple.

The doors to an elevator slid open, and Lawless was about to enter when he heard his name called. He stepped back.

It was O'Hara. His usual ruddy face was ruddier. "Glad I caught you. There's a call for you. Barbara?"

CHAPTER 34

Instead of going outside, Barbara had called Lawless from the homicide squad room. All she had said was "They found out about my posing," and Lawless suggested they meet immediately. "I'm all for that, Joe," she said. "This thing has me shook."

They decided to meet at her place.

On the train, traveling the rather circuitous route that took him from Foley Square downtown to her apartment on 72nd Street, Lawless immediately discounted the pimp, Walker, as having exposed her. The night Lawless had approached him, Walker had believed what Lawless had said.

There was a good reason, Lawless thought. It was true.

They arrived at her house at around the same time. Wordlessly, Lawless followed her down the steps to the apartment door. She opened it, and they stepped inside to the shady coolness. Barbara closed the door, then turned and put her arms around Lawless.

"Just hold me," she said.

He did, and could feel her trembling a little. He held her until the trembling stopped.

They went into the living room.

"Want a drink, Joe?"

"Sure."

Barbara got them a couple of cold cans of beer, and they sat down on the couch.

She explained what happened, how she got the feeling they were trying to con her, and how she said exactly nothing, remembering what Lawless had said when Barbara had told him of Walker's blackmail try.

"You did exactly the right thing," Lawless said when she had finished. "And the reason you got the feeling they were trying to con you was because they were.

"The first thing we have to do," he said, "is to get you back on the payroll."

"I was suspended."

"Yeah, but there's a mechanism in the Department called modified assignment. You have to wait twenty-four hours after the suspension before applying for it. It's up to the PC, but he usually grants it, unless there's a strong reason not to—like it would be politically unwise."

"Where are you assigned?"

"You do work a monkey could do in some precinct other than the Five Three. But you draw a full salary."

"You know a lot about the workings of the Department, don't you?"

"A fair bit. I've spent some time on the wrong side of the tracks," Lawless said. "We also want to try to take careful steps, and know what we're stepping into."

"How are we going to do that?"

"Get a good *consigliere*. Like Leo Grady. He spent all his time on the job as a clerical man at headquarters."

"You give me hope."

Lawless held up his can. "Empty," he said.

She went and got them both new cans. "Do you think this will be in the papers?"

"Maybe," Lawless said. "Probably." He took a sip of beer and put his arm around Barbara's shoulder. "I think we should follow the philosophy I've developed on this. Don't think about yesterday—there's nothing you can do about it—and don't think about tomorrow. Live for now. We'll cross the mountains as we come to them."

She put her beer on the coffee table and snuggled close to his chest.

CHAPTER 35

Mark Dawkins, the art director for the New York *Telegram*, had once wanted to be an oil painter, so he appreciated beauty. And there was beauty lying on the easel before him. Never mind that it was a woman—it was still Beauty.

The Beauty was on page 74 of *Big Ones*. It was the picture that the city editor, Sam Mosholu, had told him to use with the big story on the "Sex Cop." Dawkins was surprised, this time, at the city editor's taste. Secretly, Dawkins considered him a clod, expert only on bad cigars and bars that smelled of loos.

The cop was beautiful. The picture showed her from the waist up, her head bent forward ever so slightly, her eyes wide and darkly made up, electric with sensuality. The other woman pawing her was hardly noticeable.

The CE's memo had instructed:

(1) Use the pix on p. 74.
(2) Use plenty of tit—but in taste.
(3) Bring magazine back to CE under pain of death.

Dawkins looked at her nipples. He wished he had them that size. He wished he had the tits, too! Magnificent. His problem wasn't showing plenty of tit; it was how not to show plenty of tit!

He set the page up squarely on the easel, then slowly raised his T square higher and higher until it touched the nipples, then covered them. He went another inch, stopped, waffled, and went up another inch and stopped. He drew crop marks, horizontal and vertical.

He placed plain white sheets of paper at the crop marks and eyed it. It would be exactly how the picture would appear in the paper. He would wrap the copy around the pix, and use 18-point Caledonia Bold for the headline:

SECOND COP IN SEX - PIX SCANDAL

Dawkins stood there, imagining his handiwork on page 3. Magnificent.

CHAPTER 36

The story of Barbara's posing broke in the *Telegram* five days after she was suspended.

The story was basically only three paragraphs long—detailing that the alleged model was Barbara, her precinct, what she did there, the name of the magazine she posed in, and her address. Seven subsequent paragraphs were a rehash of the Consuela Fernandez case.

Lawless and Barbara knew someone had the story the day before, because at night her phone started to go off the hook with everyone from the *New York Times* to *New York* magazine wanting to interview her.

Lawless had a simple suggestion: "Move into my place—or someplace else where they can't find you. Otherwise they'll hound you to death."

Barbara was all for that, because after the first five calls she found herself upset and embarrassed. She remembered the Fernandez case. It seemed to be in all the papers every other day.

They got a break. The PC had acceded to Barbara's request for modified assignment. Three days after she applied she got word that she had been reassigned to the 101st Precinct in Queens. It was way out in the boondocks, but she was on payroll.

Late the night before the story broke, she moved into Lawless's apartment in the Pelham Bay section of the Bronx.

"It's still pretty good here," he said. "Almost like it was thirty years ago. You get an occasional shark swimming in, but there are a lot of Italian families living in the area, and they seem to have their own police force."

After settling in, Barbara had made a call to Laura at the restaurant, and asked her to call back as soon as she could. Laura returned the call ten minutes later.

"Tomorrow," Barbara said, "a story is going to come out in the *Telegram*—I wanted to tell you about it."

She did, as briefly as possible, and ended by saying, "We don't think it was Walker who told the newspapers—but whoever, there it is. I just wanted to tell you that as far as I'm concerned it changes nothing. You're going to stay out of the life, and this guy is going away."

During the conversation Laura had dropped some change in the phone to continue talking, and when Barbara had finished and Laura didn't respond she thought that her time had run out and she was disconnected.

"Laura?" But there was no dial tone. "Laura?"

"I'm here," she said in a low voice. "I . . . I just wanted to say . . . thank you for what you did."

"You're worth it, Laura," Barbara said. "You deserve to live."

The day the story broke, Barbara worked a regular tour in the new precinct. And Lawless worked his regular tour—fifteen hours. He got home to his apartment at around eleven o'clock, laden with Chinese food.

"My philosophy," he said as they sat in the living room, eating the food off the coffee table, "is the same as·George Carlin's: 'I never eat anything from my refrigerator,' he says, 'that I don't recognize.' "

Barbara laughed. "I'm surprised I'm so relaxed," she said. "I felt like I was in a goldfish bowl today."

"It'll settle down a bit. People like to focus on other people's problems—it takes them away from their own."

"Yeah?"

"I think down deep they don't really care that much. They can only care about their own problems."

"You think so?"

"Most people," Lawless said.

"It's sad."

"It's just the way it is."

"You're not only good-looking; you're smart."

"You're smarter than I am—and a lot better looking."

Barbara didn't say anything for a while. Then: "I never thought about that. I always got good marks—honors and all that, but so many times I felt I wasn't seeing things just exactly the way they were."

"That's because you're an idealist, a dreamer. You want things to turn out with a storybook ending, so you bend things so they do."

"You see things just the way they are, don't you?" she asked.

"I guess. But I like storybook endings too."

"I love you, you know that?"

"I see that clearly," Lawless said. "And I love you too."

Later, in bed, Barbara was snuggled in Lawless's arms. "This is known as regression in the service of the ego," she said. "A return to the womb."

"I'm here," he said.

CHAPTER 37

The man sat by the living room window and sipped iced tea.

He remembered the way it had been with Mary Baumann. It was early May when she had started to mock him. No words. Just the way she looked at him with her dark, cruel eyes.

It had angered him, made him angrier than he could ever remember having been.

He had put her in a sexual fantasy, one that he had been having all his life with various women. She was tied up, helpless, and he was working on her, hurting her. As usual, he stimulated himself to orgasm with it.

It relaxed him.

She continued to mock him; he continued to fantasize and stimulate himself more frequently.

But the anger steadily increased, and around the third week in May he realized that he needed a woman, that the fantasy was not enough. He had had them before, and they had lived his fantasy, but there was simply no one available at the moment.

He went to Manhattan and hired a dark-haired, dark-eyed, lushly built prostitute for two hundred dollars. They went to a sleazy hotel in the Times Square area. He tied her up and worked on her.

After he had paid her she said to him, "You're a fucking freak."

Then he found himself getting angry at odd, inappropriate times. At work, in transit, just eating dinner. He had trouble controlling himself so that no one would notice.

He developed physical problems: headaches, blurred vision, upset stomach, tiredness. He went to a doctor.

"Are you," the doctor asked, "under some kind of stress?"

"Yes."

"That's your problem," the doctor said. "Relax."

He went to another doctor. He prescribed Valium, 2½ mg. every few hours. The man took that, then 5 mg, then 10. Ten worked, except it made him function like a zombie, and even with the ten in him, enough tranquilizer to sedate an elephant, he could feel the anger growing.

Mary Baumann did not help. She mocked him even more as May turned to June, and did not waste any opportunity to preen and parade her big tits in front of him. Of course, she continued to be the whore she had always been.

He stimulated himself multiple times every day, and to a fantasy that was rougher than he had ever had, even worse than with the whore. He thought about getting another hooker, but it scared him. He didn't know if he could control the anger. Actually, it wasn't anger anymore; it was rage.

Then one day, lying in bed one early morning, imagining her dark, glistening eyes mocking him, he realized he wanted to kill her.

And then he decided to do just that.

In quick order he knew where he would do it and how he would do it. It was as if he had been thinking about it his entire life.

Busily, excitedly, he went about the task of preparing things. He bought the cord and everything else he needed in Newark, New Jersey, far from his home. Untraceable.

He visited the room in the cellar twice. First to make sure that the building was empty at night.

The second time was to clean it. He made it sparkling fucking clean.

162

Then he was ready. Calmness reigned. The rage was controlled, like water behind a dam.

He was clever. He had no trouble getting her into the building and into the room.

Once inside, he warned her to be quiet. She said she would be. That turned out not to be completely true.

He had placed two battery-powered lamps in the room. It was very important for him to follow the sequence of reactions she would have, the looks on her face.

Once she saw the room, with the sheet spread in the center of it, she started to cry. There was no cruelty in her eyes anymore. Just terror.

It turned him on, and the dam opened, and he let the rage flow out, controlling it.

As she sucked him, the first act, he exhorted her to do better, told her that as a little whore with such training she could do better. She worked on him in a frenzy, and as he looked down at her head going he couldn't help but smile inside. She didn't know what was in store for her.

As he tied her, she started to whimper and beg. It was too much.

He told her everything was going to be all right. How he enjoyed fooling her! How he loved making her think that after a little sexual escapade everything would be okay!

He went at her in a frenzy, the cord alternately straining and relaxing. It worked beautifully. One highlight was when he entered her anally. He drove himself into her very hard.

The feeling was good, but it was near the end of his time with her that she let loose the gagged, muffled cry that thrilled him most: *Mommy,* she cried. *Mommy . . .*

Later, when it was over, he felt hollow, calmer than he had ever felt in his life. He knew what he had done. He had an alibi prepared. There was no way anyone could connect him to the crime. And he would never do it again. Why should he? There was no need.

But he was wrong. The feeling started again—almost immediately.

Now he drained the last of the iced tea and went over to the sink. He dumped the remnants of the ice out, washed the glass, and put it on a dish rack.

Then he went and looked at the open New York *Telegram* on the table. His eyes narrowed as he looked into the dark, cruel eyes of Barbara Babalino.

CHAPTER 38

While Barbara went off to spend another day in the goldfish bowl at the 101st, Lawless gathered Grady, Piccolo and his partner, Ed Edmunton, in the squad room.

Grady had been working constantly on the Baumann squeal while Edmunton and Piccolo were on a couple of grounders—drug-related hits.

Edmunton and Piccolo were not alike. Edmunton, age about fifty, was a bear of a man, weighing in at over three hundred pounds. Piccolo, thirty-five, was five feet six and weighed one thirty. Edmunton was at Fort Siberia for grass-eating—taking small gratuities; Piccolo was there because of innumerable brutality charges.

"We're going nowhere on the Baumann case," Lawless said, "and this guy could kill again. We have to come up with something."

Grady got a clear image of Mary Baumann, tied up, eyes open, dead in a dirty cellar. He didn't want to go through something like that again.

Lawless reviewed the major investigative details of

the case, pausing a number of times to answer questions from Piccolo and Edmunton.

"We're left," he said, "with only one connection to the killer—his pubic hair."

He opened a folder on the desk and took out some sheets of paper. "On here are the names of the people, twenty-two, who have blond hair, or some blond hair."

He passed the sheets out to each man. "I've included all of the names. All were interrogated and gave alibis. I want the alibis checked."

"Why don't we just take hair samples," Piccolo said, and Edmunton laughed gutturally. Edmunton thought Piccolo was a scream.

Grady did not hear the comment. He was focused on a name on the list. It had Lawless's initials after it, meaning he would check it out himself.

"You have her father's name here," Grady said.

"He has grayish blond hair."

"But her father?"

Piccolo looked at Grady. "Hey, Leo. If there was a murder in St. Patrick's Cathedral, the first guy we'd suspect is the cardinal."

Edmunton laughed. Lawless did not.

"You have to consider everyone, Leo," Lawless said. "I really don't know what his relationship to his daughter was. Also, alibi-wise, the father said he was painting on Eighty-sixth Street during the time the girl was gone. That has to be checked. Also, his wife works nights. He could have sneaked away."

To Grady the thought was repellent. He did not want to explore it, figuring Lawless could back it up with other examples.

"Let's go over the names," Lawless said.

He took out another folder. As he read each of the names he handed out the DD 5's and whatever other material there was on the particular individual.

"Study the DD 5's before you recheck or requestion people. Run all the names through BCI to see if they have yellow sheets. We're particularly interested in something related to sadism or bondage. And you know what else, right? A lie, an inconsistency. Good luck.''

Grady went to the bathroom, where he took a long swig of vodka. Then he went back to the squad room, sat down at one of the desks, and read the DD 5's. There were four people to check out: Arthur Gleason and James Horan, both fourteen-year-old students; Raymond Scott, a thirty-two-year-old guidance counselor; and John Farris, a forty-six-year-old administrative assistant.

He read and reread the DD 5's. The students said they were at school during the day and at home at night during the time Mary Baumann was missing. Farris had the same story: at school, at home. Raymond Scott was at the movies the night of the fifteenth and in school the sixteenth.

Grady put their names through BCI and decided to wait for the results before doing anything. If they had sheets, he wanted to know that before proceeding. Indeed, maybe Lawless would want to know it first.

Lawless was treating him almost as if he were a seasoned detective. That was flattering—but Grady didn't want to make a mistake. A mistake here really meant: overlook a murderer.

He thought about Lawless assigning himself to talk to Mary's father. It was something no one could relish—except maybe the madman Piccolo. It was just a little thing, Lawless taking that job, but it was one more little thing Grady realized about Lawless, one more reason why he had such a hardworking squad of detectives.

CHAPTER 39

Arnold Gertz stood in the darkness near the entrance to the roof of Jiminez's house and looked down.

Since the moon was out, he had a good view of the goat pen and the bombed-out area behind it.

It was around midnight, and as usual the cowbell-trumpet-piano cacophony pumped from the streets and windows as far as the ear could hear. He could hear the jabber of people talking in Spanish, punctuated by laughter, an occasional angry shout, and the clank of a tool: a bunch of people were changing the transmission on an old Chevy in front of an adjacent house.

The night was hot, as usual—there had been only three days of rain since he started the stakeout—and occasionally he could catch the whiff of dog crap. While Jiminez's roof was clear, other roofs were not: people commonly walked their dogs on them. None of the dogs were small, and Arnold had observed one male Hispanic walking a thing that he thought was a Gila monster. He had seen it in a zoo once. It left a load like a dog.

Occasionally he would witness—or be aware of—sex acts being performed on adjacent roofs. The roof was an important part of living in Fort Siberia.

The action was either on the roof, in the hallways (lovemaking, urinating, defecating, shooting up), or on the street. The only activity behind the building was the aimless meandering, interrupted by an occasional call to nature, of Jiminez's goats in the pen. Jiminez would come out once or twice a night to check them, but he would not look up at Arnold, though he knew he was there.

There was usually no sign of life in the area behind the pen, except once in a while someone would come back to urinate, and twice during the stakeout young people had gone into the gutted structure where he had first set up the stakeout, probably to make love.

But there was no sign of the perps.

If it was going to happen—if they were going to come— they had to come fairly soon. Rather than go back to the assignments—the empty assignments—that Bledsoe had given him, Arnold had taken leave. He could sleep in the day, which is what he was doing, and be in position on the roof before the night came. Jiminez kept his eye on the goats during the daylight hours.

But the leave would end soon, and if he had to go back to the precinct and do things—work in the day, stake out at night—he didn't know if he could. When would he sleep? He could probably do it for a while, but even though he was in top-notch physical condition he knew it would catch up with him.

And, oh God, he didn't want to be asleep if the perps came.

He stayed at the post constantly. Only twice did he leave it.

Once, around three in the morning, there was a loud fight down on the corner involving maybe a dozen people, but Arnold did not get involved. A few blue-and-whites eventually showed—and an ambulance—and things calmed down.

Another time he heard gunshots. But they were far away and he did not get involved.

If they came, Arnold figured he could be down the stairs in less than a minute.

Occasionally, Arnold would count the goats—one, two—and he would sometimes get a gripping sensation in his stomach if one was out of sight—even though he had seen it go into the shack. He would only get relief when the goat reemerged.

Once something happened that scared him a little. He thought he saw the perps, tiny and bushy-haired, coming across the lot, but then he realized he had made them up from the shadows.

He tried to think back to what Lawless had said to him, how he had complimented him, how he believed they might come.

Now Arnold looked across the lot at the bank of abandoned buildings separated by dark alleys. A few of the apartments had squatters in them.

They might come from one of the alleys. Arnold glanced to his left. Just more rubble-strewn lot; to his right the same thing. Any way they came they would be in the open a long time.

Arnold didn't care which way they came. As long as they did.

CHAPTER 40

The investigation into the alibis of the possible suspects with blond hair was going nowhere. Piccolo and Edmunton had not come up with anything. Lawless had checked out Mary's father. On June 16 he was painting an apartment on 86th Street, not murdering his daughter.

None of the people Grady checked through BCI had yellow sheets, not even a Dis. Con.

After receiving his reports, Leo Grady took the next investigative step. He put a couple of swigs of vodka in his belly. Then he called Wade Junior High School, on 170th Street and the Concourse, where Mary had gone to school, to find out if the people on the list—who all said they were in school on June 16—had in fact been there. The man on the line turned out to be a Mr. Oliver Prendergast, assistant principal.

"Is there something wrong?" Prendergast asked.

"Oh, no," Grady reassured him. "Just need to verify some whereabouts in the Baumann case. Strictly routine."

"All right," Prendergast said.

And Grady could have added: we also want to see if one of these folks is a murderer, but don't let it bother you.

The following day Grady got to the school at nine-thirty. He parked his unmarked radio car about a block away.

It was a huge red brick building heavily marred with graffiti and filth. Bars and chain mesh covered many windows. What a difference, Grady thought, between this place and the school, St. Aloysius, where his girls had gone.

He had an image of them running to him one day, prettily dressed in white dresses, so small, ribbons in their hair. They must have been twelve or thirteen.

He scanned the side of the building. He wondered where Mary Baumann had spent her time. He wondered if someone had ever come to meet her. Probably not.

He touched his beads. He hoped she was in Heaven.

Before getting out of his car, Grady glanced around and in the rear-view mirror and took a long pull on his flask, followed by some expertly administered spritzes of Binaca.

He wasn't going to enjoy this. This wasn't just asking someone about ropes and knots. This was real police work.

Now, in summer, the school was relatively empty—no students in sight. Grady found Prendergast's office on the first floor and went in.

Prendergast came out from an interior office to meet him. Grady smiled. Prendergast, a tall, thin, bald, bespectacled man in his mid-fifties, nodded back. He led Grady into his office and motioned him to sit down in a chair next to his desk.

"How can I help you, Detective?" he asked.

Grady smiled, reached into his jacket pocket, and

took out an envelope. He took the list of names—there were twelve; eight were window dressing—and handed the sheet to Prendergast.

"That's a list," Grady said, "of individuals we haven't double-checked as to whereabouts on June sixteenth. Could you tell me where each was on that date?"

Prendergast got up and went to a bank of nearby file cabinets. Within a minute he was back at his desk with two folders. From the serrated edges of the paper Grady thought they might be computer printouts.

Prendegast took out a mechanical pencil and leafed through the printouts, every now and then making a check mark against the list. He went through all the names in less than three minutes.

"They were all in school that day," he said, "except for Mr. Scott. He was at a symposium of guidance counselors in Manhattan. At the Aylward House."

"I see," Grady said, not missing a beat. "You're sure of the symposium date?"

"Certainly," Prendergast said.

Back in the car, Grady took another slug of vodka, this time because his stomach was fluttering badly.

The guidance counselor had lied. He had told Jake Aarons, the detective who wrote the DD 5 on Scott, that he was in school on the sixteenth.

Back in the squad room, Grady checked further. He called Aarons and then six other people, and finally got to the person who could definitively tell him if Raymond Scott was at the symposium.

When Lawless got in, Grady told him the results.

"He wasn't at school, and he wasn't at the symposium. He lied."

"Good work, Leo," Lawless said. "Run him."

CHAPTER 41

Once caught in a lie, Raymond Scott qualified for special attention by the homicide squad. "Basically," Piccolo said to Grady, "we look up his ass with a microscope."

Scott was rechecked through BCI. They contacted the Army for his service records, sent a special memo to the FBI, and a request for information from the New York State Department of Motor Vehicles. They examined his records at New York State Tax and Finance and city tax, the IRS, and, though it was illegal, whatever Social Security—through a contact of Lawless's—had on him.

That was for openers.

Lawless also met with Jake Aarons.

"I remember him," Aarons said. "Good-looking. Well-spoken. Smooth."

"Anything unusual?"

"Not that I could see."

At Lawless's instructions, Grady also called back Prendergast.

"I'm sorry to bother you, sir," Grady said, calm and articulate from the vodka swimming in his belly, "but I forgot to ask you about the backgrounds of a couple of people on the list—Mr. Farris and Mr. Scott. We'd like to know their employment before Wade."

"Farris," Prendergast said, "I can tell you right away.

He came from District Eighty-nine in the Bronx. He's been here ten years. "Scott," he continued, "I don't know. Just a moment."

He came back with the efficiency Grady anticipated, within a minute.

"Before his assignment here," Prendergast said, "he was a guidance counselor at Franklin High School in Philadelphia."

"Do you have an address?"

"Certainly." Prendergast gave it to him.

"Thank you."

Grady had made the call from the squad room. He gave the information to Lawless.

Lawless pondered what to do over a cup of coffee and a cigarette. Then he dialed Philadelphia information and got the number of Franklin High School. He dialed it.

He was bucked to three different people before James Hayden, principal of the school, got on the other end of the line.

"My name is Joe Lawless. I'm a police officer in New York," he said. "We're checking out the backgrounds of some people involved here in a crime. One of them is a man who worked at Franklin High. Raymond Scott."

There was the slightest hesitation before Hayden answered. But to Lawless, a trained listener, it was pregnant, obvious.

"Sir, I don't even know you are who you say you are."

"I'm a detective with the Fifty-third Precinct in the Bronx. You can call me back."

"I don't want to talk to you about anything. Not on the phone."

"Can I come down there?"

"When?"

"I can make it today."

"What kind of case is this?"

"Homicide."

Pause.

"Murder?"

"Yes."

Pause.

"All right, I can meet you later," Hayden said.

Hayden held the line while Lawless called Amtrak on another line. They arranged to meet at six-thirty at the information booth at the 30th Street Station.

By four o'clock, the train with Lawless on it was softly running across New Jersey on its way to Philadelphia. Lawless looked out the window at the "meadowlands," a public-relations man's euphemism for swamp. To Lawless, it was neither. It was a Mafia bone orchard.

He lit a cigarette and inhaled deeply. He wondered what Hayden would have to say—because he would have something to say. If he didn't, Lawless throught, he simply would have said, "Don't come—I have nothing to say," or its equivalent. But he didn't.

At the station, Lawless recognized Hayden right away from the description he had given: a short, conservatively dressed, wiry-looking man with glasses and gray hair. He looked like he spent a lot of time playing golf or doing something outdoors. He was in good shape.

Lawless shook hands with him.

"May I see your identification?"

Lawless took it out and handed it to him. Hayden examined it. He handed it back.

They went out of the station and walked a couple of blocks to a small gray station wagon.

"I would like to take you to my house," Hayden said when they got under way, "but to tell the truth I want to tell you something that I don't want young ears to hear."

"No problem," Lawless said and he thought that he, too, had something to say that young ears shouldn't hear.

"I thought we'd go to a diner I know on Market," Hayden said, smiling slightly. "The food is terrible. We'll be able to find a table that's isolated."

A few minutes later the two men walked into the Champion Diner. There were only a few diners at tables and a couple on counter stools. They took an isolated booth in back.

The service was terrible too. It took three minutes for the waitress to show up. She looked like she resented their presence. She took their orders for coffee and went away.

174

"What's this murder case?" Hayden said. Lawless sensed he was nervous.

"A thirteen-year-old girl was assaulted and asphyxiated."

Some of the color went out of Hayden's face. "You think Scott did it?"

"I don't know. That's where I thought you could help. All we know is that he lied to us about his whereabouts during the time the girl was killed."

The men paused in their conversation when the waitress came over with the coffee. They sipped. It was lukewarm and bitter.

Hayden looked at Lawless. When the waitress was out of earshot he said, "Scott was a son of a bitch. He should have been tarred and feathered."

"Why?"

"He was guidance counselor here for a year—first year as assistant," Hayden said, "and he had an affair with one of the girls who came to him for help. Debbie Williams. She was fourteen."

As usual, Lawless had a poker face. He remembered what O'Hara said about similarities among victims.

"What does she look like?"

Hayden paused. "Dark hair. Dark eyes. Very well built. She looked like a full-grown woman.

Something gripped Lawless's stomach. His face showed nothing. "How do you know he was having an affair?"

"One of the teachers—Mr. Morris, who teaches history—spotted the two of them going into a motel in Cherry Hill. We confronted him, but he denied it. The girl denied it too. She was hung up on him."

"Do you have any idea what the details of the relationship were?"

"No," Hayden said. He paused. "We were able to force him to resign. But we couldn't bring formal charges without proof. We would have had a strike on our hands. It all just got pushed under the rug."

Hayden sipped the coffee. His statement dripped with regret.

"Can I talk with Debbie Williams?" Lawless said. "Do you know where she is?"

"She's dead."

"How?"

"Car accident. Intoxicated. About six months after Scott left. I blame him. After he left she came apart at the seams.

"Son of a bitch," Hayden continued. "She was a disturbed young girl. She goes to a guidance counselor for help . . ."

"Do you know what school Scott was at before Franklin?"

"Sure. Jackson High in south Baltimore. He was there two years."

"Did he have problems?"

"I never checked—at least not thoroughly."

"What do you mean?"

"We took everything at face value. Or rather, I took everything at face value." Hayden looked down at the coffee, and Lawless sensed an immense sadness.

"I hired him," Hayden said softly.

Before they parted, Hayden brought Lawless back to Franklin High, where they looked at a yearbook that showed some pictures of Debbie Williams. There were no pictures of Scott. The formal picture of Scott had been pulled just before publication. There were no candid shots of either the girl or Scott.

Later that night, in his motel room on the outskirts of the city, Lawless thought about Debbie Williams. She had the same general looks as Mary Baumann. And, like Mary, she looked older than she was.

Lawless had been down false roads too many times to vault to Scott's guilt. But it was not unpromising. What he needed was a pattern, or a more direct connection.

And he thought about Scott. Nice guy.

He called Barbara about ten.

"Hello." Her voice was subdued.

"How are you doing?"

"Better, now that I hear from you."

"What's the matter?"

"Nothing. I just get tired of people regarding me like the leper who walked Queens. Sneaking looks at me and all. And those reporters. I had a reporter from the *Telegram* slip into the seat opposite me in a place I purposely went to because I thought no one would find me. I felt like pouring my soda on his head."

"You should have."

"Next time I will," she said. "Sorry to wail. How's the case going?"

"Looking up a little. Scott was involved with a girl down here who has the same physical description. I have more checking to do."

"When will you be back?"

"I don't know yet."

"Oh."

"I'll call tomorrow night. Okay?"

"I miss you badly. I find myself doing obscene things to your pillow."

Lawless laughed. Then: "I love you." It was beautiful. He got it out without feeling that his stomach went with it.

"You don't know how good that makes me feel. I'll be okay. I got Joe Lawless on my team."

"Believe it, baby."

CHAPTER 42

At eleven the next morning Lawless entered the "Round Building" on 8th and Race streets, headquarters of the Philadelphia Police Department. He had arranged to meet with Captain George MacLeish, head of the Intelligence section. Scott had lived in the area, and Lawless wanted to see if there were any similar bondage-style murders, particularly in 1982 and 1983, the years Scott was at Franklin High.

MacLeish, a big, ruddy-faced man in his mid-fifties, met Lawless in the lobby, then led him to a back conference room.

"Computers make this fairly easy," MacLeish said with the trace of a brogue. "They spit up fifteen homicides I'd say are in the area you're interested in. Here they are."

There was a thick pile of folders on one end of a large conference table.

"I'll leave you with these. Need any help, holler."

Lawless sat down, lit a cigarette, and began.

He went through the files twice, reading the Philly version of DD 5's, examining photos, trying to pick up something similar.

In a few cases the girls looked like Mary—and Debbie Williams—dark hair and eyes, softig figure. In a couple of cases death was asphyxia by ligature. And in three cases panties and/or bras were stuffed in the girls' mouth as gags.

Three of the girls were under fourteen. One was ten. In two cases the tying was fairly elaborate. But in no case were there marked similarities between these victims and Baumann, and in no case did the tying come remotely close to the way Mary Baumann had been bound.

Lawless drove back to the motel, then called the Baltimore PD. He told them who he was and what he was interested in, and they promised to break out the files.

He got in the car and drove south.

CHAPTER 43

At twilight on the day Joe Lawless drove south toward Baltimore, Barbara Babalino sat on the couch in his living room and looked around. It was all so empty. It looked like a suite of hotel rooms, which is probably all it meant to Lawless. What she couldn't do with it!

She got up, went over to the old-style stereo, and looked at the records in the racks beneath Beatles. Creedence. Rolling Stones. Chuck Berry and all the old-time rock-style stars of the fifties. Nothing of the current groups.

She stood for a moment. She missed him badly. Much more than she had said on the phone.

She went into the bedroom. He had told her she could go through his things—"My house is yours"—and she wanted to, again. She enjoyed looking at them. Better than anything else, the things showed, in some silent, profound way, what he was like. And this was a way she could touch him, though he wasn't there.

She went over to the dresser, picked up the framed picture of his father, and looked at it. He was in uniform, and she could see Lawless in his face, particularly in the eyes. She put it back and glanced at a photo of his mother. He resembled her even more.

On the wall there was a framed picture of Lawless's graduating class at the Academy—all young men, many smiling, dressed in summer blues. She hadn't had any trouble finding Lawless the first time she looked. His face showed the fifteen years he had been on the force, but she liked it better than the young man's face. It had been lived in.

Lawless was smiling slightly, and she could read inside him. He felt proud. It was a proud day for all of them. A quick thought: Even now, at Siberia, she knew, he was still proud. He could still smile.

She opened the top dresser drawer, touched his clothing. It made her heart beat faster. She smelled things. They smelled of the laundry, but she throught she could smell him. She inhaled sharply. God! He could get her going even when he was two hundred miles away.

From the bottom drawer she picked up a small box and opened it. There was a stack of black-and-white pictures from Vietnam. Shots of Lawless alone, in groups, his arms draped around the young guys that flanked him, all of them smiling, all so young. Were these the men who fought wars?

She put the box back. Next to it, just lying on the bottom of the drawer, was a silver star, the second-highest award the military could give.

Someday, she thought, she would talk to him about Vietnam. But not now.

There was one other box. She opened it. Inside were Mass cards commemorating the passing of his father and mother. And beneath them, a bunch of letters written to them when he was in Vietnam. She did not want to read them now.

Near the bed was a bookcase. It was filled with books on history, World War II, technical books on police work, some of which she had herself.

In a silver cup was a tiny American flag. He had sounded so anti-American in talks she had had with him, but when she thought about it she realized he wasn't anti-American. He didn't swallow everything like Pavlov's dog just because someone waved an American flag and implied it was patriotic.

Now, as she stood in front of the bookcase, she had a sense of something missing in his life. A sense of modernness. No, he was not against modern things. But . . . something. He liked old things . . . he liked . . .

180

Her mind went back to the dinner at her house. Something she had asked him: "Where are you from, Joe?"

And his answer: "Where I'm from is gone. They call it Bedford-Stuyvesant now."

That was it. Where he was from was gone.

And then she realized exactly what it was, and she articulated why she loved him. It was his value system, the living core of his existence, and the courage to live by it.

There was a place—wasn't there?—where men like Lawless came from. Yes, there was, but now it was mostly gone, gone from America. People paid lip service to value systems, but they lived in fear, they got greedy, they . . . yes, Lawless had said it: they lose their way.

Oh yeah. That was a place. Her heart swelled with love; her eyes filled with tears.

Where I'm from is gone.

She went back into the living room and sat down on the couch. The very last rays of twilight illuminated the room. She realized that she, too, had a value system, and that she would have to go.

She wasn't sorry that she had come to his apartment, but to stay would be a mistake. Ultimately, she knew, everyone faced everything alone. And the longer she stayed here, the harder it would be for her to leave, to face whatever it was she would have to face.

Her mother had taught her that. When her father had gotten sick, her mother had been devastated and for a while had run away, sort of dropped out. But then, as time went by, she had come around, and during the last desperate days of his illness she was right there with him, as she had been for months.

The last thing he saw before he died was her mother's loving face looking down at him.

If Lawless called tonight, she would tell him. He would understand. Maybe. Whatever, it was the way it had to be.

Lawless called at ten-thirty.

"How's the investigation going?" she asked him.

"I'm in Baltimore. Tomorrow I'm going to check out similars and visit another alma mater of Scott's."

"Good luck."

"How are you doing? You sound better."

"Joe, I have to go home."

There was silence, the only sound the slight ocean noise of the long-distance connection.

"Why?"

"It's better. I have to face the music myself, really. I'd love to lean on you totally—spend some time in your watch pocket, say—but I can't."

"I . . . I need to help you," Lawless said, "as much as possible."

"Count on it."

"When are you leaving?"

"Right away. Tonight."

"It's getting kind of late, isn't it?"

"I'll be all right. If not, I'll call a cop." There was a pause.

"I'm going to miss you," Lawless said.

"I'm expecting you over at my place anytime you can make it."

"It's not the same thing."

"I know," Barbara said.

"Okay," Lawless said. "I'll call tomorrow."

"You better."

"You're some piece of work," Lawless said. "I love you."

"I love you too," Barbara said.

Barbara emerged from the subway stop near her home about midnight.

She was tired, and more nervous than she realized now that she was going home to an empty apartment. She tried not to think what might lie ahead.

Still, she was not sorry she had done it. It was the only way.

The man sitting in the front of a car parked across the street and down the block a bit was out of the orbit of light thrown by a street lamp. And he was on the passenger side so that in case he was spotted it would seem as if he were waiting for the driver.

He was still. Nothing moved except his eyes. They moved in tiny increments, following Barbara as she lugged her suitcase down the block.

She turned into her apartment building and was soon out of sight.

He wondered who she had been whoring with.

CHAPTER 44

The Baltimore Police had come up with eleven bondage-style murders for Lawless to look at. As in Philadelphia, he looked at them quickly. They included a couple of unusual ones, but there was nothing similar to the Baumann killing.

Lawless got directions to Jackson High from one of the Intelligence guys who had helped gather the files, then drove out.

He didn't call the school before he left. Whenever he could, he tried to arrive on a scene cold, so people would not have time to think and to formulate answers. You almost always got a better reaction that way, one more likely to be truthful.

As he drove, he fantasized that Barbara was with him. Just sitting next to him, in a summer dress, the two of them laughing and talking. And in the fantasy she was drinking a can of soda, and as he glanced at her once, her hand around the can, he saw the ring. His ring. They were married.

He felt a little crawl of panic. Inevitably, he knew,

that's where the relationship would lead him. One day, he would ask her.

It could work. This time it could. They were both cops. It was not like him and Karen. They were from different worlds. But he and Barbara were from the same world. She knew that being a cop was something that got inside you and wouldn't let go. She understood.

Yes, it would be different. He wanted kids. He and Karen had always said they would have kids one day, but that day never came. Now he was thirty-seven. Physically he could father children for a long time, but he wanted to be a father to them. To—yeah—do all the things with them that his father had never done with him. Go to ball games, play together, talk—that would be nice.

Again, a crawl of panic. Who could say Barbara would even marry him? Who could say whether she wanted children? Who could say . . .

For the moment, he thought, he should be satisfied with love. Every time he thought he would be seeing her fairly soon, a warm sensation permeated him.

Love. Without love . . . He smiled at the ghoulish thought. Without love they wouldn't need many people working homicide, because it was love gone wrong that produced most of them. The knifings, the shootings, the stranglings, the suicides . . .

His mind shifted to Mary Baumann. Those dilated, staring eyes.

She would never have a chance at love. Thirteen years old. She had had a right to life. Sure, maybe, if you looked at her life, it wouldn't have turned out too well. But that was her right too. Taking it away was the right of only one being, a God. Lawless had long ago given up on organized religion, but he still believed in God, and only God could shut you down.

He thought again of those dark, staring eyes.

We care, kid, and we're going to make someone pay.

CHAPTER 45

Lawless had never been to Baltimore, but he found
Jackson High School without difficulty. It was a mod-
ernistic one-story building, very wide, set on carefully
tended suburban lawn that was a little brown now in
August.

There were kids all over the place. They had summer
school. Lawless asked one of the students, a boy about
fifteen, where the principal's office was. He was directed to it in an accent that was distinctly Southern.

As he walked down the hall toward the office, students walked past him from behind him and in front.
The place had a very high energy level. He caught
odors: perfume, sweat—and emotion.

The sign took him by surprise. It was on an open
door: GUIDANCE. He wondered if Scott had had an office
in there.

He stepped through the doorway. There were a couple
of desks flanking three more doorways. The doors were
closed on two of them, and the names of the counselors,
he assumed, were on the doors: Mr. Meagher, Mr. Freda.
He couldn't see the name on the corner office because
the door was open. He approached it. There was someone inside.

The name on the door was Dr. Cortissoz. Sitting behind the desk was a slim, attractive woman whom he took
to be around forty-five. She looked at him suspiciously.

"Can I help you?" she said.

Lawless smiled, took out his tin, and showed it.

"My name is Joe Lawless," he said. "I'm down here

from the Fifty-third Precinct in New York City, looking into the background of a former employee of the school who worked in this department."

"Did you get cleared at the principal's office?"

"No. Were you here in '80 and '81?"

"Yes, but I can't talk with you."

"One way or another you will," Lawless said. "Because I'll go back to the principal's office and he'll clear me—and probably send me here. Or he won't, and I'll pick up the phone and call the City Desk of the Baltimore *Sun*."

"What do you mean?"

"Tell them that you people hired a guidance counselor who may have murdered a thirteen-year-old girl in New York City."

Lawless saw that he was getting through.

"What man?"

"Raymond Scott."

"Oh," Dr. Cortissoz said. She had an expression on her face as if Lawless had dropped something rank on her desk.

Lawless was inside the office.

"Why don't you just talk to me," he said, sitting down, "and I'll be out of your hair very quickly."

She lit a cigarette. Lawless lit one too.

"What do you want to know?"

"Did he have any problems?"

"Like what?"

"Doctor, let's not play games. Was he involved with any of the students he counseled in, shall we say, an unprofessional manner?"

She glanced toward the doorway. She got up, closed the door, and sat back down.

"Yes," she said. "He was involved with one of the students. At least one."

She paused, then continued.

"We suspected more, but we couldn't prove it. We couldn't even technically prove the one."

"What do you mean?"

"There were rumors near the end of the time he was here that he was involved with various girls. But he was definitely involved with a girl named Bonnie Atkins— that's her maiden name. Her married name is Plotnik. He was seen twice going into motels with her. And after he left, she told me he had had sex with her."

"Was he fired?"

"Forced to resign. He's very cool. We confronted him, but he wouldn't quit until six months later."

"Do you," he asked, "know where she lives?" And he thought, *If she lives.*

Dr. Cortissoz shook her head. "No, but a couple of months ago they had a party, a reunion party."

She picked up a phone, tapped out a number.

"Penny," she said, "do you have Bonnie Atkins's address? I mean Plotnik." She paused. "Thanks."

Dr. Cortissoz held her hand over the phone. "Penny organized the party," she said. She took her hand away from the phone, listened, and wrote something on a slip of paper.

"Thanks," she said, hanging up as she handed the paper to Lawless.

"How old was she when she was in school?" Lawless asked.

"Thirteen, fourteen. I can find out exactly."

"No, that's okay. What'd she look like?"

"Dark hair, dark eyes. Very pretty. The prettiest girl in her class, maybe the whole school."

"Mature for her age?"

"Very."

Lawless looked at her.

CHAPTER 46

The sky was growing dark and threatening rain as Lawless started out for Bonnie Plotnik's house. With the aid of a couple of passersby he found it without too much difficulty.

The area she lived in reminded him of a cleaned-up version of Fort Siberia. It was down by the railroad station, one of a long line of run-down, three-story brick buildings. The streets and sidewalks were dirty, with graffiti everywhere. It was Baltimore's slum.

All of the tenements had short stoops. Just before he stepped up and went inside, Lawless glanced at a little black kid sitting on a battered tricycle on the street. The kid was eyeing him, and the eyes were not friendly. He was Whitey, the Man.

Lawless rang the bell and was buzzed in. He went through a short hall, then through a dirty glass door to the foot of a long, narrow set of stairs. He glanced around the hall. Paint was peeling from the dingy walls and ceiling, and there was a heavy smell of urine. Shades of Fort Siberia.

A heavyset woman loomed at the top of the stairs. She was about thirty, with bleached blond hair.

"Yeah," she said. She was wearing a tight-fitting skirt that showed rolls of fat, and a sweater that showed, large, sloppy breasts.

"I'm looking for Bonnie Plotnik," Lawless said, starting to climb the stairs.

"What do you want?"

"I'm from New York," he said softly. "I'm looking

188

into a case involving a young girl. I'm a detective, and I was told Bonnie might be able to help us."

"How?"

Lawless reached the top. He looked at her. He showed his tin. "Is she here?"

"I'm Bonnie."

Lawless recalled what the guidance counselor had said: *the prettiest girl in the class, maybe the school.*

"What do you want?"

"Can we talk inside?"

She looked at him expressionlessly for a moment. He could smell beer on her. Then she turned and he followed her through the open door of an apartment directly opposite the stairs. She closed the door. They passed through an unkempt, run-down living room where a small child was watching cartoons on a badly out-of-focus black-and-white television.

She stopped.

"Go to your room," she said, and the boy immediately turned off the TV and toddled off without complaint or comment. Lawless got the sense that he didn't want to make Bonnie mad.

"What's this all about?" she said.

Lawless looked more closely at her. She was still pretty, but there were lines on her face, and the end of her nose had broken blood vessels. It was hard to believe she was only nineteen or twenty.

"A thirteen-year-old girl," Lawless said, "was found murdered in New York. Raymond Scott is a suspect."

Her eyes narrowed. "Oh, that bastard. Now he's murdering girls."

"What do you mean?"

"You want a beer?"

"Sure."

Lawless followed her into the kitchen, a cramped little room with a badly worn linoleum floor, a sink full of dishes, and greasy walls. A roach scampered out of sight behind the stove.

She took out two sixteen-ounce cans of Oasis beer

and put one on the kitchen table. She pulled the top expertly off her own and flipped it toward a full bag of garbage. It went in.

Lawless sat down opposite her at the table. He took the top off his can and laid it on the table.

They drank from the cans.

"What about Scott?" Lawless asked. "You knew him?"

She glanced out the window adjacent to the table. The sky was very dark. Her face softened. She looked younger. She spoke, and Lawless got the feeling she was talking about a different person. She probably was.

"I had just turned fourteen when I went to see him," she said. "To ask his advice, get his help. My mother and father were getting a divorce, and I was upset. I asked him what I should do.

"He was nice at first. Very, uh, 'supportive,' I think the word is. And then one day when I was feeling very low he came over and sat down next to me. 'You need love,' he said. 'You need love.'

"He put his arms around me, and before I knew it that's just what the bastard was giving me. After that we did it all the time. Every now and then I think about the fact that I was fourteen. What a bastard!"

"Can I ask you a question, without meaning any disrespect?"

"Yeah."

"Did he try anything sexually offbeat?"

"Kinky? Not at the beginning."

Suddenly she tipped the can up and drained it. Lawless had never seen a woman drink like that. She got up and went to the refrigerator.

"Another?"

"Sure."

Lawless chug-a-lugged the rest of his can. He suppressed a belch.

She got two cans, opened them, put one in front of him, and sat back down at the table. She flipped the tops toward the garbage can. Both disappeared.

190

She took a long slug.

"I was mature," she said, "But I was four-fucking-teen. And he was a full-grown man. He was rough—very rough."

"You mentioned kinky."

"Sure," she said. "He was."

"Did he ever tie you up?"

"He tied me up and he fucked me up."

"How did he tie you? I mean, where were the ropes?"

"Around the wrists and ankles. To the bed. He screwed me front and back. He liked to hurt."

"Did he ever tape your hands, tie something around your neck?"

"No."

Lawless took a long slug. "How did the relationship end?" he said.

"He broke it off. He just told me one day he didn't want to see me anymore. That it would be better for both of us."

"What was the real reason?"

Bonnie Plotnik, née Atkins, smiled bitterly. "You're smart," she said. "The real reason was that he found someone else. Even younger."

"Do you know who?"

"No, I just heard about it a few years ago. I was young and naive back then. I believed it was better for both of us. I loved him."

She smiled, and for the first time Lawless saw her teeth. Two were missing, and one was dead.

"But let me tell you," she said, "being involved with a shit like that and married at sixteen to a guy who doesn't work makes you old fast."

"Thanks for your help."

"I hope he's the killer," she said. "I'd like to come up and pull the switch."

"Take care," Lawless said.

When he emerged from the tenement, a light rain was falling.

He got into his car, which was parked on the other

side of the street, pulled out, and slowly drove down the block. As he went, he glanced in the rearview mirror. Through the rain-beaded rear window, the tenements were thrown completely out of focus.

He thought about Debbie Williams, the young girl Scott had been involved with in Philadelphia, and who died a DWI at thirteen. Scott killed her, Lawless thought. He thought of Bonnie Plotnik. He had killed her, too.

CHAPTER 47

The next morning, Lawless met with Grady, Piccolo, and Edmunton in the squad room. He brought them up to date on what he had learned about Scott. Then: "We need to know where he was during the time Mary Baumann was done, the night of June fifteenth and sixteenth. We have two choices. We can bring him in or shadow him."

"Let's bring him in," Piccolo said flatly. Edmunton looked at Piccolo and laughed gutturally.

"Isn't it," Grady said, "uh, shadowing him, kind of dangerous? What if he is the killer and gets away from us?"

Or, Grady thought, gets away from *me*.

"It's a point," Lawless said. "There's always a risk. But if we catch him prepping for a job, we should be able to stick him good. Or he might lead us to something concrete. And we have nothing on him right now."

Lawless, who had been sitting, got up and walked over to a position opposite the window. He inhaled deeply on the cigarette he was smoking.

"Let's shadow him for a few days," he said, disappointing everyone.

"We'll use two-man teams—Leo and I will take nights, Ed and Frank days—twelve-hour shifts. Our first step," he added, "is to get an ID on him."

A couple of hours later, a plain battered brown van with mirrored porthole windows pulled up and parked across the Concourse and down about fifty yards from Adams High School on 174th Street. Inside the van were Lawless, Grady, Piccolo, Edmunton, and Aarons. They watched through the windows, which were one-way.

They were waiting for Raymond Scott. An innocent call to Wade had determined that he was doing counseling work at Adams for the summer.

At two o'clock the school disgorged. Kids came running out of the building, young girls and boys. Occasionally an adult emerged.

Aarons's eyes were glued to the entrance. So were everyone else's.

"There he is," he suddenly said. "Blondie."

The man he referred to looked as though he had just stepped out of the pages of *Gentlemen's Quarterly*. It was a hot, sunny day, but he looked cool in the extreme, like he didn't have or need sweat glands.

He was tall and well-built, very good-looking, his blond hair styled. He had on a light cotton suit, sports shirt, no tie, and shiny light shoes. He wore mirrored sunglasses. Grady found it hard to believe that this man could assault and kill a little girl. Why?

As Scott walked, Edmunton squeezed off twenty exposures with a 35mm camera with a zoom lens on it.

Scott crossed the Concourse diagonally. He got into a sporty red Honda Prelude, started up, and headed south down the Concourse. Immediately, Edmunton passed through the door into the driver's compartment, started the vehicle up, and followed. Lawless got into the passenger seat.

At 138th Street the Honda hung a left, then a right.

193

"He's heading for the Drive," Lawless said.

Scott was. He made a looping turn after crossing the Willis Avenue Bridge and headed downtown.

He got off the F.D.R. Drive at East Houston Street and headed west.

"I think he's going home," Lawless said.

Edmunton had no trouble keeping the Honda in visual contact on the drive across town, but he briefly lost it in the maze of Greenwich Village streets. Then he picked it up again.

Scott lived on Barrow Street. When he turned into it, Edmunton went by, losing the Honda. He went around the block and down, then pulled into a space around the next block. Scott was squeezing his car into a small parking space on Barrow.

They watched him go into his building, a five-story red-brick structure similar to other buildings on both sides of the block.

"Okay," Lawless said to Piccolo and Edmunton. "We'll see you tonight." Lawless, Grady, and Aarons waited for an opportune moment, then slipped out a side door and headed for the subway. Piccolo and Edmunton trained their attention on the building entrance.

They took turns watching. One would watch while the other would sleep, or read, or do crosswords, or talk about this or that but mostly about Piccolo's pets: a monitor, white rats, a python, and a tokay gecko, a lizard that is the only natural enemy of the roach.

Edmunton loved hearing Piccolo go on about them. So interesting.

At six, adrenaline surged. Scott appeared. He was dressed in sports clothes and carried an overnight bag. He headed up the street, in the opposite direction from where his car was parked.

"I'll take it, Ed," Piccolo said.

He exited from the rear door and was soon about fifteen yards behind Scott on the other side of the street.

194

As he walked, Scott was eyed by a number of fags, Piccolo noted, but he did not look back.

Three blocks from his building he turned into the Embrac Fitness Center. Piccolo wandered to the end of the block, where he stood in the shade, lit a cigar, and waited.

Scott came out of the center an hour and a half later. Piccolo followed. Scott went back to his apartment, and Piccolo got back into the van.

"Where'd he go?" Edmunton asked.

"A fucking gym."

As it got dark, Lawless showed up. He came down Barrow in a sedan and, by prearranged signal, flashed his lights once, then continued down the block and parked on the next block over.

He and Grady walked back to the van and slipped in when they could.

Piccolo detailed Scott's activities for the day—one trip to the Embrac Fitness Center.

"Okay, me and Leo'll take him to the school. We'll see you there about nine. Okay?"

Lawless gave Piccolo the keys to the sedan, and when he and Edmunton could, they slipped out and went up Barrow to the car. Lawless watched until they drove away.

Five minutes after they left, it was completely dark.

Lawless said, "I'm going to see what kind of rear exit the building has. Okay?"

"Okay, Joe," Grady said, but he shifted a little inside. He would be alone—and he had very little vodka in him. By a stupendous act of will he had gone dry most of the day because the last thing he wanted to do was let Lawless down—either by inattention or maybe by falling asleep.

"You'll be back soon?"

"Shouldn't take more than ten or fifteen minutes."

Lawless left the van a few minutes later. Grady watched him cross the street, then disappear into the building.

The hall was clean, with no graffiti. It had double-frosted glass doors flanked by lines of bells. Lawless checked. Scott lived in apartment 3-C.

Lawless tried the front door. Closed. He pressed the bell of a fifth-floor apartment and a few seconds later was buzzed in.

The lobby was small, clean, well maintained. Someone was cooking steak.

Straight ahead was an elevator, the car at the floor. To the right were stairs, or a door to them. He went over and tried the door. It was locked.

He pressed the button to the elevator. The doors slid open and he got on, then pressed "B." The car descended.

He stepped out into the basement.

It was well lit and freshly painted, the ceiling and walls sparkling white, the floor gray enamel. It was a far cry from the place where Mary Baumann had died.

And much smaller. To his left was a hall that led he knew not where. He started down it, and turned back immediately. Directly ahead was the super's apartment.

The hall to the right of the elevator was more productive. He went down it, past a series of storerooms, then hooked a left and saw what he wanted: a rear door. It was wood with individual inset windows.

He tried the knob and was surprised to find it open. Maybe they weren't super security-conscious down here.

There was a bulb burning over it. He closed the door behind him and walked quickly out of the radius of light. He stood in the darkness a moment. He heard the sounds of a love ballad, canned laughter, a plane droning, far in the distance. He got his bearings and knew he had to make his reconnoiter fast. If someone spotted him they might call the cops.

It took him only a minute to traverse the entire backyard, and then he understood why the rear door was open.

There was no way out. The walls to the yard were sheer concrete about fifteen feet high and topped by a Cyclone fence topped with barbed wire. And there was no way in.

Lawless felt something relax inside himself.

Five minutes later he was back in the van with Grady. Grady felt something relax inside himself too.

"Anything?" Lawless asked.

"No," Grady said. "But a lot of gay men."

"This is the area for it."

He detailed to Grady what he had found, and then both men turned their attention to the front entrance of the building, waiting for Raymond Scott to show—or not show.

CHAPTER 48

Piccolo and Edmunton relieved Lawless and Grady at nine the next morning. The van was across the street from the school.

"He went in at eight-thirty," Lawless said. "His Honda's parked on the next block."

"Why don't you let Ed and me talk to this fuck?" Piccolo asked. Edmunton giggled.

Lawless shook his head. "No," he said. But he thought, It might come to that. No way was there going to be another dead girl if Scott was the killer.

Lawless and Grady left, and Piccolo and Edmunton settled in to watch the school. They had an ice chest full of cold drinks and water, portable fans, and both men wore shorts and light shirts.

It was hot already, and as the day wore on the heat would build up in the van, so that by the time Grady and Lawless arrived to relieve them it would be like a sauna. The only relief they might have would be trailing Scott home—or wherever he went when he left school. Then they could open the windows as they drove.

The hours dragged. By noon it was so hot in the van that the men weren't talking anymore—they didn't have the energy. Piccolo kept stationed at one of the windows, and Edmunton did an imitation of a man trying to sleep.

Nothing happened. There were the usual comings and goings one might expect at a school, but nothing extraordinary and no sign of Scott.

At two, school let out, as it had the day before. And Scott came out just as he had the day before, except clad differently: he had on a light gray suit and dark shiny shoes, but his mirrored shades were in place.

Piccolo, who thought he must have sweat a tubful that day, turned to Edmunton, who, he thought, probably sweat a river, and said, "A real sweetheart, isn't he?"

Edmunton didn't react. Too washed out.

They watched Scott go to his car, get in, and start to drive south. They followed, Edmunton driving.

As they went, they rolled down the windows. The warm breezes coming in felt like arctic headwinds.

Scott went left at 138th, then wove his way to the F.D.R. Drive just as before.

"I wonder," Edmunton said as they got onto the Drive, "why he doesn't take the West Side Highway downtown. He lives on the West Side."

"He's a weirdo," Piccolo said.

Again, Scott got off at the East Houston Street exit, drove across town, then threaded the Honda through a series of complicated streets to his building on Barrow. Piccolo and Edmunton kept him in sight all the way.

Scott parked close to the spot he had taken the day before. Edmunton pulled into a completely different spot on the next block. They would watch the building with glasses. The last thing they wanted was to take a burn; the more tired you were, the more possible that was.

Nothing happened. This time Scott stayed indoors. Piccolo and Edmunton sweated and watched.

Lawless and Grady showed up at dark.

"He's been in since he got here," Piccolo said.

"Tomorrow," Lawless said, "we're going to change vehicles. I'm going to try to get us something with air-conditioning."

Lawless and Grady watched the building all night with glasses. Scott stayed inside.

CHAPTER 49

Lawless was unable to get an air-conditioned vehicle. What he did get was another van even more dilapidated than the first, and just as uncomfortable.

Piccolo and Edmunton were in position the following day at two o'clock when school let out. They waited for Scott to emerge as he had on the two previous days, but he didn't.

First there was a crowd of kids outside the school, then clusters, then just a few stragglers.

"Where the fuck is he?" Piccolo hissed. The van was directly across the street. He was at one window, Edmunton at the other.

"I don't know," Edmunton said.

Piccolo was considering what to do—go in the school or contact Lawless—when Scott appeared at the door.

"You fuck," Piccolo said.

Scott, dressed, as usual, like he had walked off the pages of a fashion magazine, crossed the Concourse and got into his car. Piccolo and Edmunton waited until he was immersed in southbound traffic before following. It promised to be another boring seven or eight hours.

At around 165th Street, traveling in the right lane adjacent to Macombs Dam Park, the Honda's flashers suddenly went on. Piccolo, driving, made an instant decision. He kept going.

The van went by the Honda. Edmunton caught a glimpse of Scott. His head was turned toward the park. Then Edmunton looked in the side rear-view mirror.

"Hey, Frank, there's a broad getting into the car. She just came from the park!"

"What'd she look like?"

"I can't see. Too far away."

Gently, Piccolo pressed on the brakes as he approached a green light. It turned amber, then red.

"The flashers went off. Here it comes," Edmunton said.

The light was long enough. The Honda pulled up next to the van. Edmunton could see, and Piccolo strained to see, the bottom half of the woman who had gotten into the car. She had big tits and nice legs encased in sausage-skin jeans.

Piccolo let Scott get ahead, then dropped in behind him. It was impossible to see the face of the woman, but she had dark hair.

At 161st Street, Scott hung a right. Piccolo followed.

At Jerome Avenue, he hung another right. Piccolo followed.

At Jerome Avenue, he hung another right and headed north, back uptown.

. Piccolo and Edmunton rode in silence. They were unaware of the weather, their sweaty bodies, cool breezes, or anything. It was that moment you wait for in a stakeout: something could be going down.

At Fordham Road another right. The Honda tooled east. Piccolo was in his element. He loved action. He felt totally alive. He always thought what the high-wire guy, Wallenda, had said when asked if he would go back up on the wire after a near-fatal fall: "Go back?" Wallenda had said. " Life is the wire. All else is waiting."

All right, you fucker, let's do it! Whooeeeeee!

The traffic on Fordham was fairly heavy. Piccolo had no problem keeping the little red car in sight.

Maybe, he thought at one point, he should apprehend, or ask for backup. But why? He had no proof any crime had been committed, was being committed, or would be committed. But his gut spoke to him. A gut honed over fourteen years on the street. The guy was late coming out the building; he met the girl in what really could be considered a secret rendez-fucking-vous. Yeah, something was going down.

He felt the weight of his .38 in his pocket. And there was a shotgun in back within easy reach. He was ready, Eddie!

The Honda continued east across Pelham Bay Parkway. Traffic thinned. Piccolo hung back. Scott had no idea they were up his ass.

Near Southern Boulevard, Scott's right blinker went on, and Piccolo and Edmunton knew where he was heading: to the Zoological Motel, a popular hot-bed facility more popularly known as the Zoo, which was, as one vice cop put it, "A condom's throw from the Bronx Zoo" across the street.

The Zoo had been built by a consortium of Mafia biggies who had transplanted some of California's architectural delights. It was a big pink stucco job topped by an orange-tiled roof and surrounded by a Cyclone fence topped with razor wire, the latter an idea transplanted from Fort Siberia and designed to make sure everyone who entered the motel went through the front gate and paid. The Zoo made a tremendous amount of money, understandable when considering that the average stay was around an hour and a half.

The Honda had stopped by the entrance kiosk adjacent to an electronically operated gate. Piccolo made another quick decision.

"We're going in, Eddie," he said, "as a loving fucking couple."

Edmunton giggled.

The gate opened and the Honda went through. Piccoo pulled the battered van up to the kiosk.

The attendant, a young, macho-looking dark-haired dude, seemed on the verge of saying something to the skinny little man in shorts next to whom sat a big fat man in shorts, but something in Piccolo's eyes told him not to.

"Films," the attendant said.

"No," Piccolo snarled.

"Seventy dollars. Suite seventeen."

Piccolo handed him the money, got the key, and went through.

"They went around the back, Frank."

Piccolo drove up a cobbled driveway flanked by plastic palm trees, then made a right at a fork. The road led to a block of rooms on an extremity of the property.

The detectives saw the car as soon as they got to the back, and spotted Scott and the woman going into the room at the end. She was not only built; she was pretty, with dark eyes as well as dark hair.

"I better call Joe," Piccolo said.

He went to a freestanding phone booth at the opposite end of the bank of rooms from where Scott had gone in.

Lawless answered after the fourth ring.

Piccolo detailed it.

"I'm on my way," Lawless said.

CHAPTER 50

It was, Barbara learned later from Lawless, just a case of bad luck. While she was trying to call him, he was on his way to the Zoo.

Her call to Lawless had been prompted by one she had received at the Nine Four.

At the time, she was in a conference room containing a huge table on which were spread foot-thick stacks of papers, and she was being bored to distraction as she stapled them together. They then would be distributed to all Queens commands, and she would start on new stacks.

Calls to her were being forwarded to the conference room. When she picked up and heard the voice, it grabbed her stomach. It was official, guarded.

"Officer Babalino?"

"Yes."

"This is Deputy Inspector Macgruder at the commissioner's office. It is my duty to inform you that after a complete investigation by the Internal Affairs Division it has been concluded that a departmental hearing will be conducted in your case."

Barbara went hollow. She thought of Lawless.

"You will be notified of the time and place."

"Thank you," she stupidly said.

After she hung up she immediately tried Lawless at home, because she knew he was on stakeout, and then at the station. No luck.

Then she started to think of the departmental trial. Ninety-nine percent. She had no chance.

One percent. Not even Lawless could help.

But it was no time for panic. She smiled. What else was she to do?

When in doubt, she thought, go back to basics. She dialed the number. It was the first telephone number she had ever learned. She had learned it when she was six years old.

"Hello." The voice had a slight Italian accent.

"It's me, Ma."

CHAPTER 51

As it happened, Lawless only lived ten minutes from the Zoo. He paid his way in. He hadn't decided how to handle it, so he didn't identify himself.

When he pulled his car around to the back, Piccolo and Edmunton got out of the van. He got out of his car and went up to them.

"They've been in there fifteen minutes, right?"

"Yeah," Piccolo said.

This seemed an unlikely place for murder. Still, the girl had the same physical description, and who could predict what a head case would do.

"Let's go in," he said.

The three men went up to the door. Lawless motioned Piccolo and Edmunton to flank it. He tapped softly on the door. There was no answer. He tapped louder. He heard steps.

A muffled voice came though the door.

"Yes?"

"This is the manager. May I speak with you, sir," Lawless said.

The door opened a crack. Scott looked out, squinting. Lawless put his tin at Scott's eye level.

"Open up."

The eyes unsquinted.

"Do you have a warrant?" Scott said smoothly.

"Certainly."

"Just a minute."

"No," Lawless said, and pushed his way in, knocking Scott back.

Scott was in sort of foyer. He was dressed only in black bikini underwear.

Lawless went past him into the bedroom. The girl was on the bed, nude, face up, tied by each wrist and each ankle to a bedpost. She was alive—and terrified. Her head was off the bed, looking at Lawless. She could have been the sister of Debbie Williams, or Bonnie Plotnick when she was young—or Mary Baumann.

Lawless turned and walked back to the foyer. Edmunton and Piccolo were in and had closed the door.

"Listen," Scott said. "You can't do this. My lawyer will have your badge. Where's the warrant?"

"Shut up," Piccolo said, "or I'll tear your head off and shit in it."

Scott looked at Piccolo as if he were crazy.

"Cuff him," Lawless said.

Lawless went back to the girl. He picked up a sheet that had been neatly folded and placed on a chair, shook it out, and covered her. He started to untie the knots. They were square knots.

"Who are you?"

"Lynn!" Scott yelled. "You don't have to—"

There was a thumping sound, followed by a series of gasps.

"Shut up, fuckhead," Piccolo hissed.

Lawless glanced at the girl as he worked.

"Lynn Jacobs."

"Where do you live, Lynn?"

"178 East 174th Street."

"What do you do?"

"I . . . I go to school."

"Where?"

"Wade."

Lawless was finished untying her hands. She was sitting up, holding the sheet over herself. He started to untie her legs.

"How old are you?"

She hesitated. Lawless said nothing.

"Fourteen."

"What're you doing here?"

"Just making love."

"Why are you tied?"

The girl said nothing. She glanced toward the foyer. Lawless went into the foyer. Piccolo and Edmunton were standing over Scott, who was sitting on the floor, hands cuffed behind his back.

"Take him in the bathroom."

Piccolo grabbed Scott by the hair, lifted him up, and pushed him into the bathroom, which was right off the foyer. He closed the door and started the shower.

"Why?"

"He just . . . just liked to make love that way."

Lawless completed the untying.

"Did he do it any other way?"

"I . . I don't know what you mean."

"From the back? In the backside?"

She lowered her head. "Yes."

"Tied?"

She nodded.

"How? Like this?"

"Yes."

"Did you have a rope around your neck?"

"No."

"Were you hurt?"

"A little, but he loves me." Her eyes teared.

"How long have you been seeing him?"

"June."

"How long you been fooling around?"

"July."

"Get dressed."

Lawless went into the foyer while the girl dressed in record time.

He knocked on the bathroom door.

The door opened and Edmunton looked out.

"Take the girl to the car," Lawless said, "and wait. Okay?"

Edmunton came out of the bathroom and escorted the girl, fully clothed, out of the room.

When they left, Lawless said to Piccolo, "Bring him out."

Piccolo pushed him into the room. Lawless still sensed a certain cool defiance, but a certain wariness of Piccolo too.

Lawless grabbed a straight-backed chair and put it near Scott. Facing him.

"Sit there."

Scott sat down.

Lawless looked at Piccolo. "You got a knife?"

Piccolo produced a switchblade from his pocket and snapped it open.

A wave of fear passed across Scott's face.

"Pull down his underwear."

"What are . . . are you doing?" Scott said. Piccolo had a wolfish grin.

He pulled down the bikini underwear to Scott's knees.

"Get some tissue paper and cut off some samples."

Scott's eyes widened.

Piccolo went to the bathroom, got some toilet paper, and returned. He bent down, grabbed a few strands— Scott shied back—of Scott's pubic hair—it was blond— and cut it off. He folded the paper up and put it in his breast pocket. He stood nearby with the knife open.

Lawless sat on the bed. He looked at Scott.

"Do you know why we're here?"

"No."

"Don't lie to me again, Mr. Scott," Lawless said. "You think we're here because you're cohabiting with a fourteen-year-old student. But that's not why. You know the real reason why, don't you?"

Scott looked at him. Lawless tried to read his face for some glint of recognition. He didn't see any.

"I want to find out if you're a murderer."

Scott smiled.

"Why are you smiling, scumbag?" Piccolo hissed. "Let me work on him," he said to Lawless.

Lawless did not respond. "What does the smile mean?" he asked Scott.

"It's bizarre. Murder who?"

"Mary Baumann."

"I didn't kill her. That's absurd." He half smiled again. But this time Lawless saw something else. A glint of fear.

"I'm going to ask you a question," Lawless said. "Remember what I said about not lying." He paused. "Why did you lie about your whereabouts on the day Mary Baumann was murdered?"

"I wan . . . want to see a lawyer. What about the Miranda warning? What about it?"

Piccolo held the knife so the point went up Scott's nostril. "We got the Piccolo warning," he said. "Right here. Speak, you fuck!"

Scott hesitated. "I didn't want anyone looking into where I really was."

"Where?"

"I . . . I was at an orgy."

"Can you prove it?"

"No. It was just a bunch of people who got together after drinking all night."

"You were at this orgy from the night before?"

"Yes, it went through the next day."

"I would suggest you find someone who can prove you were there."

"I'll try."

"Did you know Mary Baumann?"

"Yes. She came to me for counseling." Scott glanced down, then up.

"Did you ever make it with her?"

"No," he said, shaking his head.

Lawless looked at Piccolo. "Get the phone book over there."

"Right."

"You have a pipe in the car?"

Piccolo nodded.

"Get it, will you."

Piccolo folded the knife and left.

"What are you doing?" Scott said.

208

"I told you not to lie. You lied. We're going to put a phone book on your abdomen and then beat it with a pipe. It hurts like hell but doesn't leave any bruises."

"Hey, wait . . ."

Piccolo returned with the pipe. And the wolfish grin had returned.

"All right," Scott blurted. "I had an affair with Mary. Back in April. But I didn't kill her. She was troubled. She came to me for help. I loved her. I care so much about these girls. I love them. I counsel them."

"Did you ever tie her like Lynn?"

"No, I wasn't even counseling her when she . . . got killed, and we only had sex a few times. I . . . I didn't kill her. You have to believe me."

"We're going to need more than your word, Mr. Scott," Lawless said.

"I'll try to find someone from that, uh, party I was at. I will. Can I go?"

"No," Lawless said, getting up. "You can't."

"Why not? You have no proof either, do you, that I killed anyone."

"No," Lawless said. "But I have plenty of proof of statutory rape. We're going to book you for that, if nothing else."

CHAPTER 52

Lawless got Barbara's message when he got back to the squad room. He called and was told she had gone home early. He called her at home.

"Hello."

"Barbara, what's the matter?"

"They're going for a trial. I found out today."

"I'm off stakeout. I'll be over tonight."

"Oh, good," she said intensely.

When he hung up, he called Grady. The phone rang a long time before Grady, sounding like he had strep throat, answered.

He told him what had happened.

"Okay," Grady said. "I'll see what I can find out. The real solution to these things is political. A strong rabbi downtown." He added, "And I'll contact Wendell Lansford to see if he can represent her. He was a trial commissioner."

"I know him," Lawless said evenly.

"He's not one of my favorite people either. But if you're going to have anybody, one of the wolves is best."

"Thanks, Leo."

After speaking with Grady, Lawless went to a small room on the top floor of the station house. Inside were Edmunton, Piccolo, and Scott. They would question him until an assistant district attorney arrived and a decision was made about what to book him on.

The interrogation, after the ADA, James Stacy, arrived, went much longer than expected. Lawless did not get to Barbara's house until after ten o'clock.

She had the door open a millisecond after he rang the bell. He went inside, and she closed it quickly and put her arms around him. He kissed her on the mouth. He felt like enveloping her, protecting her, keeping her from harm. At the same time he knew he couldn't. Not completely.

"I need you, baby," she said, still holding him tight. "I hope you can sleep with me attached like this."

He said nothing. He held her close.

After a while, she broke away and led him by the hand into the living-room.

"Drink, Joe?"

210

"Sure."

"Beer?"

"That's good."

"Okay," she said, and smiled. "Walk me to the kitchen."

He followed her in and watched her get the beers. She handed them to him. There were wisps of hair sticking out from her head and her eyes were red.

They went back into the living room and sat down on the couch.

"I'm scared, Joe. I don't know how I'm going to get out of this."

"I talked with Leo," Lawless said. "He's contacting a lawyer named Wendell Lansford to see if he's available. You may want him. He's a former trial commissioner."

"That sounds good," Barbara said.

"But the real way to handle these things is politically. From inside. Leo's going to find out what's going on. Then we'll see what we can do, who we can reach."

"That sounds promising."

Lawless nodded. He sipped his beer.

"It just," Barbara said softly, "it just hit me hard. I know you said how hard it is to beat something like this. I want to stay a policewoman."

Lawless kissed her hand.

"I even called my mother," Barbara said. "Christ! We both started to cry on the phone!"

Lawless smiled, but inside it was hurting him.

They were silent for a while, then she leaned over and kissed him on the ear. His arms flashed with gooseflesh.

She looked him. "I've been talking about myself so much, I forgot about you. How come you're off the stakeout?"

"We arrested Scott."

"You did!"

Lawless explained about finding him in the motel with the underaged female, and about the questioning.

211

When he was finished, Barbara looked at him with a curious expression.

"What's the matter?" he asked.

"It just struck me that those girls and . . . and Mary Baumann . . . I fit their description quite well. Kind of creepy."

Lawless shook his head.

"Assuming that's the connection to the killer," Lawless said. "Do you know how many other women in this city fit the same description?"

Barbara nodded. "But how many of them," she said, "had their picture in the *Telegram?*"

Lawless took her hand. "I think you're under a lot of pressure," he said.

"You're right," she said. "Anyway, you got Scott locked up. Assuming he's the killer."

"Well," Lawless said, "we do have him, and the DA thinks he did it, but he's not going to book him until we get the report from the lab on his pubic hair."

There was a pause.

"You don't think so, do you?" Barbara asked.

"He's got the pedigree," Lawless said. "A history of working on females who fit the same physical description and are in the same age bracket. He's kinky—a little sadistic. Even the knots are right, and he's got no alibi yet for June sixteenth. But"—Lawless looked at her—"I don't think it's him. None of the girls he was involved with was tied like Mary Baumann, and I'm simply not getting the right vibes. But that doesn't mean," Lawless said, taking her hand, "he isn't the killer."

"My mind is raw," Barbara said. "My defenses are down. We're having a great day, aren't we."

He put his arms around her and held her tightly.

At eleven o'clock, Barbara's phone rang. Lawless picked up on the first ring.

"Hello."

"Joe? Vic Onairuts."

"What have you got."

"The hair's not even close," Onairuts said. "The hair on Mary Baumann did not come off Raymond Scott."

"I appreciate you working late on it, Vic."

"I know. Sorry."

Lawless hung up. He looked at Barbara, asleep. He made no attempt to awaken her.

CHAPTER 53

August 10 was an unseasonably cool day in Fort Siberia. By the time Turner finished roll call it was only fifty-seven degrees. The weatherman predicted it would not get above eighty.

Turner could sense the uplifted mood of the group in front of him. As the mercury lowered, so did the violence. But not all was Nirvana.

"Anyone," he said, "who's cadged one of these ices from the vendor at Webster and Tremont, be wary of a cough. The proprietor"—he glanced at his clipboard—"one Ignacio Serrano, has active TB."

There was nervous laughter.

"There is a rumor," he continued, "that this facility is going to be painted. You know what that means in terms of the way the city operates. Six months after painting it will be torn down."

More laughter.

"We'll have the citizenry tear it down," someone yelled.

"Faster than a wrecking ball," someone else chimed in.

"Today," Turner said, "I'd like to demonstrate something we've covered before. But it's very important. Instinct shooting."

"Oh shit," someone in the back said softly.

But Turner heard it. His face turned to granite. "Who said that?"

A young patrolman in the back raised his hand. His cheeks were abnormally red.

"This may be boring to you," Turner said, his voice like a knife, "but one day you may die out there because you don't know it. If you don't want to know it, get out."

The cheeks got redder, but the patrolman stayed.

Turner waited a few seconds, then picked up a sheaf of papers on a desk behind him and handed them to a patrolman in front for passing out.

"It's all there," he said. "Read it, and practice it."

For five minutes following this, he demonstrated the procedure. Then, without further comment, he left the room.

CHAPTER 54

The night of August 10 was cooler than the day, and Arnold Gertz, camped on Jiminez's roof, was relatively comfortable. The sound of the music had diminished a decibel or so. The jabbering was less than fever pitch. No gunshots could be heard.

But Arnold was not particularly aware of the weather. He was turned inward, and a disturbing idea was growing in his mind. He had not seen the perps in so long he wondered if they really did exist. Maybe he had never seen them.

And maybe, he thought, it was the uppers he was eating like jelly beans to keep himself going on very little sleep. Still, he had fallen asleep twice at the desk in the station. Sleep—that's all he seemed to want or need to do. On the train home, at home—he and Naomi had not made love in ages—and he had almost fallen asleep on the roof. Almost.

When he was awake, his relationship with Naomi was testy, and that bothered him. He wondered just how much longer he could take it. Or Naomi could.

He looked out over the edge of the roof. In the pen, the goats stood motionless. The rubble-strewn fields were empty, no sign of life from the alleys across the field. Nothing.

Just yesterday he had spoken to Lawless about whether he should stop the surveillance.

"That's the way a stakeout is, Arnold," Lawless had said. "Ninety-nine and nine-tenths nothing. We watched a guy for only three days and it paid off. You can watch three months and come up empty."

"What do you think I should do?"

"Listen to your instincts."

His instincts said stay.

Arnold took the lid off a Styrofoam cold case and took out a protein drink. He replaced the lid, put the drink on it, then took out a small bottle of uppers, popped one in his mouth, and washed it down with the drink.

After a few minutes he felt like he had slept a hundred hours. He was raring to go.

CHAPTER 55

On August 11, Leo Grady attended the seven o'clock Mass at St. Aloysius. When it was over, most of the people left, except for some elderly ladies and Leo, sitting in a pew in the back. He was saying his rosary.

It was his habit to go to church every morning, but he usually didn't say the rosary. What was on the eleven o'clock news the night before had prompted that.

There had been two homicides and a suicide of the kind that defined Fort Siberia. Grady wondered if he was going to be involved in either but, more important, whether he would be able to continue.

The first involved a pregnant seventeen-year-old girl who threw her three-month-old son to his death from a fourth-story window, then followed out the same window.

The second was the killing of an eighty-eight-year-old woman. She had been battered to death. She had been living on food stamps.

The reports had given Grady a severe case of the flutters, and he started to remember what Iron Balls Callahan had said about him—that there was no way he could make it through to thirty-five. He had started to believe that he could make it. And now this.

Two months. That was all he had to do, and the summer would be over soon.

But, oh, it seemed like two years.

Last night he had talked about it, over half a bottle of vodka, with Rita. Now he needed Jesus to help him. Jesus would have to help him make it.

A knifing thought. Of Rita. St. Aloysius was where

her funeral had been. He had prayed to Jesus to save his darling, but Jesus had taken Rita home.

Grady squeezed his eyes shut. He was thinking blasphemy. There had been many times in his life when Jesus had helped. So many, many times.

And there had been times when he hadn't. And Grady could not explain why—or why not. It was beyond human thinking. Jesus was God, the Savior, the Lord. You believed in him or you didn't. He believed in him. He believed in him now.

Grady's fingers grasped the rosary beads tightly.

Help me, Jesus, he thought. Help me make it through the day.

Hail Mary full of grace, the Lord is with thee . . .

Hail Mary full of grace, the Lord is with thee . . .

Lawless was not at Fort Siberia when Grady arrived. Benson, another squad member, said he was on the old-lady squeal.

"Did he say anything about me?" Grady said.

"No."

Grady nodded. He felt relief and elation sweep through him. He almost glanced upward.

He got himself a cup of black coffee, spiked with vodka, sat down at one of the desks, and dialed a number. It was of a friend down in headquarters who had been on vacation and was due back today.

"Officer O'Toole."

"Let me speak," Grady said, "to the best clerical man on the best police force in the world."

"You got him," O'Toole said. "How the hell are you, Leo? How are you surviving?"

"God knows," Grady said. "God knows. How's old Iron Balls?"

"Out sick."

"Nothing trivial, I trust."

O'Toole laughed.

"How's your fine boy, Tommy?"

"Fine."

"And your lovely wife?"

"Lovely." Pause. "What do you need, Leo?"

"You're so smart, Tommy. I want to know why Barbara Babalino is going to stand trial."

"You mean Fernandez Two?"

"What?"

"That's what they call it around here. Fernandez Two."

"Oh. Can you do it?"

"Hey, Leo! That'll take me at least an hour!"

Grady chortled. "I know it's asking a lot, Tommy. But if you don't do it I'll put in a 57 requesting you be reassigned here."

"Don't even joke about it."

"I'm not joking."

"Ha-ha," O'Toole said. "What's your number?"

"They don't have phones here. They communicate with drums."

'O'Toole laughed. Grady gave him the number.

"Leo, don't be a stranger. I'd like to see you before . . .." And he laughed. "I owe you that."

Grady looked the other number up in the Manhattan directory. He dialed it.

"Lansford, Jeffries, and Lowell," the clipped, syrupy voice said.

"Mr. Lansford there?"

"Who's calling?"

"Leo Grady."

Grady spent five minutes on the phone with Lansford, who said he would be more than happy to help Officer Babalino. Grady knew why. The publicity, and the fact that Grady had once referred some valuable business to him—and might to it again.

The conversation ended with Grady saying that Barbara would likely call Lansford.

Less than an hour later, O'Toole called Grady back.

"Is she a friend?" There was no joviality in O'Toole's voice.

"She's close with a guy who's been a real friend to me."

"There's a problem. They want her out. LaPalma's behind it."

"Oh."

"He's telling the PC that the Department image, and the PC's image are in decline. That examples must be set to raise the moral standards. You know, the whole long sideburn—moustache—cops-with-yellow-sheets syndrome. His real reason, of course, is that he's nuts."

"What do you think the PC will do?" Grady asked. Of course he knew the answer.

"What's expedient. She's gone."

"No way to reach LaPalma?"

"You know the answer to that, Leo."

Yes, he did. He also knew that everyone was afraid of LaPalma, like they had been afraid of Hoover.

"Who will sit?" Grady asked.

"It doesn't matter," O'Toole answered. "Leo, you know all this. You taught me, remember?"

"Yeah. Thanks. Keep in touch."

"I'm sorry, Leo."

Grady hung up. He hated telling Lawless this. It was going to hurt. And this on top of the Baumann case, which was at a complete standstill.

Grady buried himself in paperwork the rest of the morning, then went to a local deli for lunch. It had never been held up. It was owned by an ex-concentration camp victim who was as adroit at cooking lean pastrami as he was at handling a sawed-off shotgun. He had a sign taped to the register: STICKUPMEN SHOT. SURVIVORS PROSECUTED.

Grady had pastrami on rye and a Lite beer, then went back to the station. Lawless had not returned.

There was a phone message for Grady.

"Call Ernest Brown."

Grady remembered right away. How could he forget? The girl with the see-through blouse, the little lock on her neck, the black guy with the shaved head.

Why would he be calling? Could he have something? Please?

He dialed the number.

"Ernest Brown Studios."

It took him only ten seconds to be connected to Brown.

"Officer Grady," Brown said, "I showed those pictures of the girl around. Someone has recognized that method of tying."

Grady froze.

Just like that. Just like that.

"Who?"

"A member. He'd rather not be identified. But he will talk to you or Joe."

"When? I can be there in forty-five minutes."

"Just a minute." Brown went off the phone, then came back. "Come ahead."

A minute later, Grady was on the street, walking toward the subway entrance on Fordham Road. He hadn't walked so fast in ten years.

CHAPTER 56

Thirty-five minutes later Grady emerged from the subway station at 34th Street. He kept up the pace, and five minutes later he was stepping off the elevator into Brown's studio.

There was a different girl behind the desk. She was pretty and was dressed normally, except for a thick spiked collar like one that a Great Dane might wear around her neck. Grady only gave it passing disaffection.

"Leo Grady," he said when she approached him.

"Oh yes. Please come with me, sir."

The girl led him to the studio proper. Brown was there, busy taking photos of a woman who looked like a skeleton in a shiny dress. A wind machine blew her hair as she struck various poses.

Nearby, a conservatively dressed man with silvery hair—in his mid-fifties, Grady guessed—watched the proceedings.

Brown caught a glimpse of Grady and waved. "I'll be with you in a minute."

A minute later he finished the shooting and came over to Grady. The conservatively dressed man followed.

Brown shook hands with Grady.

"This is John, Officer Grady. That's not his real name, but that's what we'll call him. Okay?"

"Sure." Grady blinked. He hoped his surprise didn't show too much.

Brown led the men into his office. They all sat down, Brown and "John" facing Grady.

"Brew?"

Grady nodded. John shook his head. Grady sensed John watching him. John was nervous. Grady was too.

Brown picked up the phone, punched a button twice. "Two beers," he said, and hung up.

"How's Joe?" Brown asked.

"Okay. We've been busy."

"So I read."

"Didn't work out."

"I know."

The girl came with the beers, which were opened. Brown tersely directed her to the place- one in front of him, the other in front of Grady; she did and left. Brown took a sip. Grady took a slug which he tried to make look like a sip.

"Okay," Brown said. "What John says here is between me, you, Joe, and John, as far as its source goes. He will never have to testify. Okay?"

"Okay," Grady said. He was sure Lawless would go along with it.

Brown nodded. He looked at John.

John reached into his jacket pocket and withdrew what Grady recognized as the Xeroxes of the Baumann pictures. He handed them to Grady, who put them in his suit jacket.

"I haven't seen that tying method in thirty-five years, and I only saw it once, but that was enough."

Grady, riveted to the words, was aware of the surprising timber and resonance of John's voice. And the nervousness beneath it.

"During 1951 and 1952 I was in Army Intelligence, in Korea. And we received reports in early '52 that American POWs were being mistreated by the North Koreans. We couldn't confirm or deny, but someone got the idea to raid one of the camps, take it over, and see.

"One summer night—I don't remember the exact date—we mounted an attack and succeeded in doing just that.

"We were shocked. The conditions," he continued, "were abysmal. No sanitation, little or no food, no protection from the elements."

John's voice lowered. "But the worst thing we found," he said, "was this method of tying. The exact method used on the girl. It was used as a way to discipline or brainwash the prisoners, and we"—he hesitated, his voice lowering further—"found two skeletons where the ropes were still intact."

"God," Grady blurted.

"The name of it in Korean is Daeji Bu-jap-da. Roughly translated that means 'tying the pig.' We wanted to publicize it, but it got suppressed."

Grady's mind was being pulled back to the cellar again. The little girl in the cellar. He slugged his beer, wrenched his mind away. He had to be a cop.

"Was there any sexual thing?"

"No," John said. "Just the tying."

"How about her hands. Are they part of it?"

"No, I've never seen that before."

"Anything else?" Grady said.

The men shook their heads. Grady drained the can.

222

"Another beer?" Brown asked.

"No, that's okay."

Grady stood up. He shook John's hand, then Brown's. "Thank you," he said.

"Glad we could help, Officer," Brown said.

Grady looked at Brown, then John. "Why don't you call me Leo," he said.

CHAPTER 57

Lawless was sitting in the squad room when Grady got back. Lawless looked washed out. Grady approached him.

"I talked with a friend downtown, and Lansford," he said.

Lawless looked up sharply at him. Grady told him what he had learned.

"I appreciate it, Leo," Lawless said.

"But there is some good news," Grady said. "I talked to Brown. We've identified the way the girl was tied."

Grady detailed his meeting with Brown and "John." As he talked, Lawless took out a cigarette, lit up, and smoked.

When Grady was finished, Lawless said nothing.

"I was thinking," Grady said, "it may be an Oriental we're looking for."

Lawless nodded, but he thought, Orientals don't have blond hair.

He got up and went to one of the file cabinets. He pulled out a file, put it on a desk, leafed through it. Grady watched. He was looking for something. He found it. A single sheet of paper. Grady recognized it. The list of suspects with blond hair.

Lawless glanced down at it, then looked up.

"If we assume," he said, "that this method was learned in Korea, by a person who first of all is old enough now to have been there, and who has blond hair—"

Oh no, Grady thought.

"—then it had to be her father. He's the only person old enough."

Grady's mind recoiled against it.

"But anyone could have learned it later. And you said, Joe, that he had an alibi. You checked it out yourself."

Lawless nodded. He was puzzled. June 16. Baumann was painting. His daughter was being murdered. How could he be in two places in the same time?

"I know. We're going to have to recheck—and call the Army. Let's do that right now."

Lawless called Army Headquarters and got off a confirming teletype to St. Louis, where the military records were kept, asking a rush reply on Baumann.

Then they pulled an unmarked car and headed downtown. It started to rain lightly.

Lawless parked the car on 86th Street and Second Avenue, practically in the same place he'd parked when he first checked Baumann's alibi.

They went to the super's apartment.

"Painter's gone," the super, a middle-aged man of Slavic extraction, said. "Work 'round block. 1823 First, I think."

Lawless and Grady walked through the rain to the address. Outside there was a pair of green vans with yellow lettering, SUNSHINE PAINTING, on the side. It was the company that Baumann, a subcontractor, had done the work for at the other building.

They walked through the freshly painted basement, but there were no painters in sight. It occurred to Lawless that a painter could get to know a cellar, however

224

mazelike, like the back of his hand if he painted it. He felt something start to come together.

The super's wife directed them to a room in the back of the cellar where the painting foreman was. It was he Lawless had spoken to.

The foreman, a young dark-haired guy named Russo, was in the room when Lawless and Grady went in. Russo was using a big stick to mix beige-colored paint which almost overflowed a new garbage can.

Russo glanced up. "Oh," he said.

"How you doin'?" Lawless said. "I talked with you before, I just wanted to double-check the whereabouts of someone on June sixteenth. You said that Mr. Baumann was painting that day."

"That's right," Russo said. He had stopped stirring. "He worked on Second Avenue that day."

"Can you be sure?"

"Absolutely," Russo said.

"How come?"

"I pay the subs by the room. He did two rooms that day."

"Yeah?"

"Yeah. Two bedrooms. He had a fair amount of prep, and it was a two-color enamel job."

"What do you mean?"

"The walls were painted with flat, and the woodwork enamel was a second color. He's a pro, but he was there all day doing it."

"You remember all this stuff in your head? The date, I mean."

"No way. I write it down in a book. I need it for insurance, taxes, and the like."

Lawless was still puzzled, but there was no place else to go. "Have you seen Baumann lately?" he asked.

"No."

"Well, I'd appreciate you keeping this quiet. Don't mention it to anyone, okay?"

Russo nodded, but something was on his mind. "Can I ask you a question?" he said.

225

"Sure."

"He's the murdered girl's father, right?"

"Yeah."

"How come he's being questioned? How could he kill his own daughter that way?"

CHAPTER 58

Driving uptown, Lawless discussed it with Grady.

"In my gut, Leo," Lawless said, "I know it's him. But I don't understand it. I believe the foreman. Baumann was painting that day. He couldn't be in two places at the same time. And he also was home, at least part of the night, on the fifteenth. He made all those calls he said. I looked at the mud sheets."

"Huh? What are they?"

"Records of all local calls not detailed on the bill. The printing is unclear, hence the name."

"Oh."

"I don't understand it. Any ideas?"

"Maybe Dr. Onairuts made a mistake."

"I doubt it. He's the last guy to write his words in stone. I've taken a lot of what he's said to the bank."

They were near 124th and Lenox, Harlem, when Lawless pulled the car over.

"Let's get a drink."

Twist my arm, Grady thought.

Grady was a bit puzzled as to why they had stopped in Harlem—maybe it meant nothing—but he followed Lawless into a bar, the Torchlight, right on the corner. Every person in the bar was colored. It looked like a neighborhood place.

The barmaid, a heavyset black woman wearing bright red lipstick and shiny earrings, came over. She smiled.

"Hey, baby," she said to Lawless. "How you doin'?"

"Okay, Fae. How are you?"

"Not bad. When you gettin' married?"

"You never know," Lawless said.

"Hey, that's serious."

"This is Leo Grady, Fae."

"How you doin', Leo. On the job?"

Leo nodded.

"Siberia?"

"Yes."

"Then you'll like Harlem." She laughed, showing large, glistening white teeth. "What'll it be?"

"Screwdriver for me," Grady said.

"The same," Lawless said.

Fae brought the drinks and went away to wait on other customers.

"I used to come here a lot when I first went into homicide," Lawless said.

He sipped his drink.

"And I learned a lot right here, too. We used to drop in and kick cases around. Clancy, my first sergeant, he was born to the job. He taught me plenty.

"I sometimes come back here, just to think about a case. I half expect to see Clancy walk out of the men's room and join me."

He smiled.

"One thing he always said was that when a case is going nowhere you have to reexamine your assumptions to make sure they're sound. You could figure something with the logic of a philosopher, but if your assumptions are wrong, your case isn't worth anything."

Lawless was quiet for a long time. In the background, playing low, was a song that to Grady sounded more like someone talking than singing.

Then the song ended, and Grady heard someone say, "Holy shit," and he realized it was Lawless. It was the first time he had ever heard him utter an obscenity. He looked at Lawless. There was a tremendous intensity about him.

"It's so simple," he said. "It's always so simple once you figure it out."

"What?"

"We had assumed that the killer was with her on June sixteenth, right?"

"He was, wasn't he?" Grady said.

"No," Lawless said. "No."

"She was reported missing June fifteenth, found June seventeenth. Onairuts said she was dead—what? ten, twelve hours when she was found? In other words we assumed the killer had her alive for twenty-four hours. And during that time sexually abused her five or six times."

"Yes," Grady said. "So?"

"So," Lawless said, his voice low, "that's the trap! Because she was *alive,* I assumed he was with her. But he wasn't! He just worked on her for that one night—after making a grandstand play to find her."

"And then . . ." But Grady could not finish the sentence. Something was breaking inside him. Jesus.

". . . left her to die," Lawless said. "He was painting an apartment while she was struggling to live, struggling all those hours to keep from choking."

Grady's eyes misted. He whacked down the screwdriver. And then something else boiled up inside him, something he didn't even know was there: rage. Inexorably his mind focused on details—the knots, her eyes—feeding the rage. He wanted to smash something, break something. He wanted to kill something.

He swallowed. His voice was husky. "We've got to get that bastard," he said.

"We will," Lawless said.

CHAPTER 59

The next morning, a copy of Richard Henry Baumann's service record was delivered by messenger to Joe Lawless.

He had gone into the service in October of 1950 and had been honorably discharged in September of 1953, a corporal. He had spent a year in Korea in 1952, three of those months as a prisoner of war.

Lawless immediately gathered the entire squad: Grady, Edmunton, Piccolo, Benson.

It took him five minutes to recap the case, culminating in the report from the Army.

"I don't think there's any doubt," he said, "that Baumann is the killer. But right now, all we've got is a scenario on how he did it. We haven't got a particle of physical evidence."

"Why don't we just talk with him?" Piccolo said.

Edmunton laughed.

Lawless shook his head.

"What I want to get is a sample of his pubic hair. If we can get that and it matches what we found on Mary Baumann, I'll go to the DA."

"How are we going to get that?" Benson said.

"Let me do it," Piccolo said. "I'll just rip off a handful."

Edmunton laughed. Grady looked at Piccolo. The idea didn't disturb him.

"We're going to go into his house and take it. Once we get it, and it matches, then we'll get a search warrant and get it proper."

Grady realized he was hearing cops talk about committing a felony. He didn't care.

"Frank," Lawless said. "We'll set you up to go in. You're going to need your picks."

"When am I going in?"

"As soon as possible, but not today. It's too late. And not tomorrow or Sunday. When Leo and I first went there their schedule was that he worked during the day, she at night. The only gap we have when the house isn't occupied is late afternoon."

"What about the meantime?" Grady asked. "He'll be loose, won't he?"

"No," Lawless said. "We're going to watch him with the full squad until we can bust him. And we have to be sure we never lose him. This guy killed his own daughter. We're talking about a maniac, and a clever one."

No one said anything.

CHAPTER 60

The stakeout was in place on Richard Baumann Friday afternoon. Lawless called Barbara at the 101st, explaining what had happened. "We're watching him around the clock, and it shouldn't be long before we get him off the street."

"Okay," Barbara said softly. "By the way, I had my number changed."

"Good," Lawless said. He took the number. "I can't make it today. I'll see you as soon as I can."

On Friday evening Barbara checked that the closed-circuit alarm system that covered all the entries to her apartment was working okay.

She also checked the .38 snub-nose she kept in the closet to make sure it was loaded. She had that and her service revolver.

Lawless was able to get to her apartment at around ten on Saturday. The story of her trial had broken in all the media.

They sat down on the couch. She was perturbed.

"I had my number changed yesterday night," she said, "and today the phone has been going off the hook. I called the phone company, and of course they say no one could possibly get it. Sometimes I think reporters are lower than pimps. By the way," she added, "I called Laura. She's doing fine."

"Good."

"How's the surveillance?"

"Tight. Baumann just goes about his business. We're going to go in Monday to get the hair sample."

Barbara looked at him. She did not like that. But it was not the time to argue police ethics or morality.

"Who?" she asked.

"Piccolo."

"He's a madman."

"He's a good cop, too. Learned a lot from Turner. Never misses a roll call."

Lawless wanted to keep talking. He didn't want Barbara to ask the questions he didn't want to answer. "You've picked up a lot from Turner, haven't you?" he said.

"Believe it. Guy's great."

"Do you know why he's at the Five Three?"

"No. Do you?"

"Yeah," Lawless said. "I do."

"How come?"

"I know a cop, a guy named Charlie Ryan, who knows the whole story."

"What?"

"About six years ago," Lawless said, "Turner was riding a sector car in mid-Manhattan with a kid who was just out of the Academy. They got a gun run, a liquor store.

"Turner was driving, and when he pulled up near the store, the kid just jumps out, John Wayne style, gun drawn, and goes into the store, and immediately is fired upon. Turner jumped out of the car, and when he gets there the kid is down. He fired, got one of the perps, got hit in the leg himself, but the other got out the back.

"Another car came to the scene—this one with Charlie Ryan driving—and they scooped up Turner and the kid, put them in the back, and made a beeline for Roosevelt. The kid had a pulse, so Turner, leg and all, gave him mouth-to-mouth, but by the time they got to Emergency he was DOA.

"Later, Charlie told me, he visited Turner and all Turner said was, 'I can still taste his blood, Charlie. He's too young to die. They're all too young to die.'

"Charlie told me he heard Turner ended up in South Oaks. It burned him out. I guess his being at Siberia helps him. Maybe knowing that he can prevent something like that. I don't know. He doesn't talk about it."

Tears were streaming down Barbara's face. "Christ almighty! How terrible. I'm worrying about my career, and here's a guy probably trying to hold his sanity together."

"I know," Lawless said. "But while you're experiencing your own problems it's hard to take solace from other people's."

"I guess you're right. It just seems selfish."

"I don't think so," Lawless said. "Just human."

There was a silence.

"Speaking of my problems," Barbara said. "Was Leo able to find out anything?"

Lawless lit a cigarette. He had to be honest. Without the truth, they were lost. "Yes," he said.

She stiffened. "Let's have it."

Lawless explained about LaPalma, and immediately felt the heat coming off her.

"It's just what you've been saying," she said. "They

think about the goddamn Department image, the goddamn image of the PC, or they worry about a guy who
jerks off over sin! They think about everything except
justice, about me! My life. Fucks! I should go to the
newspapers. I should tell them!"

"They'd deny it."

"Liars, too, the fucks!"

Barbara got up. "Let's have a drink."

He watched her go toward the kitchen. As she passed
the nightstand, the phone rang. She picked it up.

"Fuck you," she yelled into it without trying to learn
who it was. She slammed it down, then threw it on the
bed.

Lawless laughed. She was some piece of work.

She brought two beers back, gave one to Lawless,
then sat back down on the couch. They sipped the
beers.

"Do I have any chance?"

"Sure. There's always a chance. Grady will guide us.
The lawyer could do something."

She snuggled close to him. She rubbed the inner part
of his thigh softly with her hand.

"You're lucky," she said. "I'm super horny when I
get depressed."

CHAPTER 61

On Monday afternoon, Frank Piccolo, disguised as a
plumber—complete with one-inch cigar stub jutting from
his mouth—waited in the surveillance van across the
street from Baumann's house for Mrs. Baumann to leave.

At around four o'clock, she did, grabbing a bus on the

corner. Benson, one of the dicks in a camper who had followed Baumann to an interior paint job on Allerton Avenue in the East Bronx, gave the go-ahead.

"He's still inside," Benson said. Piccolo had plenty of time.

He exited the van, toolbox in hand, went across the Concourse, and three minutes later was standing in front of Baumann's front door.

He rang the bell. No one answered. He went quickly to his toolbox and withdrew a ring of picks. Two minutes later he was standing inside the Baumann apartment.

He was tempted to toss the place to see what he could come up with, but he had his orders.

He located the bathroom and went inside. He took a large screwdriver from the toolbox and used it to take out the big chrome screw holding the tub strainer in place. He lifted out the strainer, then used a small hooked piece of wire to probe the trap. A moment later he hoisted out a dripping wad of hair and debris.

"Beautiful," he said softly. There were many blond hairs entangled among the dark and gray ones.

He cut the wad in half, put one half in a plastic envelope, and dropped the other half down into the trap. He put the envelope in his pocket, cleaned up, and refastened the drain.

A few minutes later he was giving the okay sign to the van, and a short while after this was in the subway on his way down to Bellevue, where Onairuts waited.

It didn't take long. Onairuts came out of one of the labs, his normally poker face threatening to smile.

"You got yourself a killer," he said. "As much as hair is a match, this is a match."

Then Piccolo was on his way back uptown. A half hour later he was inside the van.

"A match," he said.

"Good," Lawless said. "I'm going to the DA tomorrow to see if we can get a warrant and get this guy off the streets."

CHAPTER 62

On Tuesday, another scorcher, and the fifth day of the surveillance, Frank Piccolo made a mistake. He and Edmunton had parked their surveillance van, labeled Department of Highways, up the block from the building on Allerton Avenue where Richard Baumann was working.

Around ten o'clock, thirst upon them, Piccolo realized that he and Edmunton had forgotten their cold chest. They would have to go through the entire day without a drink.

"Hey, fuck that," Piccolo said. "There's a deli a couple blocks away. I'm going there."

"He might see you," Edmunton said in a rare burst of assertiveness.

"No way. He's inside painting. How's he going to see me?"

Piccolo exited from the back of the van and went up the block.

Unknown to Piccolo, he took a burn. Baumann was painting a front window, and he noticed Piccolo get out of the truck. It puzzled him. He got out of the back. There was no one in the front.

Baumann waited by the window, and his eyes narrowed when he saw Piccolo, laden with cold drinks and ice, get into the truck from the back. And stay there.

Later, after work, Baumann loaded up his own van and drove slowly down Allerton. He felt empty. The van followed.

He took the same meandering route home that he had taken that morning. The van stayed with him all the way, and as he went about the business of straightening out inside his van, a white one in pristine condition, he became aware that the Highways van had parked across the street, slightly down the block.

He was definitely being watched.

He went upstairs and went through the motions of making supper. But he could not eat. He was trying to think about what to do. When it started to get dark he went into the master bedroom. Through heavy translucent curtains he looked out.

The van was still there.

He tried to watch TV, to listen to music, to do a crossword puzzle. He could not concentrate.

At around eight-thirty, just after dark, he checked again and saw some movement. Then he realized he was witnessing the changing of the shifts.

At nine o'clock, he took a walk to a newsstand at Kingsbridge Road and the Concourse. As he crossed 197th Street he unobtrusively glanced down it. Another van. They were watching the back of his building too.

Later, Baumann lay on his bed in the darkened master bedroom.

How did they find out? He had been careful. Very careful. No one had seen him take her out of the building or into the other building. He was sure of it. The night had been particularly dark. And she had not made a sound. He had tricked the little whore.

"Where are we going?"

"A surprise, Mary. A surprise."

She had gone forward almost willingly, and there had been no one in the building.

How?

He did not know, but he knew he could not get to the cop. She would laugh and think: Just because you can kill a little girl doesn't make you anything. You're still a little nothing.

Baumann closed his eyes and squeezed his hands into fists. He had to get to her.

How?

It would have been so easy. It was all planned. The hard part, the risky part, would have been getting her from her apartment to the van. Once in the van, she was his. He had had another abandoned building all picked out, a room inside where no one could find them.

Now he could not even get out of his building without being watched.

He inhaled sharply and felt an anger oozing into him.

But he might, he thought, get out in a disguise. He could change the plan. Travel the subway to her apartment, tie, fuck, and kill her—but quickly—and they would not even know he had been out. They couldn't know about her. And when they discovered her, they would not accuse him. They would be his alibi. He was in his apartment all night. They would have to think it was someone else.

Then he felt a blackness, a depression settling over him. It was too risky. They would be looking extremely closely at anyone coming in or out. There was no way he could disguise himself well enough to fool them.

He saw her face, her eyes mean, her mouth laughing, and it echoed through his mind.

And then, unknown to him, Richard Baumann's mind clicked off and returned to another time, another place.

It was dark, in a living room somewhere. A basement apartment. The furniture was old-fashioned. And worn. It was sometime in the thirties.

There was a boy. He was about seven, thin, with curly blond hair. He was looking up at someone. He was feeling a fullness in his bladder, though he did not have to go. He was very scared.

The woman was the boy's mother. She looked down at him, her dark hair bobbed, her cheeks and lips very red, the smell of her perfume making him gag, her chest enormous in a low-cut dress, her dark eyes mean and hard, looking through his inconsequential soul.

She was going out again, he thought, with someone.

"I want you to have this place sparkling clean by the

time I get back, you hear? The last few times you didn't do it right. And be a good boy. If you're not a good boy, Mommy may not come back. I've got my suitcase in the car."

The boy could not talk. He just looked up at her, and then she was gone, up the stairs, her high laughter and the deeper laughter of the man she was with enveloping him, shrinking everything inside him to nothingness. Then the little boy sat on the edge of the couch and started to cry, terrified, as only a child can be terrified, that Mommy would never come back. . . .

Richard Baumann snapped back. Tears streamed down the side of his face. Not from terror, not from sadness.

From rage. He must get at that fucking cunt. He must ask her, as he asked the first little whore, "Are you coming back?"

But how, how, how, how, how, how, how . . . ?

Something occurred to him. A simple idea. Very simple.

But it might work. It was worth a try. Tomorrow.

CHAPTER 63

The next night, Richard Baumann waited for the darkness. He was in his master bedroom, watching the horizon. The sky was red, the horizon brownish, like the edge of an old page. The sun sank; the sky darkened.

Conspicuously, he passed in front of the living room window so he could be seen by someone looking up from the van.

Then, just before darkness, he went back into the master bedroom and changed his clothes: dark jersey, pants, and a baseball cap. The overnight bag had already been packed.

He took a last look down at the van, then went to the front door.

He opened it and listened. Nothing. Quickly, his steps silenced by the short sneakers he was wearing, he went to the stairs, opened the door, and went—up.

At the roof, he opened the door, peeked out, then gradually opened it all the way. There was no one in sight.

He crossed walls with the grace and fluidity of a man years younger—years of housepainting had left his body wiry, surprisingly strong—until he was five roofs away from his own—a good half block away.

He had brought a prybar, but it wasn't necessary. The door was open. He listened. Spanish music and cooking smells mixed with a faint smell of urine wafted up. He descended quickly and quietly.

He took the stairs to the small lobby and looked out the entrance door. There were Spanish on the street; they were drinking, jabbering. They would not remember.

He could see the van, half hidden by parked cars. He exited the building.

He walked toward the subway entrance at Kingsbridge Road and the Concourse, and started down it.

On the way down, he passed Leo Grady, who was late.

Leo Grady had a face everyone forgets, and Baumann did not remember where he had seen him.

Baumann did not have a particularly distinctive face either, and when Grady glanced at him, his face didn't register.

It half registered when he got to street level.

Was that Baumann? He thought. No, it couldn't be. One of the guys would be on his tail.

Still, he looked an awful lot like him.

Grady walked as fast as he could to the van and got in the front. Lawless let him in the back through the compartment door.

"Joe," he said, "is Baumann still up there?"

"Yeah. Why do you ask?"

"I just saw a guy go down the subway who looked an awful lot like him."

"Yeah?"

Lawless patched through to the van watching the back. Benson picked up.

"Ray. Any sign of Baumann?"

"No."

"How was he dressed?"

Grady described what he remembered—in black, with a baseball cap.

"I don't like it. Let's call him."

A moment later, Grady and Lawless climbed out of the van and walked quickly to a phone on the corner. By some miracle, it worked.

Lawless let it ring . . . and ring . . . and ring. No one answered.

Lawless hung up and dialed Piccolo's number. He hoped he was in. He felt an urgency to get in the apartment, and if Piccolo wasn't in to get the door open, he might have to force it. Since they hadn't gotten the warrant—it was due tomorrow—it could jeopardize the case.

Piccolo was in.

"Get here fast, Frank," Lawless said. "I think Baumann has slipped out. I want to look in his apartment."

Precisely four minutes later Piccolo—who lived on Bainbridge and 204th—pulled his souped-up Trans Am behind the van.

"Let's go," Lawless said with low urgency.

They went across the street quickly and were in front of Baumann's door a couple of minutes later.

They rang the bell. No one answered.

Piccolo, on the wire, was living life to its fullest. The door swung open a half minute after he stuck a pick in the lock. They surged inside.

"Toss the place gently," Lawless said. "We want to find something that will tell us where he might be."

Benson, Grady, Piccolo, Edmunton, Lawless, and Marcella fanned out into the various rooms.

Two minutes later, Grady, in the master bedroom, called out, "Hey, Joe. You want to come in here?"

Lawless came in and Grady showed him a small metal trunk. It was in the bottom of a closet Baumann used for tool storage; there were tools on pegs on the wall.

"Open it, Frank."

Piccolo had the lock undone in no time. Lawless opened the lid.

"Holy fuck," Piccolo said.

They had found cancer. There were rolls of tape, a large coil of polypropylene cord.

"Look at this!" Piccolo said. "Look at this shit!"

But Lawless was thinking of what was *missing*. The scissors. And . . .

"Leo," Lawless said urgently, "was he carrying anything?"

"Yes. Yes, he was. An overnight bag."

Then, underneath the tape, he saw it. A folder, a manila folder of some sort.

Lawless picked it up and opened it.

On top was a color picture of Richard Baumann's daughter. She was dressed in a sultry way. She looked far older than she was.

Then he leafed through other pictures, and in each she got younger and younger until . . .

There was a picture of Mary Baumann when she must have been five years old or so. She looked like she had on a costume, a European-style dress.

Lawless turned it over. On the back was written, *Christina Maria Della Noce, cinco.*

Lawless was puzzled, then he got it.

She's adopted. Mary Baumann was Christina Maria Della Noce. She was a little Italian girl. That's why she didn't resemble Baumann or his wife.

He looked at her for a moment. A pretty, little dark-haired, dark-eyed girl, and then the horrific thought fought into his mind. It stripped the years of armor off Lawless, and suddenly he was two months on the job walking into his first crime scene.

Oh Jesus. Oh Jesus Christ. It couldn't be. Yet it could.

He picked her . . . he adopted her . . . to raise her . . . to kill her. Like a lamb to the slaughter . . .

An envelope within the folder.

He opened it. Newspaper clippings and then . . .

"Oh my God."

Barbara looked at him from page three of the *Telegram*. Barbara, pretty, dark-haired, dark-eyed, softig Barbara.

It rocked him, but he forced himself to look at one final envelope. He reached in and took out a single picture.

It was old, brownish. The picture of an unsmiling woman, pretty, dark-haired, dark-eyed—and he remembered what O'Hara had said about the killer, and he knew who she was. The source. Where it all began.

Calmly, he handed all the material to Grady.

The phone was in the kitchen.

He went to it and dialed Barbara's number.

Busy. He tried again. Busy. She had it off the hook. Reporters.

He stood there. He knew that what he did next might mean life or death to her. In moments like this you had to not care about consequences, just act.

It had been at least twenty-five minutes since Baumann was spotted. No, more. Closer to thirty-five.

There was only one way to go. He dialed Central Communications.

"Central K."

"We got ten-thirteen at 127 West 72nd Street, basement apartment."

"Repeat the address."

"127 West 72nd Street, basement apartment. Female police officer."

"We got it."

Lawless started running for the door.

Piccolo yelled, "C'mon, Joe. I got a rocket waiting in the street."

A minute and a half later, Piccolo was moving the Trans Am through its gears as it approached eighty miles an hour.

"Sorry to go so slow," Piccolo yelled above the roar of the engine. "I'll let this fucker go on the Drive."

Piccolo was a tremendous driver, and all Lawless could think was that maybe, by some miracle, he would be on time. Probably not. But he had given a 10–13, which was "Officer Needs Assistance," and there was no signal on earth would galvanize cops more. If he didn't make it there in time, some cop on the 10–13 would.

But he was wrong.

CHAPTER 64

Baumann made good connections and was standing in the rear yard adjacent to Barbara's apartment while Lawless was still in Baumann's.

He knew he would have to be more careful than with the other one. She was a cop. He would assume she had a gun.

He stood motionless and watched her windows, which had the shades pulled. He glanced around, then walked onto a shallow brick wall and dropped noiselessly into the yard.

This had to be quick. If he was spotted, someone might call the cops.

He went up to one of the windows. Through a space between the jamb and shade he saw her. She was asleep, on her belly, ass up. Ready. He felt a fullness in his groin. He ground his teeth. He left.

Three minutes later, Barbara Babalino heard the door-bell ring. She rose sleepily from the bed. It's Joe, she thought. Good. Good.

For just this moment, softened by sleep, her defenses were down.

She opened the door.

The light was behind someone tall. She couldn't see him that well. She was about to ask who he was when she saw the knife, a long, wicked knife. It was in his right hand, pointing out from his naval. Suddenly, she was awake, her heart hammering. She knew who it was.

He pushed his way in and closed the door behind her. She felt helpless. She tried to think. If she screamed, he might stab her. She couldn't outrun him. Her guns were in the closet.

He led her to the center of the room.

Maybe she could talk to him. No. Dangerous. He was a maniac; she might set him off. She needed time.

"On your stomach."

She was thinking of what she told other women about how to react in rape situations. She hesitated.

"I'm not going to hurt you, Barbara. I just want to tie you up."

She wanted to believe him.

He put the overnight bag on the floor and unzipped it. He reached in and pulled out the yellow polypropylene cord. She saw tape.

"See?"

He's going to kill me, she thought. Just like his daughter.

She was on the verge of tears. Not a cop anymore. Just terrified. Then, from nowhere, she remembered the hard granite face of Turner and what he had said at one of the roll call meetings: *When you're under stress, you'll go back to who you are, what you are, and what you've really learned.*

What was she?

Baumann moved the knife an inch toward her. She dropped to her knees. She was trying desperately to think.

Back to who you are . . .

She thought of Joe. Poor Joe. He wanted her so much. She . . . she had to live for him. She . . . she had to live for herself. For herself!

Then an idea. It was a chance.

She started to lie down, whimper a little, and then totally without warning she pulled the plug wire of the lamp. The plug popped out of the wall. The room plunged into darkness. She was aware of Baumann moving, but she rolled out of the way as he thumped on the floor. He was too late.

There was no light in the room. She could not see him, or he her. It was black. Totally black.

She lay motionless, breathing through her mouth, hoping he couldn't hear the staccato thumping of her heart.

Seconds passed. Her eyes were starting to adjust to the darkness. So, she knew, were his.

If she could get to the rear door. No. She remembered Turner saying, *Never have the light behind you. It silhouettes.* And the windows were lighter than the room.

The front door. She could not make it there, either.

She fought the panic, tried not to think who was in the room with her, but couldn't. She was alone in a dark room with a maniac. It was a nightmare.

She remembered something. She had been drinking a Pepsi at the end of the bed. From a goblet.

Her hand searched. Where? Where . . . ? Where . . . ? She touched it, cold and slick, she grabbed it. And then with one sweeping motion she hurled it toward the windows.

Glass shattered, and a moment later the closed-circuit alarm on her windows started to waken the dead.

She heard, beneath the screeching of the alarm, movement, or maybe just sensed it, because then the front door was open and Baumann was out it, and she saw his shadow vaulting up the stairs.

Barbara put her face in her hands.

Thank God. Thank God. I'm safe. Thank God. I'm . . . I'm . . .

I'm a police officer!

And then she was up. She ripped open the closet door and grabbed her snub-nose.

She had on pants and shirt but was shoeless. There was no time for that. There was just time for pursuit.

She ran up the stairs and out the door. She turned left, then right. Baumann was trotting toward Central Park.

She started to run after him. He saw her. He crossed the street, and then went into the park.

In the distance, she heard a siren, then another. Maybe she should get backup. No. There was no one else now. He could not be allowed to kill again.

He had taken a footpath into the park. But the path was well lit; she would be easily seen. She vaulted onto a bench, then onto a short stone wall. She looked, then dropped into the park. It was dense with bushes and trees.

Where was he? He was mad. He might go for her even if she drew on him.

She was vaguely aware of the other side of the park, the tops of buildings, some illuminated, looking down. Through trees light glittered on water.

She felt like an animal, all her senses totally alive.

The sirens got closer. Good, they covered the sound of her feet. What sound? Crazy.

It happened, as she really knew it would, without warning. First there was light in her left peripheral vision, then it blinked off.

She turned as if in slow motion and Baumann was springing at her from behind a tree, his head tilted, somehow only the whites of his eyes showing.

For a millisecond she thought of Turner and then simply brought up the .38 in a short arc, as if bringing up her finger to point at Baumann, and squeezed the trigger and there was an explosion and at the same time she realized that the knife was going to go into her but she kept squeezing—that's what Turner had said you do in instinct shooting—and the gun roared deafeningly again and again and the impact knocked Baumann back as the knife went into her shoulder and he staggered, and she kept squeezing until she realized the gun was clicking and Baumann was down.

She went over to him. He was spread-eagled on the ground, face up, blood coming out of his mouth. The overnight bag lay nearby.

Barbara was aware of a riot of sounds and sirens and doors slamming. Some cops came over. Then she turned and saw Lawless leaping out of a Trans Am. He was running toward her. She held up her hand.

"I'm okay," she yelled.

Lawless slowed, came close. She had never seen his face like this. It was raw, naked, sick. . . .

Barbara started to cry. He had tears in his eyes. They embraced.

"Now you can hold me," he said.

CHAPTER 65

Arnold Gertz was alone on the roof in the darkness.

It was five days after Barbara Babalino had shot Richard Baumann dead. She was fine, and Arnold had heard a rumor that because of her actions with Baumann all charges against her were going to be dropped. It would be hard prosecuting a hero.

Arnold thought of the song. What a difference a day makes. It had made a big difference in her life. It would make a big difference in his. One day, two days more. And then he would leave the roof forever. It was destroying his health and hurting his relationship with Naomi and the twins.

Yes, he was at the absolute end. And it wouldn't be so bad. Life would go on. He had his health, he had Naomi, he had the twins, he was a police officer.

No, it wouldn't be so bad.

But . . .

It was two in the morning, and three roofs over they were barbecuing a pig. He could smell it. He could hear the music, the laughter. He glanced over. They were a nutty people, he thought.

He looked back, down, across the field.

He turned to stone.

There, fresh from one of the alleyways, were two men. Two bushy-haired perps.

He ducked. Were they real?

He scrambled on all fours to the roof door, then he was inside and going down the stairs like a man possessed, because that's exactly what he was.

Suddenly he was on the street. He looped around and went down Jiminez's alley. He went to the end of the building and peeked. They were real.

One of them had a pair of bolt cutters, and Arnold watched as he carefully clipped a big section of fence away. When both perps were inside the pen, Arnold stepped out from behind the building, his .38 up.

"*Buenas noches*," he said, using two of the dozen or so Spanish words he knew. "You're under arrest."

Arnold was able to get the cuffed perps away from the pen before Jiminez had a chance to kill them, and by three o'clock they were in the station lockup.

Then he went up to the dormitory room and sacked out.

He awoke at seven and called Naomi.

He told her what had happened.

"Oh, Arnold, I'm so proud of you. Why don't you go stick it to that Bledsoe!"

"I don't think so," Arnold said. "I don't think he

248

could ever understand." And he knew, too, that he might not get his street job back. It didn't matter. It was Bledsoe's problem, not his.

Lawless came in at eight o'clock and Arnold told him what had happened.

"Congratulations, Arnold. Nice work."

"I'll tell you. That call to me that night. That was the difference."

"That's okay. That's the way it has to be," Lawless said. "Cops have to care about each other, or we're gone."

"Thank you."

CHAPTER 66

The day after Arnold Gertz made his collar, Lawless called Barbara at home, where she was still recuperating a bit from Baumann's assault.

"I just got word," he said, "that Walker's dead. Someone worked him over with an ice pick."

"Oh," Barbara said softly. But she felt relief. "Do you have any idea who?"

"No, a guy like Walker you start off with lists of suspects."

And Barbara knew that Lawless was going to do exactly nothing.

She immediately called Laura and told her.

"I'd be lying," Laura said, "if I didn't say I was glad. Good riddance."

Barbara promised to meet with her the following week to discuss Laura's plans.

* * *

Two days later, the same day she got the doctor's go-ahead to return to duty, the rumor became official: all charges were being dropped, and she got the feeling that she could go to any precinct in the city.

The next morning, she returned to Fort Siberia. She stood in the back of the assemblage of cops and watched Turner do his morning thing. As she did, she remembered the story Lawless had told her about him, and she remembered something else. That was why she was here today, just to say it.

Then Turner was finished and he started to limp away, like he always did.

"Hey, Turner," Barbara yelled.

Turner stopped in mid-stride. Faces turned toward her.

"I just want you, and every cop in this room, to know something." She was filling up, so she got it out fast. "I'm alive," she said, "because of the things you taught me in this crummy room."

Turner's face softened. He nodded.

And then he was gone, and the men and women of Fort Siberia dispersed to start yet another day.

Delgado and O'Malley, as usual, stopped at Nick's Family Restaurant. Delgado got the order this time, and then they drove to a spot to eat it.

"Hey, man," Delgado said. "They bringing in an embyologist or whatever they call the dude to study the roaches in Fort Siberia. They got special kinds developed here. Some of these suckers have two heads, and some are pure white and eat the fucking insecticide that's supposed to kill them."

"No shit," O'Malley said, munching on his sandwich.

"Well, I'll tell you something even stranger. Did you see Turner today? He smiled."

"No way. That dude never smiles."

"Not only smiled," O'Malley said, "had tears in his eyes."

Delgado laughed.

"This fuckin' place, we should all have tears in our eyes."

And then he bit into a loathsome pepper and egg sandwich.